Beneath a Dying Son

New Testament Short Stories

This book is dedicated to the memory of Pandora.

Beneath a Dying Son
New Testament Short Stories

Laughton J. Collins, Jr.

Table of Contents

Introduction

This book contains stories set in first-century Judea reimagined through the lens of the American Old West. Don't expect pristine robes and solemn temples alone—this is a world where the lines between scripture and saga blur—where the spirit of the American frontier rides hard through the ancient hills of Galilee and the dusty streets of Jerusalem, echoing with the tension of a lawless border town. That may be a slight exaggeration—but only slightly.

The stories gathered here are *fictional retellings*, inspired by narratives found within the New Testament. They are *not* intended as accurate interpretations of sacred texts, nor do they seek to put forth theological theories or claim historical precision. Think of them more as tall tales spun around a campfire—campfire tales spun from the bones of scripture, recast as gritty frontier sagas where prophets speak like hardened marshals, zealots carry the weight of the world, and the desperate populace are homesteaders caught between empires.

My aim was simple but audacious: to recast these foundational tales as Westerns, transforming them into gritty frontier sagas. Some, more so than others. Picture the parched landscape of Judea as arid frontier territories with harsh desert landscapes and an unforgiving sun. Envision prophets and teachers as wandering preachers or lone, principled lawmen; Roman centurions as territorial cavalry; Temple authorities as corrupt sheriffs or cattle barons. The tension, the moral struggles, the stark choices between justice and survival, faith and doubt, the clash of kingdoms—heavenly and earthly, Roman and Jewish—mirror the struggle between civilization and wilderness, law and chaos, that defines the Western mythos.

To achieve this Western tone, *deliberate anachronisms* are woven throughout. You'll encounter elements that feel more at home in a John Ford film than in ancient history: the pacing of a tense saloon standoff, the laconic grit of a weary drifter or desert wanderer, the sudden violence of a frontier skirmish or justice, the symbolism of the open trail and the looming fortress, the echoes of saloons in crowded taverns, and even the occasional wide-brim hat and bandanna. These are not oversights; they are essential tools to evoke the specific atmosphere, pacing, and moral landscape of the Western genre. The goal was never historical recreation, but *tonal translation*. That being said, I did try to keep as much historical accuracy as

I could while trying to maintain the western feel and tone to the stories. So, there are no guns, trains or stagecoaches—instead there's knives or swords, carts and caravans.

Within these pages, you'll ride through a Judean Frontier and witness:

- Joseph and Mary undertake a desperate trek to Bethlehem, not just against imperial decree, but through bandit-haunted passes and under the watchful eyes of suspicious Roman patrols—a perilous cattle drive of a different kind.
- Jesus of Nazareth grows up in the carpenter's workshop, but the shadow of the cross he helps build feels less like ancient punishment and more like the harsh, inescapable frontier justice meted out by a distant, powerful authority.
- Encounters at wells, in temples, and on hillsides carry the weight of tense saloon confrontations or pivotal moments on the open range.
- The clash of kingdoms—heavenly and earthly, Roman and Jewish—mirrors the struggle between civilization and wilderness, law and chaos, that defines the Western mythos.
- The final days of Jesus reimagined as a high-stakes showdown. The upper room feels like a lamplit saloon holding its breath. Disciples become a loyal, sometimes quarrelsome posse, navigating betrayal and loyalty in a landscape where trust is scarce. Betrayal hangs thick as gunsmoke, and the crucifixion unfolds with the brutal inevitability of frontier justice meted out by a distant, tyrannical power. Witness Gethsemane's anguish as a midnight duel with despair, the trial as a crooked kangaroo court, and the cross as a stark gallows on Skull Hill.
- Saul's transformation into Paul becomes a supernatural desert odyssey. Haunted by the ghosts of those he persecuted—vengeful spirits marching like a phantom posse—Saul confronts a bitter, disillusioned Christ and the terrifying face of a wrathful deity: a story of cosmic horror and hard redemption.
- The birth of the name "Christian" plays out in a dusty, volatile frontier town. Believers face down hostile mobs and corrupt officials, their declaration "Jesus is Lord!" echoing like a defiant challenge shouted in a saloon brawl, culminating in a brutal ambush where faith collides with violence.
- An outsider philosopher navigates treacherous politics like a stranger in a lawless territory, witnessing Jesus' scathing denunciations (reminiscent of a lone gunslinger calling out corrupt

sheriffs), the weight of Roman occupation, and the torn Temple veil as a stark, violent punctuation.

- Paul's fervent letters, penned under threat like urgent dispatches, crackle with Western urgency, warning of impending judgment and a sudden rescue ("caught up...in the twinkling of an eye") with the desperate energy of a man evading a posse.
- Peter's moment in Gethsemane is a classic Western quick-draw gone wrong—flash of steel, spray of blood, crushing failure. Shifting to Malchus, the maimed servant, his thirst for vengeance mirrors the cycle of retribution fueling countless Western feuds, unfolding against Jesus' trial and execution.

The desert wind howls like a lonesome harmonica. The weight of prophecy hangs as heavy as those crucified, their blood soaking its pages and obscuring its meaning. Choices are stark, often violent, demanding a grit that transcends centuries. These are tales of hope wrestled from despair, light piercing profound darkness, and sacrifice made against overwhelming odds—themes etched deep into the landscapes of both ancient Judea and the mythic American West.

So, tip your hat to scripture and history, but don't be shackled by literalism. You can draw your own conclusions about the man from Nazareth and those who rode beside him—these stories aren't meant to change any minds as to who that man was. Most of these stories assume as common knowledge who that man was not—the messiah—savior—son of God but they are not being presented as facts. They are merely fictional stories to amuse and entertain—mostly me—but hopefully also you, the reader. Most of all, settle in and enjoy the trail through a Judea where miracles feel like moments of stark clarity in a brutal land, and the struggle unfolds under a sun as unforgiving as any hanging over Monument Valley.

So, welcome to the Judean Frontier. The sermon's about to begin, somewhere beneath a dying s☉n.

The Bethlehem Run

Joseph's knuckles whitened on the rough wood of his workbench. The news hit him like a blow to the gut. Mary, his betrothed, was with child but not his child. The air in his small Nazareth workshop thickened with dust and sand. Plans for their life together—the modest house, the family they'd raise—shattered. Betrayal mixed with a deeper, colder dread. The Law was clear. Adultery meant public disgrace, stoning. Mary's life hung by a thread. He was a man who sought justice, but this? To expose her meant death. He couldn't do it. His jaw tightened—he would break the betrothal quietly and send her away. He'd protect her and let the shame fall on him alone, if it must. He would sign the papers, tomorrow. He lay down on his pallet, the weight crushing his chest. Sleep was a distant thing, chased away by visions of Mary's frightened eyes and the harsh judgment of the town.

Then the dream came. Light—fierce and pure, flooded his mind, banishing the shadows. A figure stood within it, radiating an authority that pinned Joseph where he lay. The voice resonated, not in his ears, but deep within his bones. "*Joseph, son of David. Do not fear.*" The words cut through his panic. "*Take Mary as your wife. The child she carries is conceived by the Holy Spirit. She will bear a son. Name him Jesus. He will save his people from their sins.*" The light pulsed, etching the command into his soul. The prophecy echoed: *A virgin will bear a son. Emmanuel. God with us.* Joseph awoke gasping, sweat soaked his tunic, but the crushing dread was gone—replaced by a terrifying certainty. He rose before dawn and found Mary. He took her hand, his own calloused and strong. "I am with you," he said, the words simple, heavy with the burden and the promise. He took her into his home as his wife. He did not touch her—the child she carried was sacred—they would wait.

The Emperor's decree arrived like a plague—a census. Everyone must return to their ancestral town. David's line meant Bethlehem, a hard journey south through Samaria. "This makes no sense," Joseph said "why must we travel to the hometown of an ancestor from a thousand years ago for a census." Joseph secured a donkey, it was sturdy but slow. He packed minimal supplies: bread, dried fish, water skins and tools. Mary's time drew near. Each jolting step of the donkey on the rocky path tightened the knot in Joseph's stomach. He walked beside her, a hand steadying her when the trail grew steep. Robbers haunted these hills and Roman soldiers patrolled the area with sharp suspicion. The sun beat down hard during the day but the nights were cold. Mary bore it silently, her face pale but determined. They reached Bethlehem exhausted. The town overflowed with descendants of David. Every inn and every spare room were packed. Joseph knocked on door after door, his plea growing desperate. "My wife...she is near her time." Nevertheless, shutters closed and heads shook as they were left out in the cold Bethlehem night. Finally, a gruff stable keeper, seeing Mary's pallor, gestured wordlessly to a cave cut into the limestone behind his crowded inn. Joseph and Mary entered the cave and thanked the stable keeper. They looked around at their temporary accommodations, animals shifted in the gloom, hay covered the dirt floor and the smell of dung and damp earth filled the air. It wasn't much but it was shelter. That night, amidst the lowing of beasts, Mary cried out. Joseph helped as he could, fetching water, tearing cloth. Then the infant's first wail pierced the stable air. Joseph wrapped the tiny, squirming boy in clean swaddling cloths and laid him in Mary's arms. She looked at the newborn with an exhausted smile. *Jesus. Emmanuel. God with us.* Here?—In this place?

Weeks later, Joseph was repairing a stool outside the stable-turned-dwelling when the strangers appeared. They stood out like jewels in a dust storm. Three men, travel-stained but richly dressed in eastern silks and wool. Their camels, laden with packs, snorted nearby. Their eyes scanned the humble dwellings with an unsettling intensity. They asked questions— their accents thick. They sought a child born King of the Jews. They spoke of a star, they followed to the very spot. Unease tingled on Joseph's neck— kings and Herod didn't mix. As far as Herod was concerned, he was the king of the Jews. Joseph feared for his son's life, he remained silent but the fear was welling up inside him. He led them silently to the stable where Mary sat nursing the baby near the small fire. The men stopped, their faces transformed—wonder, reverence and a deep humility. They knelt on the earthen floor, bowing their heads low before the infant. Joseph watched, rooted to the spot. They opened their packs. Gold gleamed in the firelight. The rich, complex scent of frankincense filled the space. The bitter aroma of myrrh followed. Gifts fit for royalty—prophecy. The men stayed only a short time. They spoke little, their eyes fixed on the child with an unnerving focus. When they left, a chill settled over Joseph despite the fire. Something felt wrong.

Herod's palace in Jerusalem was a mountain of gleaming stone. Inside, the air was cold, scented with incense that couldn't mask the underlying tension. The magi stood before the throne. Herod smiled—his eyes were small, shrewd pits of endless darkness. He leaned forward, his

2

voice smooth as oil. "A new king, you say? Born in Bethlehem? How...fascinating. Tell me, when exactly did this star first appear? I am eager to worship him myself. Go. Find the child. Report back to me. Then I too may pay homage." He waved a ringed hand, dismissing them. The moment they were gone, the smile vanished. Herod's fist slammed onto the arm of his throne. "A king?" he hissed to his advisors. "In *my* kingdom?" His face purpled. Fear, cold and ruthless, twisted his features. "Bethlehem," he spat. "Find him. Eliminate him." He called for the captain of his guard. Orders were given in a low, venomous tone—plans were made.

Back in Bethlehem, the magi moved quietly. They gathered their camels under cover of twilight. "We leave tonight," their leader murmured to Joseph. "Do not return to Herod. We are warned. His heart is black." They mounted. "The child is in danger. Great danger." Without another word, they turned their camels—not north towards Jerusalem, but east, vanishing into the gathering dark. Joseph stared after them—the warning echoed. *Danger*—Herod. The cold dread returned, sharper than before. He barred the crude stable door that night, listening for every sound. He was tired but sleep was impossible. When it came, it was thin and fractured. Then the light returned—the same figure, urgent, blazing. *"Joseph! Rise! Take the child and his mother! Flee to Egypt! Herod seeks the child to kill him. Go NOW!"* Joseph jolted awake, the command ringing in his ears. He had no time to waste, he shook Mary gently. "Get up. We must leave. Now." There was no explanation needed, the fear was in his eyes, in his voice—she understood. She bundled the sleeping infant close. Joseph moved fast, he gathered the remaining bread, the water skins and he stuffed the magi's gold deep into his belt pouch. The frankincense and myrrh were left behind— they needed speed, not scent. He saddled the donkey and Mary climbed on, clutching Jesus. Joseph led them out into the cold, starless night. Bethlehem slept, unaware.

They took back streets, avoiding the main road. Every shadow held a threat—every distant bark of a dog made Joseph flinch. He pushed the donkey hard, heading south and west, towards the coast, towards Egypt— only 430 miles stood between them, and the desert loomed ahead. Behind them, back in Bethlehem, Herod's patience snapped. The magi had mocked him and his spies reported nothing. Fury consumed him—he summoned the captain. "Bethlehem. All of it. Every boy child two years and under. Kill them. Kill them all." The order was extreme—final. Soldiers marched and Bethlehem awoke to screams. Doors splintered—Mothers wept, clutching infants. Their blades flashed in the dawn light. The wailing rose, a terrible sound that seemed to shake the very stones. *Rachel weeping for her children.* The prophecy screamed in the silence left by the departing soldiers. Blood soaked the dirt streets—the innocents slaughtered. Herod sat in his cold palace, satisfied. The threat was gone—or so he believed.

Joseph, Mary, and the child were already deep into the wilderness. The sun rose like a hammer pounding on the arid land. The trail was rough, marked only by rocks and the occasional thorny bush. Water was scarce—Joseph rationed it carefully, his own throat was parched. He scanned the horizon constantly, dust plumes could mean traders, or Herod's horsemen. Roman patrols guarded the roads; they needed the empty places. Mary endured, her face drawn. She sheltered the baby from the sun under her shawl. Days blurred into nights. They slept fitfully under the open sky, listening for the scrape of claws or the jingle of harnesses. Joseph traded a sliver of gold with a desert nomad for goat's milk and dates. They avoided villages. The fear was a constant companion—Egypt felt impossibly distant. Yet, step by plodding step, the land changed. The desert grudgingly gave way to scrubland, then the green fringe of the Nile delta. They found a town, it was small and anonymous—Joseph used more gold to rent a room. They settled, they were strangers in a strange land. Joseph found work with his hands, building, repairing—he was a carpenter again. Days turned into months. They lived quietly, listening for news from Judea. The name Herod brought only silence, or stories of his cruelty. They waited—the magi's gold bought time, safety and anonymity. Jesus grew, learning to crawl on a floor far from Bethlehem.

The news came years later, whispered in the marketplace. Herod the Great was dead. The tyrant who had slaughtered Bethlehem's children was gone. Joseph felt a release, a loosening of the knot that had lived inside him since that first flight. That night, the dream returned—the familiar light, the commanding presence. *"Joseph. Rise. Take the child and his mother. Return to the land of Israel. Those who sought the child's life are dead."* Relief washed over him. Home—they could go home—finally. He packed quickly. The journey back was long, but lighter. Their fear was replaced by hope. For the first time in years, they felt safe. They crossed the Sinai and entered Judea. Joseph aimed for Bethlehem, their ancestral home but news traveled ahead of them. At a well near Hebron, travelers spoke in hushed tones. "Archelaus," one man spat. "Herod's son. Worse than the father, they say. Already bloodies his hands in Jerusalem." Joseph's blood ran cold. Judea under Archelaus was a trap. The fear surged back—where could they go? Where was safe? He lay down that night near Bethel, his mind churning.

That night, the light returned, it was gentle, but firm. "*Joseph. Turn aside. Go to Galilee. Settle there.*" Galilee—under Herod Antipas, another of the old king's sons, but known as less volatile—safer. They would be away from Jerusalem and Archelaus's reach. Joseph obeyed without hesitation. He turned the donkey north and they traveled through the hills, avoiding the main roads again. They reached a small town nestled in the hills of Galilee—Nazareth, Joseph's own town. It was familiar ground, a safe place to live and raise their son. He found a house, it was smaller than the one he'd once planned but it was perfect for them. He built a small workshop behind teir house and took up his tools again. He built tables, doors, yokes and crosses. He built a life for his family. He watched the boy, Jesus, play in the dust of the Nazareth street. The danger had passed—for now. The run was over. The carpenter's son was home.

The Carpenter's Son

The dust of Nazareth hung thick in the air, stirred by sandaled feet and the hooves of Roman patrols passing through. It coated the simple stone houses, settled on market goods, and lined the creases around weary eyes. Each breath tasted of grit, a constant reminder of the dry land and the struggle to coax life from it. Inside one modest home, shielded imperfectly from the pervasive grime, Mary smoothed Jesus' dark hair. He was seven, all sharp angles and wide, serious eyes that seemed to absorb everything, missing nothing of the world outside or the tensions within. "Tell me again, Mother," he whispered, his voice barely audible over the familiar backdrop. The sounds of his siblings arguing over chores or clattering dishes was constant. "About the angel."

Mary glanced towards the workshop door where Joseph labored, the rhythmic sound of his mallet steady against wood, a counterpoint to the children's noise. She lowered her voice, pulling him closer. "He came in the night, Jesus. Bright, like captured lightning. So bright it hurt to look, yet filled the whole room. He called me favored. Said God was with me." Her fingers traced the line of his cheek, rough from play and sun. "He said I would have a son, conceived by the Holy Spirit. That you would be great, the Son of the Most High. That God would give you the throne of David." She described the cold fear that seized her, the crushing awe that followed, the difficult journey south to see Elizabeth, the shared wonder and confirmation as their miraculous pregnancies unfolded side by side.

Jesus absorbed this, a familiar warmth spreading through him, deep and quiet. It explained the feeling, the *knowing*, that vibrated beneath his skin like the desert wind, stronger at times—a quiet resonance when he prayed alone under the stars. He wasn't just the carpenter's son—he was *chosen*. He felt the weight of it, even then, a responsibility he couldn't name but carried like a hidden stone. "And Father Joseph?" he asked, his gaze flickering towards the workshop, drawn by the sound of the mallet—the man whose shadow fell long over their lives.

Mary's expression softened with love and a trace of sorrow, a look Jesus recognized but didn't fully grasp. "Joseph was troubled. Deeply. He thought...he thought the worst of me. That I had been unfaithful." She paused, the memory still sharp. "But an angel came to him too, in a dream. Told him not to be afraid, that you were from the Holy Spirit. That you would save people from their sins." She squeezed his small hand, her own work-roughened. "He took us in. He protects us. He works hard, sunup to sundown, for all of us." She watched Joseph's shadow move behind the thin curtain separating the living space from the workshop, a constant, solid presence, yet one marked by a quiet burden.

Joseph emerged moments later, wiping sawdust from his beard and coarse tunic. He saw Mary and Jesus talking, heads close, the boy's expression intense and focused. A familiar knot tightened in his chest. He loved the boy fiercely, taught him the craft with patient hands and treated him as his own flesh. He felt pride swell when Jesus mastered a new joint, satisfaction warmed him when the boy handed him a perfectly planed board—smooth as water. Yet, the words Mary spoke in confidence, the boy's own quiet certainty when he spoke of God, the way his eyes sometimes looked beyond the wood and stone of Nazareth…they were a thorn, a constant, subtle ache. *God is his true father.* Joseph shoved the thought down, a daily practice as ingrained as sharpening a chisel. "Jesus. Judas. Wood needs splitting. Now. Old Man Ezra's olive press repair won't wait, and he pays promptly." His voice carried the weariness of the day already half gone.

Life unfolded in the steady, unyielding rhythm of work, family, and faith. Days began before dawn with prayers recited in the cool darkness, voices murmuring ancient words. Then came chores: fetching water from the crowded well, the heavy jars straining young shoulders; grinding grain between stones, a monotonous, muscle-aching task; tending the small garden plot behind the house where herbs and a few vegetables struggled in the poor soil. The air filled with the comforting scent of baking bread and the sharp tang of olive oil. Joachim and Anna, Mary's parents, visited often from the nearby village, their faces deeply lined by sun and a lifetime of faith. They brought news from Sepphoris, shared simple meals of lentils and bread, and doted on Jesus, whispering prayers over him, their eyes holding the same awe Mary's sometimes did, a look that unsettled Joseph. They told him stories of Abraham leaving Ur for a land unseen, of Moses confronting Pharaoh with nothing but a staff and God's word, of David tending sheep before becoming king, of the Prophets who spoke with fire of a Messiah, a deliverer who would restore Israel's glory. Jesus listened intently, his gaze fixed—the pieces fitting together in his mind like the intricate joinery he learned in the workshop. They were speaking of *Him*. The conviction settled deeper each time, a quiet certainty that felt less like belief and more like memory.

His siblings noticed his difference. He worked hard alongside them in Joseph's workshop, planing wood until his palms blistered, fitting joints with careful precision, carrying heavy beams that made even the older boys grunt. He obeyed Joseph and Mary without complaint, his tasks completed thoroughly. He played games of knucklebones in the dust, ran through the barley fields at harvest and helped gather olives until his fingers were stained black. But there was a stillness about him, a gravity that felt out of place in their rough-and-tumble world of scraped knees and loud arguments. He observed their frequent squabbles over tools, tasks, or perceived slights with a detached calm, rarely joining the fray unless pressed. When disputes arose, Jesus often spoke with unsettling clarity, his words cutting through the noise to the heart of the matter, exposing pettiness or selfishness, leaving them feeling judged rather than consoled. Judas, sharp-tongued, quick to anger, and fiercely competitive, bore the brunt of this perceived superiority. He resented the implied correction, the unspoken standard Jesus seemed to embody effortlessly.

"Think you know better than everyone, don't you?" Judas sneered one hot afternoon after Jesus had pointed out a flaw in a table leg Judas had cut, a slight angle that would make the piece rock. Sweat streaked the dust on Judas's face, his eyes narrowed. "Always right, the *Son of God*." He spat the title like an insult, a challenge flung into the stifling air of the workshop thick with the smell of resin and sweat. Their other brothers froze, with their tools pausing mid-motion.

James and Simon exchanged uneasy glances, their hands still on the bench they were assembling, their faces tight. Joses kicked at the dirt floor, scuffing his sandal, avoiding eye contact with either brother. Lydia and Assia, bringing water skins to relieve their thirst, watched silently from the doorway, their young faces anxious, sensing the storm.

"I only said the leg is uneven, Judas," Jesus replied, his voice level, meeting his brother's glare without flinching. He picked up the offending piece, holding it so the weak angle caught the light slanting through the window. "See here? It needs trimming. Otherwise, the table will wobble. It's not about knowing better. It's about the work being sound. About Ezra getting a good table for his money." His explanation was practical and reasonable.

"We know what you meant," Judas snapped, snatching the leg back with a jerky motion. "Holier than thou. Too good for mistakes, are you?" His voice dripped with sarcasm. "Maybe your *real* father doesn't make mistakes, but here in the dirt, with the rest of us mortals, we do." The words hung, heavy and poisonous.

Joseph's voice cracked like a whip from the doorway where he'd been observing unseen, his own face darkening with anger. "Enough! Work, or find another roof over your head!" His gaze, as it swept over them, lingered on Jesus. He saw the boy's quiet confidence, the absence of defensiveness, and it grated like sand in a wound. It was a constant reminder of the divine claim Joseph could never compete with, the claim that made him feel like a mere custodian, a guardian, not a true father entitled to a son's simple and uncomplicated respect. The workshop fell silent except for the reluctant rasp of saws and the hesitant thud of mallets, the tension thick enough to choke on, settling over them like the ever-present dust.

The Roman presence was a constant pressure, a boot heel on the neck of the village. Taxes were heavy, levied on land, goods, even heads, collected by hard-faced publicans under the watchful eyes of legionaries. Patrols marched through Nazareth regularly, their segmented armor gleaming dully under the harsh sun, their expressions bored and contemptuous as they surveyed the dusty, impoverished streets. They took what they wanted from the market stalls – the best fruit, fresh bread, a jug of wine—their authority was absolute, backed by the glint of steel. Rebellion simmered in the surrounding hills and whispered about in hushed tones behind closed doors. Zealots preached violent resistance in hidden gullies and the Empire's brutal answer to dissent was crucifixion, a spectacle of prolonged agony designed to terrify. Demand for execution scaffolds was high. Joseph's workshop, known for solid, durable work, reluctantly secured the grim contract. It meant steady pay, survival through lean times, food on the table. Joseph took the work, his face grim, his shoulders slumped under the invisible weight. He argued the point with himself late at night: It was wood—it was craft—it fed Mary, the children and kept a roof over their heads. He focused on the grain, the joinery and the smooth finish, pouring his skill into the grim task. He tried not to think about the screams that would soon echo around these beams he shaped, the bodies that would hang from them until they rotted under the sun, a grotesque warning to others. He tried not to see the crosses as anything but timber and labor, a job like any other.

Jesus, now a young man with strong shoulders shaped by years of labor, helped his father and brothers haul the heavy timbers from the yard into the workshop. The scent of fresh-cut pine and oak mingled with the ever-present dust. The wood was unyielding, demanding effort, each beam a substantial weight. One day, assembling the rough-hewn components for a batch—the tall upright posts and the heavy horizontal patibula—Jesus paused. He ran a calloused hand over the intersection point, the place where the patibulum would be secured with ropes or nails, the place where a man's back would be pressed against the grain. The wood felt cold, impersonal under his touch, yet charged with a terrible future purpose, a conduit for unimaginable suffering.

"This looks like a terrible and painful way to die," he said quietly, the words dropping into the workshop air like stones into still water. The rhythmic sounds of sawing and hammering ceased abruptly. Judas snorted, a harsh, dismissive sound, shaking his head as if brushing off a fly. James looked away, suddenly fascinated by a knot in the timber he was planing, his face noticeably pale. Simon wiped sweat from his forehead with a dusty forearm, his eyes fixed intently on the packed earth floor.

Joseph straightened slowly, his own back aching from the unrelenting work. He wiped sweat from his brow with the back of his hand, leaving a smear of sawdust across his temple. He met his son's gaze, seeing not just the capable carpenter's apprentice, but the young man who spoke of God as his Father with unnerving directness, whose eyes sometimes held a knowledge far beyond his years. A flicker of the old jealousy surfaced, quickly drowned by a profound weariness and a deeper, colder dread. He remembered the Law, the words ingrained since childhood, recited in the synagogue. "Yes, son," Joseph said, his voice rough, like gravel dragged over stone. "Very painful. Slow. Humiliating." He took a breath, the air thick with dust and the scent of doom emanating from the timbers. "And anyone who is hanged upon a tree is accursed of God." He spoke the scripture—like a hard, immutable fact, a boundary stone marking the utter horror and divine rejection inherent in this thing they built. He saw a shadow pass over Jesus' face, a deep, unfathomable sorrow that seemed too old for his years, a sorrow that recognized the truth and the terrible contradiction it presented to his own destiny. Joseph looked away first, unable to bear that look, the weight of it was too much. He picked up his mallet with unnecessary force, the sound sharp and final in the heavy silence. "Get the pegs. This one's ready for fitting. Work to do."

The resentment among the brothers festered, fed by Judas' bitterness and the others' unease around Jesus' strangeness, his unsettling calm, his direct speech that felt like judgment. Shared meals became strained affairs, the air thick with unspoken words. Jesus's quiet presence at the low table felt like an accusation to Judas, a silent judgment to James and Simon. Joses tried to stay neutral, often disappearing to tend the family's single donkey or mend a fence. Their sisters, Lydia and Assia, moved quietly around the edges, fetching and carrying, sensing the tension like animals scenting a storm, their eyes wide and watchful. Mary remained Jesus' anchor, her faith unwavering, a quiet strength in the face of the household's slow fracture. She saw the burden he carried, the knowledge shaping him, the loneliness that came with his purpose, isolating him even within the crowded house. She argued with Joseph late at night, their voices hushed but intense in the dark room after the children slept.

"He is who he is, Joseph. We cannot change it. We were chosen for this." She touched his arm, feeling the tension in his muscles, the weariness in his bones.

"Chosen?" Joseph's voice was low and strained, full of decades of suppressed turmoil, the words scraping out. "To feel like a stranger in my own home? To see my other sons sneer at their brother? To build…those things?" He gestured violently towards the workshop wall, beyond which the cursed timbers lay stacked, waiting. "He speaks of God's kingdom, Mary. What kingdom comes from *this*? From death and curses? What kind of deliverance is born from a carpenter's shop making instruments of torture? Where is the throne of David in this dust?" The questions hung in the dark room, unanswered and echoing the doubt that gnawed at him.

Their annual journeys to Jerusalem for Passover became increasingly fraught, a pilgrimage shadowed by tension. The city teemed with pilgrims from across Judea and beyond, a noisy, jostling mass. Roman soldiers stood watchful on every corner, atop the Antonia Fortress, their eyes scanning the crowds for any signs of trouble. While his siblings mingled with cousins from the south and explored the bustling markets filled with exotic spices and fabrics, or simply rested their feet after the long walk, Jesus spent hours in the vast Temple courts. He didn't just observe the rituals; he positioned himself near the teachers, listening intently to the heated debates of the Pharisees, the intricate interpretations of the scribes, the teachings of the rabbis. He asked questions—probing, insightful questions that cut through layers of tradition and legalism, questions that astonished the teachers with their depth and understanding of scripture, questions that exposed contradictions or hollow practices. His answers, when he offered them, were simple yet profound, rooted in scripture but pointing towards something beyond the rigid letter of the Law, a spirit of compassion or justice that often silenced his elders. His siblings found it deeply embarrassing, drawing unwanted attention to their family group. "Showing off again," Judas muttered darkly as they walked the crowded, narrow streets after one such encounter, jostled by the crowd. "Thinks he's better than the learned rabbis. Makes us look like ignorant fools from Galilee." James nodded agreement, his face flushed with embarrassment. Simon kept his eyes down, shoulders hunched as if trying to disappear.

They visited Zechariah and Elizabeth in the hill country of Judea whenever possible, a welcome respite from Nazareth. The air was clearer there, cooler, the pace slower and the landscape starker. Their son John, even as a youth, was a force of nature—wild-haired, intense, his lean frame wrapped in rough cloth, burning with a fierce, uncompromising devotion that bordered on ferocity. He spent days fasting in the caves, praying aloud on the windswept ridges and walking the barren hills as if driven by an internal fire. He was drawn magnetically to Jesus from their earliest meetings. They walked the rocky paths together, talking for hours of scripture, of Isaiah's suffering servant and Malachi's messenger, of the state of Israel groaning under the Roman boot, of the corruption they both sensed festering within the Temple hierarchy, of the desperate need for purity and for true repentance before God. John's words were like fire and brimstone, his conviction absolute and his gestures were sharp and demanding. He preached repentance fiercely to anyone who would listen—shepherds tending flocks on the sparse hillsides, travelers passing near the smaller tributaries of the Jordan, his voice raw with urgency, warning of wrath and demanding change. One golden afternoon, overlooking a deep, barren valley etched by wind and time, Jesus placed a hand on John's shoulder. John flinched slightly at the unexpected contact, unused to such familiarity, but met Jesus's steady, calm gaze, a contrast to his own restless intensity.

"Your voice will prepare the way, John," Jesus said, his tone leaving no room for doubt, a statement of fact as solid as the rock beneath their feet. "When the time is full, when I begin my Father's work, yours will be a crucial task. Make the path straight. Call the people back to truth. Prepare their hearts for what is coming."

John stared at him, his eyes wide, his usual fierceness momentarily stilled, replaced by a dawning and terrifying awe. He didn't question it—he felt the truth of it resonate deep within his spirit, a confirmation of the fire that consumed him, giving it terrifying focus. He simply nodded once, a sharp, decisive movement, the fierce light burning even brighter in his eyes. "I will be ready. I will not fail. The axe is already at the root."

Time passed relentlessly, marked by seasons of planting and harvest, the rhythm of carpentry and the cycle of feasts. Joseph aged visibly under the unceasing demands of life. The lines on his face deepened into crevices, his once-strong hands grew more knotted and stiff, the joints swollen. A persistent cough settled in his chest, rattling him awake at night, leaving him breathless and weak after even moderate exertion. He worked less in the workshop, often sitting in a patch of sun outside the door with a blanket over his knees, watching Jesus lead his brothers in the craft. The skill Jesus possessed was undeniable, almost uncanny. He could look at a rough log and see the bowl, the stool, the beam within it, his mind shaping the wood before the tools touched it. He made joints seamless, invisible, as if the wood grew together. He shaped curves that flowed like water, his tools—chisel, plane, adze—an effortless extension of his will. Joseph felt pride swell in his chest watching him, a master craftsman emerging from the boy he'd taught. But alongside it grew a profound distance, a gulf widened by Jesus' increasingly frequent talk of his destiny, of the Kingdom he would bring—talk that had shifted over the years. He spoke less now of David's throne and military victory, more of seeds falling on different soils, of a shepherd leaving ninety-nine sheep to find the one lost, of a kingdom not of this world, built on love and sacrifice—concepts that confused practical Joseph and alarmed his brothers, sounding like weakness or madness.

One harsh winter—cold and wet, a fever swept through Nazareth, a ruthless sickness that claimed the old and the weak. Joseph, already weakened by years of labor and the relentless cough that stole his breath, was struck hard. He burned with heat, shivered with chills and struggled for each rasping breath. Mary and the children took turns nursing him, wiping his brow with cool cloths and forcing sips of thin broth between his cracked lips. The workshop fell silent, tools cold and unused. Jesus sat by his bedside for long hours, holding the old carpenter's work-roughened hand, feeling the thinness of the skin over bone and the fading pulse beneath his fingers. Joseph's breathing was labored and wet, his eyes clouded with pain and something else—a lifetime of unspoken conflict, love, fear, and a dawning resignation. The single oil lamp flickered on the walls, casting long, dancing shadows.

"You've been a good son," Joseph rasped, the words costing him immense effort, each one a gasp, punctuated by the rattle in his chest. "A good carpenter. Strong hands. Good mind." He paused, gathering strength, his gaze fixing on Jesus' face, searching the features he had watched grow from childhood and the face he had raised as his own. "This…path you see…this kingdom you talk of." He struggled, the words thick and laden with a father's desperate concern cutting through the years of jealousy to the core of his protective love. "Is it worth it, son? The cost? The…the pain I see ahead?" His eyes pleaded for reassurance, for a different path.

Jesus' expression was solemn, filled with a love that transcended blood, a deep respect for the man who had shielded him, taught him and provided or him, a man whose quiet strength had been his earthly foundation. Yet also present was a profound, unshakeable resolve, a certainty that filled the small room, as tangible as the chill air. "The cost is necessary, Father," he said, his voice low and clear, unwavering. "The scriptures must be fulfilled. It is the will of my Father in Heaven. The pain…it is part of the path laid out. There is no other way." He didn't look away, holding Joseph's fading gaze.

Joseph closed his eyes—a single tear tracked through the dust and sweat on his weathered cheek, carving a clean path. *My Father in Heaven.* The words, even now, at the end, were a final, quiet blow, a reminder of the claim he could never share and the ultimate distance. He squeezed Jesus' hand weakly, a ghost of his former grip, the grip that had guided small hands holding their first tools. "Then…do it well." His breath gasped, rasped wetly, then slowed, becoming shallow and uneven, each inhalation a struggle. Later that night, the house bitterly cold despite the small brazier, surrounded by his weeping family—Mary clinging to his hand, her face a mask of grief, his sons bowed with the weight of sudden responsibility and loss, his daughters sobbing quietly into their shawls—Joseph, the humble carpenter who had raised the Son of God, breathed his last, a final, soft sigh escaping his lips. The house filled with the raw, animal sound of loss, the end of an era, the breaking of a chain that had anchored Jesus to Nazareth.

The mourning period passed, marked by prayers, shared memories tinged with regret, and the stark, echoing absence of Joseph's presence. The workshop felt cavernously empty, unnaturally silent without the steady rhythm of his mallet, the familiar sound of his pragmatic voice settling disputes or instructing on a tricky joint. Dust settled thickly on his carefully maintained tools. Jesus worked there alone now. His brothers avoided the space entirely, their grief hardening into a cold barrier, mixed with resentment and perhaps fear of the responsibility Jesus now embodied as the eldest male. Judas watched him with dark, unforgiving eyes from the yard, from the doorway, never offering help, never speaking unless necessity demanded it, his presence was a constant, brooding shadow. Only Mary shared his space, moving quietly, sweeping sawdust into a pile, or simply sitting in the corner mending clothes or weaving, a silent communion of shared loss and the heavy, unspoken purpose that now pressed down solely on her son's shoulders. The air between them buzzed with things that could not be said, with prophecies recalled and futures feared.

One morning, as the first pale light touched the hills east of Nazareth, washing the stones in a cool gray, Jesus did not go to the workshop. He stood at the edge of the village, where the well-trodden path led down towards the Jordan valley, disappearing into the haze. He looked out, not at the familiar olive groves silvered by dawn or the distant bulk of Mount Tabor, but towards the river. Towards where John's voice was rising like a clarion call in the wilderness, a sound carried on the wind of prophecy. The words of the prophets—Isaiah's suffering servant bearing the sins of many, Jeremiah's lament over a faithless people, the psalms of David crying out from depths of despair—echoed in his mind, intertwined with his mother's stories of angels and stars. Joseph's dying question about the cost, the visceral feel of the cursed execution wood beneath his hands. The vengeful God of his childhood understanding, the God who demanded sacrifice, who cursed the hanged, who spoke through fire and flood. That God demanded action, obedience unto death, a cup that could not pass. The time for waiting, for learning, for the quiet, hidden life of Nazareth, was irrevocably over. The fullness of time had come, pressing upon him with the weight of the world.

He turned back to the house. Mary stood in the doorway, wrapped in a worn shawl against the morning chill, her face pale but resolute, etched with lines of profound sorrow and steely faith. She knew—she had always known this day would come. She had felt its approach in the deeper stillness of his prayers, in the new, focused intensity of his gaze—in the way he handled Joseph's tools with a sense of finality. She didn't try to stop him. She didn't plead or weep. She simply met his eyes across the small yard and nodded, a small, fierce movement, a mother's surrender to a will greater than her own. Her eyes were dark pools in the dawn light, filled with an unbearable love and a terror she could not voice—the cost laid bare before her in that single look.

Jesus gathered a small bundle—a spare tunic, his cloak, a waterskin and a little bread wrapped in cloth. He looked at his home, the simple stone structure where he'd grown from boy to man, learned a trade, known a father's rough affection and a mother's unwavering love. His gaze swept over the workshop, the place where he'd learned the craft that would one day build his own deathbed, the place of Joseph's legacy and his brothers' resentment, now silent and still. He saw Judas watching him from the deep shadow of the olive press, his expression unreadable, a dark silhouette of withheld anger and bitterness. James looked away quickly, busying himself unnecessarily with a water bucket, his movements jerky. Simon stared fixedly at the ground, shoulders hunched as if against a blow. Lydia and Assia stood behind Mary, weeping silently, their faces buried in their shawls, their grief for their father mingling with the shock of this departure.

No farewells were spoken. Words were inadequate, bridges burned long ago by resentment and the isolating, immense weight of destiny. The gulf was too wide, the understanding too fractured. He turned his back on Nazareth, on the dust and the memories and the fractured family, on the life that had shaped his body but could not contain his spirit. His stride was long and purposeful, eating up the path that led down from the hills towards the river and the wild prophet shouting repentance. He walked towards the confrontation he was born for, the work his Father demanded. The desert sun climbed higher, beating down harsh and unforgiving, like the demanding eye of the God who called him forth. The path ahead promised pain, betrayal, abandonment, and a terrible, necessary sacrifice on the cursed wood he knew so well, wood that felt cold and final in his memory. He walked into it, the weight of Heaven was heavy on his shoulders, the silence of his earthly home, the echo of his brothers' turned backs and his sisters' muffled sobs, ringing in his ears like a dirge. The reckoning had begun—the carpenter's son walked towards the cross.

False Witness

Dust swirled down the narrow street, coating the sun-bleached stone buildings. Outside the shaded colonnade, a crowd gathered, drawn by the lone figure speaking. Jesus stood calm, his simple clothes stark against the ornate robes of the men confronting him. The Pharisee leader, Zadok, stepped forward, his hand resting near the knife concealed beneath his sash. His eyes were like hard stones. "Your words poison the people," he stated, his voice low and dangerous. "You break our law."

Jesus met his gaze. "The law serves the people. It should not crush them." His quiet certainty filled the space.

Zadok's lip curled. He glanced at his companions, their faces were tight with anger. One shifted, his hand moving towards his own weapon. The crowd held its breath. "Blasphemer," Zadok hissed. The word hung in the hot air. He took another step, closing the gap. Jesus didn't move. Zadok's hand flashed, drawing the knife—not at Jesus, but plunging it deep into his own thigh. He cried out, collapsing. "He attacked me!" Zadok gasped, blood soaking his robe. Then panic erupted. The other Pharisees surged forward, seizing Jesus as the crowd scattered. Zadok's pained smile held a grim triumph.

The Third Day Draws Blood

The desert wind scraped grit against the limestone walls of Jerusalem. Inside a cramped, smoke-filled room, the air hung heavier than the despair. Thomas traced a crack in the rough-hewn table, "It's tonight. Or never. They'll move him tomorrow, seal the tomb proper, or worse, dump him in a common pit."

Peter stared into the weak flame of a single oil lamp. Shadows danced across his face, deepening the lines of exhaustion and grief. "He said three days. He promised. But the Romans..." He slammed a fist down, making the lamp shudder. "They saw him die. We all saw him die. Dead men don't rise."

"Dead men *stay* dead," Andrew muttered, sharpening a short, wicked-looking knife. The scrape of stone on metal was the only sound for a moment. "But the people...they listened. They believed him. If they think he rose...maybe it keeps something alive. Maybe it sparks something."

Mary Magdalene watched them from the corner. Her eyes, red-rimmed but dry now, held a fierce light. "He *is* alive." Her voice was low and rough. "I felt it. Before dawn yesterday...a warmth, like the sun breaking through storm clouds, but inside."

Peter turned on her, his grief sharpening into anger. "Warmth? Mary, they broke him! They nailed him up like a common thief! We buried him ourselves! Wrapped him, carried him and laid him in Joseph's tomb. Cold. Still. Dead." He spat the word. "This...this plan is madness. But it's the only madness left."

The plan was simple, born of desperation. The massive stone sealing the tomb entrance, the Roman guards doubled since the crucifixion on orders from a nervous Pilate—these were the obstacles. Joseph of Arimathea, who owned the tomb, provided details. A hidden crack in the rock face near the tomb, large enough for a man to squeeze through, known only to the quarrymen who cut the tomb decades before. They would approach under cover of deepest night, use the crack, retrieve the body, and vanish into the wilderness before the guards knew they were there. Then, they would 'discover' the empty tomb at dawn—a lie to give truth weight— a theft to create a miracle.

The Kidron Valley breathed cold air. There was no moon and clouds smothered the stars. The disciples moved like ghosts through the olive groves below the city wall. Six of them: Peter, Thomas, Andrew, John, Philip, and Mary. They carried ropes, a stretcher of rough canvas, and tools—iron bars, heavy hammers wrapped in cloth to muffle sound. Fear was a sour taste in every mouth.

"They patrol in pairs," John whispered, his voice barely audible. "Every half-hour. The main guard is four men at the tomb entrance. Torches."

They heard the measured tread of nailed sandals on the path above before they saw the flicker of torchlight. They pressed themselves into the gnarled roots of an ancient olive tree, their hearts pounding relentlessly in their chests. The light passed, illuminating the grim faces of two legionaries for a fleeting second—the sound faded.

"Closer than last time," Philip whispered.

They skirted the base of the cliff where the wealthy buried their dead. The air smelled of damp earth and crushed herbs. Mary led them unerringly to a spot where the rock face seemed seamless. She pushed aside a thick curtain of thorny scrub. A dark slit, barely wider than a man's shoulders, gaped in the stone. "Here."

One by one, they squeezed in. The passage was tight, jagged rock scraping their skin and cloth. The air inside was stale, cold, smelling of dust and something else—a faint, unsettling sweetness—myrrh. The tunnel descended, twisting slightly. After twenty feet of suffocating darkness, they emerged into a small, low-ceilinged antechamber, part of the tomb complex. Ahead, a low doorway opened into the main burial chamber—utter blackness lay beyond.

Peter lit a small clay lamp, shielding the flame with his hand. Its feeble light pushed back the gloom, revealing the arched ceiling of the antechamber. He gestured towards the inner doorway. Thomas and Andrew moved forward, hammers and pry bars ready, eyes fixed on the black void where the body should lie.

Peter stepped through first, lamp held high. The light spilled into the burial chamber, illuminating the smooth stone bench cut into the far wall.

It was empty.

The stretcher fell from Philip's hands with a soft thud. John choked back a gasp. Thomas stumbled forward, his hammer forgotten, his hand reaching out to touch the cold, bare limestone shelf. Only the stark white outlines of the burial shroud remained, collapsed in on itself like a discarded chrysalis. There was no body—no sign of struggle—just emptiness.

"Gone?" Andrew's voice cracked. "But... how? The stone…"

"They found the crack, our way in." Peter whispered, horror dawning. "They knew. They moved him. It's a trap." Panic flared in his eyes. He spun towards the entrance tunnel. "Out! Now!"

A harsh shout echoed from the antechamber. Torchlight flared, blinding after the near-darkness. "Halt! In the name of Caesar!"

Roman soldiers—two of them, short swords drawn, shields raised, blocking the tunnel exit. Their faces were hard, professional. They must have heard the noise, seen the light.

"Drop your weapons!" the lead legionary barked, his Latin accent thick. "On the ground! Now!"

The disciples froze—Peter still held the lamp. Thomas gripped his hammer. Andrew's knife was half-drawn. The stretcher lay useless. The empty shelf mocked them.

Mary stepped forward, shielding Peter slightly. "Please," she said, her voice surprisingly steady. "There is no body. See? The tomb is empty. Just as He said it would be."

The legionary sneered. "Empty because thieves like you already did your work? Move aside, woman." He advanced a step, his companion flanking him. The confined space crackled with imminent violence. The narrow tunnel offered no room for maneuver, only a brutal, close-quarters slaughter.

Peter's face contorted—the despair of the past few days, the terror of the arrest, the crushing weight of the crucifixion, the hopelessness of their failed plan—it boiled over. Seeing the empty tomb, faced with Roman soldiers, the fragile thread of reason snapped. He saw not soldiers, but the faceless power that had murdered his Lord. He saw the sneer of Caiaphas, the indifference of Pilate. The vengeful fist of a distant, uncaring God squeezing the life from them all.

"No!" Peter roared. It wasn't defiance, it was the raw scream of a cornered animal. He hurled the small clay lamp at the lead soldier's face.

The soldier flinched, raising his shield. The lamp shattered against the bronze, spattering burning oil. In the sudden flare and confusion, chaos erupted.

Andrew lunged, his knife flashing towards the soldier's exposed leg. Thomas swung his heavy hammer wildly. The second legionary shoved forward, his short sword stabbing low and fast.

Mary screamed, "Peter, no!"

It was too late. The confined space became a nightmare of thrashing limbs, grunts of pain, and the terrible clang of metal on metal. Peter, driven by a berserk fury born of grief and terror, grabbed the fallen iron pry bar. He swung it like a club, aiming for the head of the soldier blinded by the burning oil. The soldier ducked, the bar glanced off his helmet with a jarring clang. Off-balance, Peter stumbled forward.

The second soldier, recovering from Thomas's clumsy hammer blow, saw his opening. He reversed his grip on his sword and rammed the pommel hard into Peter's temple.

Peter went down like a felled ox. He hit the stone floor hard.

Thomas cried out, swinging his hammer again, but the lead soldier, blinking oil from his eyes, was ready now. He sidestepped the blow and drove his sword forward, not to kill, but to disable. The point punched deep into Thomas's thigh. Thomas shrieked, collapsing, blood instantly darkening his robe.

Andrew froze, his knife held uselessly. Philip and John stood paralyzed. The fight had lasted seconds. The Romans stood panting, weapons ready, eyes scanning the defeated group. The first soldier kicked Peter's pry bar away. The other kept his sword pointed at Thomas, writhing on the floor.

The lead soldier spat on the ground near Peter's unconscious form. "Stupid peasants." He looked towards the empty burial slab, his expression unreadable in the flickering torchlight. "Empty. Just like the centurion said at shift change. Said the ground shook before dawn. Guards fled like scared rabbits." He shook his head, a flicker of unease crossing his features. "Crazy disciples and your dead prophets." He gestured sharply with his sword. "Bind them. All of them. Pilate will want words with tomb robbers."

As the soldiers roughly tied their hands, Mary crawled to Peter—his breathing was shallow, a dark bruise already swelling on his temple. Blood trickled from Thomas's leg, pooling on the ancient stone. She looked past the soldiers, past the ropes cutting into her wrists, to the empty slab. The faint scent of myrrh hung in the air, mixed now with the iron tang of blood and the acrid smell of the busted lamp oil. The cold stone pressed against her knees. The soldiers' voices were harsh commands in the echoing chamber.

He had promised life. He had conquered the grave. But in this hollow victory, witnessed only by the defeated and the captors, death had drawn fresh blood. The tomb was empty, yet the heavy weight of the world, of Rome, of a God whose methods felt like cruelty, pressed down with suffocating force. Dawn was coming, but it brought no light, only the prospect of chains and the Praetorium's judgment. The miracle had happened. And they had missed it—utterly—tragically. The sound of Thomas's pained whimpers and the scrape of the soldiers' sandals on stone were the only answers the empty tomb gave.

The Silence of Heaven

The dust of the Jerusalem road tasted like defeat. Barak ben Levi spat, the grit grinding between his teeth. His hands, bound raw behind him, throbbed with every jolting step the Roman guards forced. The crossbeam strapped to his shoulders felt heavier than the weight of his choices, heavier than the memory of his burning village in Galilee. It seemed like a lifetime ago. He'd been a fisherman, hauling nets heavy with silver scales under a hot sun, dreaming of a free Israel. Then the tax collectors came, backed by Roman blades. His father argued—they cut him down in his own doorway. Barak watched, fourteen years old, hidden in the grain store. The fire they set consumed his mother, his sisters, the only life he knew. Freedom stopped being a dream that day. It became an oath written in ash and blood. He joined the rebels hiding in the hills near Magdala. Ambushing patrols—stealing Roman grain and planting knives in collaborators' backs. He fought for a God who demanded vengeance, a God whose silence felt like approval for the blood on his hands. Tonight's raid on the garrison stables near Jericho was meant to steal horses—it went wrong. A sentry saw them and swords clashed in the moonless yard. Barak fought like a cornered wolf, but Roman discipline was a wall, impenetrable—they overwhelmed him. Now, the road led only to Skull Hill. He'd die cursing Rome, cursing the God who abandoned His people. He'd die a rebel.

Heshvan the Quick sucked air through broken teeth. Every breath scraped like sand on stone. The rope binding his wrists bit deep. He kept his head down, watching his own shuffling feet kick up dust. Bethlehem—that's where it started—not with grand ideals, just hunger. His father carved wood—beautiful things, useless things. Heshvan craved more than dust and poverty. He tried apprenticing to a stonemason, but his hands lacked the patience. He drove carts, but the pay was scraps. He gambled, losing more than he won. Then came Rivka—sweet Rivka with eyes like dark pools. He promised her the moon, delivered only dust and poverty. When the baby came sickly, needing medicine he couldn't afford, the desperation turned sharp. He stole a merchant's purse in the market. He got away clean, the thrill was better than wine. He stole again, and again—from merchants—from pilgrims—from anyone who looked like they had coin to spare. He wasn't political, he didn't hate Rome. He just hated being poor, being powerless, watching his child cough itself weak. He became good, very good with quick hands and quicker feet. He knew every alley in Jerusalem but even the quick get caught eventually. He broke into a rich Pharisee's house with jewels glittering in a locked chest. He picked the lock, silent as a shadow. He almost made it but a servant girl, fetching water, saw him slip out the window. She screamed. The guards were faster than he expected, they broke two of his ribs catching him. Now, the jewels felt like lead in his stomach. He'd die a thief, leaving Rivka alone with a dying child. He'd die knowing he failed them utterly. He'd die afraid.

The cell beneath the Antonia fortress was a tomb cut from living rock. The air was dank, thick with the stench of unwashed bodies, despair, and old blood, it choked Barak's lungs. Iron bars separated the condemned from the guards, but not from each other. Heshvan huddled in a corner, his knees drawn tight, trying to shrink into the stone. Barak paced the small space, like a caged animal radiating fury. Their chains rattled with each turn.

"Stop that noise!" Heshvan hissed, his voice tight with fear.

Barak whirled. "Or what? You'll call the guards, thief? They already know where we are." He spat on the filthy straw near Heshvan's feet. "What pitiful crime landed you here? Stealing bread?"

Heshvan flinched. "Jewels. From a rich man's house."

Barak barked a harsh laugh. "Jewels! While Rome grinds our people into dust? You steal trinkets while they steal our land, our dignity, our lives!" He slammed a fist against the damp stone wall. "I fight them! I bleed for Israel! What do you bleed for? Shiny stones?"

"Food!" Heshvan snapped, surprising himself. "Medicine! For my son! What do you know of it, rebel? Your noble cause burns villages too, doesn't it? Or do only Roman torches count?" He saw the flash of pain in Barak's eyes, the memory of his own burning home. "We all pay," Heshvan muttered, dropping his gaze. "Just different prices."

Barak stared at the smaller man, the thief's words striking a nerve deeper than he'd admit. The fury bled out, replaced by a cold, heavy weariness. He slid down the opposite wall, silence fell, heavier than the chains. The shared doom settled over them. They were just two men, condemned to the same brutal death. Rebel and thief. Their paths, so different, had converged in this stinking pit, leading to the same Roman nails.

Days blurred into an agony of waiting. They were given scraps of food and brackish water. The mocking laughter of the guards echoed in the small cell. News filtered down: Passover crowds swelled the city. A strange preacher, causing trouble, was arrested. Barak dismissed it as just another doomed fool. Heshvan listened, hoping for distraction from the dread coiling in his gut. The sentence came at dawn—crucifixion—open to the public—on Golgotha—Calvary—the place of the skull. The words hung in the cell air, cold and final. They looked at each other then, not as rebel and thief, but as men facing the unimaginable. No words passed between them— none were needed. The shared terror was a language of its own.

The road to Golgotha was like a gauntlet. The sun beat down relentlessly as crowds jeered, spat and threw stones. Roman soldiers shoved them forward. Barak stumbled under the weight of his crossbeam, the rough wood grinding into the raw flesh of his scourged back. He fixed his eyes on the hill ahead, his jaw clenched, drawing on a reservoir of hatred—hatred for Rome—hatred for the God who allowed this—hatred for the weakness of his own failing body. He would not cry out, he would meet the nails with defiance.

Heshvan whimpered, the pain was a white-hot fire consuming him and every step was torture. He saw faces in the crowd—pity, contempt, indifference. He searched desperately for Rivka, for any familiar face, but saw none. Only strangers witnessing his shame. He wanted to disappear. He wanted it to stop. He wanted to beg for mercy he knew wouldn't come. He was drowning in fear.

They reached the flat, barren hilltop. Rough hands threw them down. Barak roared as the crossbeam slammed onto his torn back. Heshvan sobbed. They stripped them naked—the humiliation was absolute. The iron nails were cold against Barak's wrist. He braced, teeth gritted. The hammer blow was an explosion of agony. He screamed, a raw animal sound— again—the other wrist. He arched against the pain. Then the feet—each blow drove the world away in a red haze of suffering.

Heshvan's screams were higher, thinner, pure terror given voice. The nails tore through flesh and bone. The weight dropping onto them as the cross lurched upright stole his breath. He hung, gasping, every nerve ending shrieking. He saw the sky, impossibly blue and indifferent. He saw the soldiers below, casting lots for their clothes. He saw the crowd, still jeering.

Then he saw the third cross. The man in the center. He looked worse than they did—face swollen and bloody, his back a shredded ruin. Yet…

there was a stillness about him, even in his suffering—not defiance like Barak—not terror like Heshvan. A terrible, profound weariness. A sign above his head read: *Jesus of Nazareth, King of the Jews*.

Priests and elders gathered below the center cross. "He saved others!" one mocked, his voice carrying clearly. "Let him save himself if he is God's Anointed! Let him come down now from the cross, and we will believe!"

Barak, panting through the pain, seized the words. Hatred flared—he twisted his head towards the center. "Aren't you the Anointed One?" he rasped, his voice thick with agony and bitterness. "Save yourself! Save us too!" If this man claimed God's power, let him use it! Let him strike the Romans down! Let him end this torment! Where was God's power now? Only pain—only silence—only the vengeful fist of a distant tyrant demanding blood. Barak's demand was a challenge flung at the silent heavens.

Heshvan watched the man in the center—Jesus. He'd heard whispers of a healer, a teacher—a man who spoke of forgiveness. He saw no anger in those pain-filled eyes—only...sorrow? Heshvan looked at Barak, consumed by rage, he looked at the priests, smug in their cruelty. He looked at the soldiers, indifferent and Jesus, hanging broken. A terrible clarity pierced Heshvan's terror. This man was innocent—utterly innocent. He hadn't burned villages, he hadn't stolen jewels—he hung there because... because of men like them? Because of the priests? Because of Rome? The injustice burned brighter than the pain in his wrists.

"Don't you fear God?" Heshvan gasped, his voice a broken whisper directed at Barak, but loud enough in the sudden lull. "We're punished justly. We're getting what our deeds deserve." He drew a shuddering breath, the effort was immense. He turned his head, straining every muscle, to look directly at Jesus. The man's eyes met his, there was no condemnation—only an immense, unbearable depth. "Jesus," Heshvan choked out, the name a plea, "remember me when you come into your kingdom."

A silence fell across the hill—the priests stopped mocking—Barak stopped cursing—even the wind seemed to hold its breath. Jesus turned his head slowly, painfully, towards Heshvan. Blood streaked his face, mingling with sweat and dust. His lips moved—the words were faint, rasping, but clear as struck crystal in the stillness: "Truly I tell you...today you will be with me...in paradise."

A sob escaped Heshvan—not of pain, but of a profound, unexpected release. Paradise? After this? With *him*? The promise settled over him, it was a cool balm against the fire consuming his body. He closed his eyes—a fragile peace, fragile as a bird's wing, touched his shattered spirit. He hung on, the agony still present, but somehow…different—bearable.

Barak stared, incredulous. Paradise? Now? With the nails biting deep? The man was deluded, or mocking. The bitterness surged back, hotter than the sun beating down on them. He spat towards the center cross, a futile gesture of contempt. He looked away, back to the mocking priests, the indifferent soldiers, the uncaring sky. The vengeful God he knew offered no paradise—only the rope—only the nails—only the endless silence.

Hours crawled by, the agony became a constant state of being. The sun climbed higher, then began its slow descent. Barak drifted in a haze of pain and rage. Heshvan clung to the whispered promise, a lifeline in the suffocating torment. The man in the center spoke only once more, a cry that shattered the air: "My God, my God, why have you forsaken me?" Barak heard his own despair echoed in that terrible scream. He saw it as proof—proof of the abandonment—proof that God was uncaring and there was no paradise. Then, a final whisper: "It is finished." The man's head dropped.

Suddenly, the world lurched and the ground beneath Golgotha heaved violently. The crosses swayed like reeds in a gale. Rocks split with sharp cracks and dust choked the air. Barak cried out, raw fear momentarily overwhelming pain as his cross groaned under the strain. Heshvan gasped, clinging to the wood. The sky, impossibly, began to darken. Not with clouds, but as if the light itself was being sucked from the world. An unnatural twilight descended, deepening rapidly into an impenetrable, suffocating night. Panicked shouts rose from below.

In the thick, terrifying darkness, Barak felt the cold hand of absolute despair clutch his heart. The earth shook violently and the sky blackened rapidly. The center man was dead—the preacher—the messiah—the King of the Jews—the Son of Man—the Son of God. Where was the vengeance? Where was the power? There was only darkness—only the silence of the tyrant God, satisfied. He had fought, he had raged, he had demanded…for nothing. The void swallowed him.

Heshvan hung in the blackness. The pain was still there, immense, but the peace held. *Today…you will be with me…* The promise echoed in the dark. He didn't understand the earthquake or the unnatural night. He didn't need to, he just focused on the words, a beacon in the void. He waited.

The darkness lingered, an eternity passed in the suffocating blackness. Then, gradually, the light began to seep back, gray and weak. Barak blinked, his vision swimming. He saw the center cross. The man hung still—dead. He saw the priests below, they were pale and shaken. He saw the thief on the other side. Heshvan's breathing was shallow and rapid. His eyes were closed, his face strangely serene even in its suffering.

The Roman soldiers moved below the thieves' crosses. A centurion barked an order. Barak saw the soldier approach him, a heavy club in hand. Breaking the legs—hastening death before the approaching Sabbath. The club rose.

"Wait!" Heshvan's voice was a weak gasp, barely audible. He opened his eyes, looking not at the soldier, but past Barak, towards the fading light in the west. A faint, almost imperceptible smile split his cracked lips. He drew one last, shallow breath. His body went limp against the restraining nails. His head fell forward. The fragile peace remained etched on his face—he was gone.

The soldier paused, surprised. He checked Heshvan for signs of life, then thrust his spear between his ribs, just to make sure. Then he grunted, "This one's done." He turned towards Barak.

Barak watched Heshvan die. The thief had found peace—found *paradise*? While he hung here, broken and raging? The soldier stepped closer, hefting the club. Barak looked up into the bruised, indifferent sky, the vengeful God remained silent. The club rose higher. Barak drew a final, ragged breath. He had no plea left—no defiance—only the crushing weight of abandonment. The club reached its apex. Barak closed his eyes tight. The last sound he heard was the whistle of the heavy wood descending towards his shin bones. The price of the rope was paid—the silence of heaven was complete.

The Stone in Her Hand

The dust tasted like iron on Joana's tongue, kicked up by sandaled feet moving through the rocky pass. The sun hammered against the bleached stone, turning the narrow trail into an oven. Ahead, the lean figure of Jesus walked, his robes worn thin, talking quietly with Peter. Behind Joana, Mary Magdalene's quiet breathing was a steady rhythm against the harsh landscape. Joana felt the familiar pull, the rightness of being here, walking this hard ground, despite everything.

She remembered the darkness—the choking fear, the voices that weren't hers whispering lies, twisting her thoughts until her own mind felt like a prison. She remembered the day outside Capernaum, a crowd pressing close, and the desperation making her push through. Jesus had turned—his eyes met hers, he saw the turmoil inside, he saw—*them*. The ones inside her—the ones that shouldn't have been there. A simple command, spoken with impossible authority. "Go." The pressure shattered and the voices ceased. Light flooded the emptiness where the shadows had been— freedom—a debt she could never repay, only serve.

Chuza called it madness—her husband, steward of Herod Antipas' sprawling estate in Tiberias, saw only scandal. A respectable woman, *his* wife, running wild with a wandering preacher and his ragged followers? Sleeping under stars in forsaken places? It reflected poorly—on him—on his family. It endangered his position. His letters, delivered by grim-faced servants who found the group outside some dusty village, grew sharper. His last messenger stood stiffly, avoiding her eyes, delivering the words like a sentence: *Return home immediately. This folly threatens us both.*

She hadn't gone back. The pull of the road, the words Jesus spoke that cut through the noise of the world, the quiet strength beside her— Mary—held her fast. Chuza wouldn't understand—he saw only his duty, his position, the smooth running of Herod's household. He saw her absence as a personal insult and a political liability. She saw salvation—she saw life.

Mary moved closer, her shoulder brushing Joana's as the path widened slightly. No words were needed—a look passed between them, a current of understanding deeper than the desert heat. They shared water from a skin, their fingers touching for a moment longer than necessary. Joana felt the warmth spread beyond the point of contact. In the quiet nights, rolled in cloaks near the embers of the fire, they whispered. They shared their fears, fragile hopes and memories of lives left behind. Sometimes, in the deepest dark of lonely nights, their hands found each other, seeking comfort, finding something else—a fierce tenderness that felt like another kind of deliverance. A secret sanctuary within the greater journey.

Rumors swirled around Jesus, of course. Whispers about Mary Magdalene were louder because people saw her closeness to him, her unwavering presence. They saw her pour expensive oil on his feet and wipe them with her hair. They saw the way he spoke to her, with a directness and trust he didn't always show the Twelve. Joana saw it too, the profound connection, and the unspoken bond that seemed to anchor him. She felt no jealousy, only a strange resonance. Mary's devotion to Jesus was a pillar; her connection to Joana was a hidden spring. Both were essential—both were dangerous.

The landscape was miles and miles of desert—vast an unforgiving, sculpted by wind and drought. They moved through canyons that could hide bandits, across plains where dust devils spun like drunken spirits, past settlements clinging to life like lichen on rock. It felt like frontier territory, lawless and raw. Herod's soldiers, polished and watchful, were reminders of the fragile order imposed from Tiberias, an order Chuza represented. An order Jesus challenged simply by existing, by gathering the lost and the hopeful out here in the wild places.

They stopped near a dried-up riverbed outside a small, sun-baked town. Jesus began to speak, his voice carrying easily in the clear air. He talked of forgiveness, of burdens lifted. Joana listened, the familiar peace settling over her. Mary stood nearby, her gaze fixed on Jesus, a quiet intensity in her eyes. Joana watched the curve of Mary's neck, the way a strand of dark hair escaped her shawl. The desert sun glinted off the tiny beads of sweat on her skin.

A sudden commotion shattered the calm. Horses approached at a hard gallop, kicking up a plume of red dust. Three riders weren't soldiers, but men with the hard look of hired muscle, their clothes dusty but of better quality than the locals. They reined in sharply near the edge of the gathered crowd. Their leader, a man with a scar bisecting his eyebrow, scanned the faces—his eyes locked onto Joana.

"Joana, wife of Chuza?" His voice was rough, carrying over the murmur of the crowd.

A cold dread seized her—she knew that look—Chuza's reach. She stepped forward, away from Mary, away from Jesus. "I am."

"Your husband demands your presence. Now." The man's hand rested near the knife at his belt. "He's tired of sending messages. You come with us."

Murmurs rose across the band of followers. Peter stepped forward, his face set. "The woman chooses to be here. She is under no man's command while listening to the Teacher."

The scarred man spat. "She's under her husband's command, fisherman. Always. Chuza serves Herod. This…" he gestured dismissively at Jesus and the crowd, "...embarrasses his master. It ends today."

Jesus remained calm, but his gaze was sharp. "Let her decide her path. No one is bound against their will in the kingdom."

The man ignored him, focusing on Joana. "Get on the horse, woman. Or we drag you. Chuza's patience is gone. He won't have his position threatened by your…wandering." His eyes flickered towards Mary, standing protectively near Joana now, then back with a sneer. "Or your companions."

The accusation hung in the air—Joana felt the eyes of the crowd, the tension crackling like static before a storm. She saw the resolve in the riders' faces. They would use force, there would be a struggle here, near Jesus…it could turn violent. It could bring Herod's direct wrath down on them all. Chuza had calculated this—he was forcing her hand, using her devotion against her, weaponizing her love for these people.

She looked at Jesus, his quiet strength—she looked at Mary, whose eyes held fear, but also a fierce defiance. Joana couldn't let blood be spilled because of her. She couldn't be the reason Herod's men descended on this fragile gathering. Chuza wanted her back? Fine. She would go. She would face him. Maybe reason with him, somehow.

"I will go," she said, her voice surprisingly steady. "But under my own will. You will not touch me, or anyone here."

The scarred man smirked. "Sensible. Mount up."

Mary grabbed her arm. "Joana, no! You can't. He'll lock you away!"

"I have to," Joana whispered, turning to face her. She cupped Mary's face, ignoring the watching men, the crowd. "I can't bring trouble here. Not to him. Not to you." She leaned in, her lips brushing Mary's ear. "Remember the spring near Magdala? The water was so clear." It was their place, a secret spot where they had first truly seen each other. It was a promise—a plea.

Mary's eyes filled, but she nodded once, fiercely. She pressed a small, smooth stone into Joana's hand—a keepsake from that very spring. Joana closed her fingers around it, the coolness was a shock against her skin.

She turned towards the waiting horse. As she put her foot in the stirrup, the scarred man moved. Not to help her, but to grab her roughly by the waist, hauling her up with unnecessary force, his hand lingering too low. A possessive gesture—a display.

Joana reacted instinctively, years of buried frustration and fear erupting. She twisted, lashing out with her free foot. Her sandal connected hard with the man's jaw. He grunted, stumbling back, releasing her. She landed awkwardly, scrambling away.

"Bitch!" he roared, blood trickling from his split lip. He drew his knife. The other two riders closed in, with their hands on their own weapons.

Peter shouted. Men from the crowd surged forward and chaos erupted. Shouts, the clash of bodies, the panicked whinny of horses.

Joana saw Jesus step towards the fray, his hand raised. "Peace! Be still!"

But the scarred man, enraged and humiliated, wasn't listening. He saw only the woman who had defied him, and struck him. He lunged at Joana, his knife gleaming in the harsh sun. She tried to dodge, but her robe caught on a thornbush.

Movement blurred beside her. Mary Magdalene threw herself forward, placing herself between Joana and the blade. It happened too fast, a sickening thud—a gasp.

Mary staggered, eyes wide with shock. She looked down at the knife handle protruding from her chest, just below the collarbone. Bright red blood bloomed across her simple dress, shockingly vivid against the pale fabric and the dusty ground.

Silence crashed down. The fighting stopped and everyone froze.

The scarred man stared, his rage replaced by instant, dawning horror. He hadn't meant…not *her*.

Jesus reached Mary first, catching her as her knees buckled. He lowered her gently to the ground. His face was etched with a pain deeper than the desert's emptiness. Joana fell beside her, clutching Mary's hand, the stone digging into her palm. "No! Mary! No!"

Mary's eyes found Joana's. They held no blame, only a profound sorrow, a silent farewell. Her lips moved, forming a wordless breath. Her gaze shifted past Joana, towards Jesus, holding his for a fractured second filled with unspoken history and devotion. Then the light faded. Her hand went slack in Joana's grip.

The desert wind moaned through the rocks, carrying away the last whisper of her life. The scarred man dropped his knife, backing away, his face ashen. The other riders looked ready to bolt. The crowd stood paralyzed, the promise of peace shattered by sudden, brutal finality.

Joana knelt in the dust, Mary's blood warm on her hands, the small stone cold and hard in her clenched fist. The vast, indifferent sky pressed down. The path ahead, for all of them, had just vanished into a darkness deeper than any she'd ever known. Chuza's victory was barren. Her devotion had led to this. The silence—the silence was unbearable.

The Waiting

The tomb stood empty like a mouth frozen in a scream. Mary Magdalene pressed her face against the cold stone entrance, breathing in the scent of myrrh and disappointment. Three days had passed since they laid his broken body inside, three days since she had watched the Roman soldiers roll the massive stone into place and seal it with their cursed mark.

"He said three days," she whispered to the darkness within. "He promised three days."

Behind her, the other women waited in the pre-dawn shadows. Mary his mother stood like a statue carved from grief, her eyes fixed on some distant point beyond the horizon. Salome clutched a bundle of burial spices that would never be used. Joanna kept looking over her shoulder, watching for Roman patrols that might arrest them for visiting the grave of a condemned criminal.

"The stone," Mary his mother said suddenly. "It has been moved."

Mary Magdalene stepped back and saw what she had missed in her desperate need to get close to him. The great stone that had required six men to position now sat several feet away from the entrance, as if pushed aside by invisible hands.

"Romans," Salome whispered. "They have taken his body to prevent us from making a shrine."

But Mary Magdalene was already running, her sandals slapping against the limestone pathway that led back to Jerusalem. She had to tell the others, had to bring them to see the empty tomb. Perhaps this was the sign they had been waiting for. Perhaps he had kept his promise after all.

She found them hiding in the upper room where they had shared their last meal with him, twelve broken men huddled together like children afraid of the dark. Peter sat in the corner sharpening his fishing knife over and over, the scraping sound like fingernails on stone. John stared at the wall where shadows danced in the lamplight. Thomas picked at his fingernails until they bled.

"The tomb," Mary gasped, still breathing hard from her run. "It is empty. He is gone."

They looked at her with eyes that had forgotten how to hope. Three days of waiting had drained them of everything except the fear that kept them locked away from the world.

"Gone where?" Peter asked, not looking up from his knife.

"I do not know. But the stone was moved. His body is not there."

"Romans took it," Judas Thaddeus said flatly. "They want to prevent pilgrims from visiting his grave."

"Or grave robbers," Andrew added. "The burial cloths were expensive. Someone could have stolen them."

Mary Magdalene wanted to scream at their faithlessness, but she understood it. She had felt the same hollow despair growing in her chest like a cancer. Three days he had promised. Three days and he would rise again, would return to lead them into the kingdom of heaven he had preached about for three years.

Three days had come and gone, and heaven remained as distant as ever.

"We should look for him," she said. "If someone moved the body, we need to find it. We need to give him a proper burial."

"And get ourselves crucified in the process?" Matthew shook his head. "The Romans are watching us. Caiaphas has spies everywhere. We are marked men already."

"Then we are cowards as well as marked men," Mary shot back. "He died for us, and we cannot even recover his body?"

"He died because he believed his father would save him," Peter said, his voice bitter as wormwood. "He died because he trusted in promises that were never meant to be kept."

The words hung in the air like smoke from a funeral pyre. None of them contradicted him because they all felt the same way. The teacher they had followed, the man they had believed was the son of God, had died screaming in agony while his father watched from heaven and did nothing.

"His brothers are here," John said quietly. "They arrived this morning."

Mary Magdalene felt her heart sink. She had hoped never to see them again, those skeptical faces that had mocked their teacher throughout his ministry. His own family had thought him mad, had tried to drag him home when the crowds grew too large and the danger too great.

"Where are they?"

"Speaking with his mother. They want to take her back to Nazareth."

Mary Magdalene found them in the small courtyard behind the house, four men who shared their brother's dark eyes but none of his fire. They stood around Mary his mother like buzzards around carrion, speaking in low voices about practical matters. Funeral arrangements. Family obligations. The need to return home before the Romans decided to arrest everyone who had known the dead prophet.

"Sister," the eldest brother said when he saw Mary Magdalene approach. His name was James, and he had the weathered look of a man who worked with his hands and trusted only what he could touch. "You should come with us. There is nothing left for you here."

"There is everything left for me here," she replied. "This is where he will return."

The brothers exchanged glances that spoke louder than words. They thought her mad with grief, broken by loss into fantasies of impossible resurrection.

"He is dead," James said gently. "We saw the body. We helped Joseph of Arimathea prepare it for burial. Our brother is not coming back."

Mary his mother looked up at them with eyes that held depths of pain no human should have to bear. "He told me once that a sword would pierce my heart," she said quietly. "I thought he meant sorrow for his suffering. I did not know he meant the agony of hope that refuses to die."

"Mother," James reached for her hand, but she pulled away.

"Three days," she whispered. "He said three days."

The sun climbed higher, burning away the morning shadows and bringing no relief from the heat or the grief. Mary Magdalene returned to the empty tomb with some of the disciples, hoping to find clues about what had happened to the body. But the chamber held only the faint scent of death and the linen cloths that had wrapped him, folded neatly as if arranged by careful hands.

"Someone was here," John said, kneeling beside the burial shelf. "Someone took time to fold the grave clothes."

"Grave robbers do not fold laundry," Peter agreed, but his voice held no conviction. "They take what they want and run."

Thomas stood in the entrance, silhouetted against the morning light. "Perhaps we are looking at this wrong," he said. "Perhaps the empty tomb is not a miracle but a message."

"What kind of message?" Mary asked.

"That death is final. That promises of resurrection are lies told to comfort the grieving. That we followed a madman who believed his own delusions."

The words cut deeper than any Roman sword. Mary Magdalene wanted to argue, to defend their teacher's memory, but doubt gnawed at her like hunger. Where was the triumph he had promised? Where was the kingdom of heaven that would replace the kingdom of earth?

"Look," Peter said suddenly, pointing toward the entrance.

A figure stood there, backlit by the sun so that his features were impossible to make out. He wore simple robes and moved with familiar gestures, raising his hand in the blessing they had seen countless times.

"Teacher?" John whispered.

The figure stepped forward, and for a moment Mary Magdalene's heart soared. The same height, the same build, the same way of tilting his head when he spoke. But as he moved into the shadows of the tomb, she saw the truth. Just a stranger, another mourner visiting another grave.

"I am sorry," the man said. "I did not mean to disturb you."

Peter sagged against the stone wall. "We thought...we hoped..."

"Many people hope," the stranger replied. "Hope is all we have left when everything else fails."

They returned to the upper room as the day grew hotter and the streets filled with people going about their ordinary business. The world had not stopped because their teacher died. Rome still collected taxes—Merchants still hawked their goods in the marketplace. Children still played games in the dust while their parents worked and worried about tomorrow.

"We should leave Jerusalem," Andrew said as they gathered around the table where he had broken bread with them for the last time. "The longer we stay, the more danger we face."

"And go where?" John asked. "Back to our boats? Back to our nets and our old lives?"

"What other choice do we have?"

Mary Magdalene listened to them plan their retreat, their abandonment of everything their teacher had built. Three years of miracles and teachings, three years of believing they were part of something greater than themselves, reduced to arguments about escape routes and safe houses.

"He will come back," she said quietly.

They looked at her with pity and exhaustion.

"Mary," Peter said gently, "he is dead. We all saw him die. We watched them nail him to the cross and pierce his side with a spear. No one comes back from that."

"He did before. Lazarus. The widow's son. The little girl who everyone thought was dead."

"Those were different," Thomas said. "Those people had only been dead for hours, maybe days. Our teacher has been in the tomb for three days in this heat. His body has already begun to…"

"Stop," Mary his mother commanded from the doorway. "Do not speak of such things."

She entered the room followed by Joseph of Arimathea, the wealthy merchant who had donated his own tomb for the burial. Joseph looked like a man who had aged years in the span of days, his fine robes wrinkled and his usually perfect beard was unkempt.

"I have spoken with Pilate," Joseph announced without preamble. "He grows suspicious of the missing body. He thinks we have stolen it to create a cult around a martyr."

"Have we?" Thomas asked bluntly.

Joseph stared at him. "Do you think I would risk my position, my wealth, my family's safety for a dead carpenter's corpse?"

"Then where is he?"

"I do not know. But Pilate is sending soldiers to search every house in the quarter. They will be here within the hour."

Panic rippled through the room. These men who had walked on water with their teacher, who had seen him feed thousands with a few loaves of bread, now scrambled like mice fleeing a cat. They gathered their few possessions and argued about which roads would be safest, which towns might shelter them.

"I am not leaving," Mary Magdalene said.

"You must," Peter insisted. "They will arrest you along with the rest of us."

"Then let them arrest me. I will wait for him here."

"Mary," John tried to reason with her, "if he were coming back, he would have done it by now. Three days was his promise, and three days have passed."

"Perhaps he meant something different by three days," she replied desperately. "Perhaps it was not meant to be taken literally."

The look of pity in their eyes was worse than Roman chains. They thought her mad, broken by grief into delusions that would only bring her more pain. Perhaps they were right—perhaps she was clinging to fantasies because the alternative was too terrible to accept.

"Come with us," Mary his mother said, taking her hand. "His brothers will protect us in Nazareth. We can grieve properly there, away from Roman eyes."

"I cannot. What if he returns and finds us gone? What if he needs us and we are not here?"

"Then we will have missed a miracle," James said pragmatically. "But if we stay, we will certainly miss the rest of our lives."

They left her sitting in the upper room as the sun began its descent toward the western hills. One by one, the disciples slipped away through back alleys and hidden paths, carrying their shattered dreams like broken pottery that could never be mended. Mary his mother was the last to go, kissing Mary Magdalene's forehead.

"If he comes," she whispered, "tell him his mother never stopped believing."

Alone in the gathering darkness, Mary Magdalene lit a single oil lamp and waited. Outside, she could hear Roman boots marching through the streets, soldiers searching house by house for the missing disciples. They would find the room empty except for her, and perhaps they would think her just another grieving woman too broken to be dangerous.

She thought about the first time she had seen him, standing by the well outside her hometown while the sun set behind him like a crown of fire. She had been carrying water jars, living the hard life of a woman with no husband and no protection except what her own strength could provide. He had looked at her with eyes that saw not her shame but her worth, had spoken to her as if she were a person instead of a problem.

"You are loved," he had told her. "You are seen. You matter."

They were simple words, but they had changed everything. For three years, she had followed him across Judea and Galilee, listening to him teach about a kingdom where the last would be first and the broken would be healed. She had believed every word because he had given her something no one else ever had: hope.

Now hope felt like a luxury she could no longer afford.

The door opened suddenly, letting in a gust of cool night air. Mary Magdalene looked up, her heart jumping with desperate anticipation, but it was only Caiaphas the high priest flanked by two temple guards.

"So," he said, settling into the chair across from her like a spider in the center of its web. "The famous Mary Magdalene. The whore who thought she could become a saint."

"I am no saint," she replied quietly. "I am just a woman who loved a good man."

"A good man?" Caiaphas laughed, but there was no humor in it. "Your good man nearly started a riot in our temple. He overturned the tables of honest merchants and claimed authority that belonged to God alone."

"He was God's son."

"He was a lunatic who believed his own delusions. And now he is dead, as all lunatics eventually are."

Caiaphas leaned forward, his eyes glittering in the lamplight. "But his followers continue to spread poison. They claim he has risen from the dead, that death itself has been conquered. Such lies breed dangerous hope in dangerous minds."

"What if they are not lies?"

"Then where is he?" Caiaphas spread his hands wide. "If your teacher has truly conquered death, why does he not appear before the Sanhedrin? Why does he not confront Pilate? Why does he not claim the throne of David and establish this kingdom he preached about?"

Mary Magdalene had no answer. The same questions had been tearing at her heart since she found the empty tomb. If he had truly risen, why remain hidden? If death had been defeated, why did it still feel so final?

"I will make you an offer," Caiaphas continued. "Tell me where his body is hidden, and I will ensure your safety. Refuse, and I will turn you over to the Romans as a conspirator in the theft of a criminal's corpse."

"I do not know where he is."

"Then you are of no use to anyone, living or dead."

The high priest stood to leave, but paused at the door. "Your teacher was not the first to claim divine authority, and he will not be the last. They all end the same way, these would-be messiahs. They die, their followers scatter, and the world continues unchanged."

"He was different," Mary Magdalene insisted, though her voice lacked the conviction she tried to project.

"Was he? Then where is the kingdom he promised? Where is the justice he preached? Where is the God who supposedly loved him enough to call him son?"

Caiaphas smiled, and it was the cruelest expression Mary Magdalene had ever seen. "Your God, if he exists at all, is a monster who feeds on suffering. He gave you hope just so he could watch you lose it. He let you believe in salvation just so your damnation would taste sweeter."

After he left, Mary Magdalene sat in the darkness and felt the truth of his words settle into her bones like winter cold. If God existed, he was indeed a monster. What kind of loving father would watch his son die in agony? What kind of merciful deity would allow his followers to be hunted like animals?

The lamp began to flicker as the oil ran low. Soon she would be sitting in complete darkness, waiting for a dawn that might never come. She thought about the disciples, probably halfway to Galilee by now, putting distance between themselves and the shattered remains of their shared dream. She thought about Mary his mother, returning to Nazareth to live with the knowledge that her son had died believing himself abandoned by heaven.

She thought about him, wherever he was now. Dead in some unmarked grave, or perhaps his body had been thrown into the valley of

Hinnom where the city's trash burned day and night. His flesh would be ash by now, his bones scattered by wild dogs, his promises dissolved into the same nothingness that awaited them all.

The lamp died, plunging the room into absolute darkness. Mary Magdalene closed her eyes and tried to pray, but the words would not come. What was the point of prayer when God either did not exist or did not care? What was the purpose of faith when it led only to betrayal and abandonment?

She must have dozed, because she woke to the sound of footsteps on the stairs. Roman boots, heavy and deliberate. They had come for her at last, come to arrest the last fool who still believed in dead prophets and empty promises.

The door opened, and soldiers entered with torches that turned the small room into a cave of dancing shadows. Their leader, a centurion with scars across his knuckles, looked around at the simple furnishings with contempt.

"Are you Mary of Magdala?" he asked.

"I am."

"You are under arrest for conspiracy against the empire of Rome."

They bound her hands with rope that cut into her wrists. As they led her down the stairs and into the street, Mary Magdalene looked back one last time at the upper room where she had waited for a miracle that never came.

The prison beneath the Antonia Fortress was everything she had expected. Stone walls slick with moisture, straw that crawled with insects, the smell of human waste and despair. They threw her into a cell barely large enough to lie down in and left her to contemplate her choices.

She could have fled with the others. She could have returned to her old life, found another husband, borne children, lived and died in the ordinary obscurity that was most people's fate. Instead, she had chosen to wait for a dead man who had promised to return and had broken that promise like all the others.

Days passed, or perhaps weeks. Time had no meaning in the perpetual twilight of the dungeon. Guards brought her moldy bread and sour water, just enough to keep her alive for whatever fate awaited her. Sometimes she heard screaming from other cells, the sound of interrogations and torture. She wondered if the disciples had been captured, if they were dying in agony while cursing the teacher who had led them to destruction.

Then came the morning when they dragged her from her cell and into the courtyard for trial. Pilate sat on his judgment seat, looking bored and irritated by the necessity of dealing with another religious fanatic. Caiaphas stood beside him, his face, a mask of righteous satisfaction.

"Mary of Magdala," Pilate said without looking up from the scroll he was reading, "you are charged with grave robbery and sedition against Rome. How do you plead?"

Mary Magdalene looked up at the sky above the courtyard. Clouds were gathering, dark and heavy with the promise of rain. For a moment, she imagined she saw a face in the shifting shapes, familiar features looking down at her with sadness and regret.

"He said he would come back," she whispered.

"What?" Pilate looked up, annoyed.

"My teacher. He promised he would return in three days. He promised he would not abandon us."

"Your teacher is dead," Pilate said flatly. "His body has been disposed of according to Roman law. There will be no resurrection, no second coming, no kingdom of heaven to replace the kingdom of earth."

"Then he lied to us," Mary Magdalene said, the words tasting like poison in her mouth. "He lied about everything."

"Yes," Pilate agreed. "He lied. As all prophets lie, as all would-be saviors lie. They promise what they cannot deliver and leave their followers to pay the price of their ambition."

The clouds opened suddenly, releasing a torrent of rain that turned the dusty courtyard into a sea of mud. Mary Magdalene tilted her face up to

44

receive the water, letting it wash away the tears she had been too proud to shed.

"He was supposed to save us," she said to the storm. "He was supposed to make everything right."

"Instead, he made everything worse," Caiaphas observed. "He gave you hope when you should have accepted despair. He promised you meaning when you should have embraced meaninglessness. He told you that you mattered when the truth is that none of us matter at all."

Lightning split the sky, followed by thunder that shook the stones beneath their feet. In the distance, Mary Magdalene could hear the city awakening to another day of ordinary suffering, ordinary struggle, ordinary death. The world would continue without her teacher, without his promises, without the kingdom of heaven that existed only in the desperate dreams of the lost and broken.

"The sentence is crucifixion," Pilate announced. "To be carried out at dawn tomorrow."

As the guards led her back to her cell, Mary Magdalene thought about the other women who had followed their teacher. Were they safe in distant towns, learning to live with shattered dreams? Were they finding new loves, new purposes, new reasons to keep breathing? Or were they like her, broken beyond repair by promises that had turned to ash?

That night, alone in the darkness, she finally allowed herself to mourn. Not just for him, but for all of them. For the disciples who had given up everything to follow a madman. For his mother, who would spend the rest of her life wondering where she had failed as a parent. For his brothers, who would carry the shame of their family's most famous member.

Most of all, she mourned for herself. For the woman who had believed in love when the world ran on hate, who had trusted in mercy when the universe offered only cruelty, who had hoped for salvation when the only certainty was damnation.

The rain continued through the night, drumming against the stone walls like the fingers of impatient gods. Mary Magdalene closed her eyes and tried to remember his face, but found that memory was already fading.

In time, she knew, even the pain would fade. Someone else would take her place in the cell, some other dreamer would pin their hopes on some other false messiah, and the cycle would continue until the sun burned out and the stars fell from heaven.

At dawn, they came for her with hammer and nails, and she went to her death still waiting for a promise that would never be kept.

Three Denials at Gethsemane

Dust coated everything. It coated the worn leather of Jesus' sandals. It coated the dry stalks of grass clinging to the rocky hillside. It coated his tongue, bitter as the thoughts churning inside him. Below, the lights of Jerusalem glimmered like fool's gold in the night, a dust-choked town clinging to the edge of the wilderness. He hated the sight of it now. He hated the path laid before him.

He sat apart from the others near a cluster of gnarled olive trees, the twisted branches stark black against the star-dusted sky. The creek bed below was dry, just a scar on the land. Gethsemane—the name felt like a mockery. This wasn't a place of oil presses—not anymore; it was a place of crushing despair. His disciples slept nearby, sprawled like tired travelers after a long journey. Peter snored softly, his face slack with exhaustion. Jesus watched him. Peter—the rock—or so he'd thought. The one who swore he'd stand firm.

A deep, sour anger tightened in Jesus' chest. Why him? Why this? He'd walked the dusty trails, healed the sick, fed the hungry, spoken truth to power. He'd done everything asked and this was the reward. A slow walk to the gallows? Abandonment—the word scraped his insides. His Father felt distant and silent as the desert night. The plan felt like a betrayal from the start. He'd accepted it, like swallowing gravel, because resistance seemed pointless. But the acceptance brought no peace, only a cold, heavy resignation that sat like a stone in his gut. He needed his men—now, more than ever. He needed them sharp, ready and loyal. Especially Peter—he'd imagined Peter leading them afterward, carrying the torch.

Judas was a known liability—a snake in the grass—just waiting for the right moment to strike. Jesus saw the greed flickering behind his eyes, the restless energy. He saw that betrayal was coming, a necessary evil written into the grim script. But Peter? Peter's denial would be a knife twist. It would be more personal—it would sting like salt in an open wound. Jesus clenched his fists, the knuckles white against the dark fabric of his robe. He wouldn't begrudge them fear. But denial? Abandonment? After all they'd shared? The campfires, the shared meals, the narrow escapes? The anger flared again, hot and sudden. He felt alone—utterly alone under the indifferent stars.

Hours earlier, in the upper room of a nondescript house, the air thick with roasted lamb and impending doom, Jesus had looked straight at Peter. The lamplight cast deep shadows. "Tonight," Jesus said, his voice flat and drained. "Tonight, every one of you will desert me. Scatter like sheep when the wolf comes."

Peter jerked upright, his chair scraping the stone floor. His face flushed. "Desert you? Never! These others might lose their nerve, Teacher. But not me! I'd die first! I'd go to the gallows singing your name!" His voice boomed in the confined space, earnest, passionate and utterly convinced.

Jesus met his gaze—the bitterness rose in his throat. He saw the fervent belief in Peter's eyes, the absolute conviction. It made the coming failure sting worse. "You'd die for me?" Jesus asked, the words heavy. "I tell you the truth, Peter. Before the rooster greets the dawn, you'll deny me. Not once. Three times." He held Peter's shocked stare. "You'll swear you never knew me."

Peter's jaw clinched. He slammed his fist on the rough table. "Never! I'd die first!" The others murmured agreement, shifting uneasily.

Jesus looked away—he felt tired, so tired. Peter's loud promise felt hollow against the vast, crushing weight of what was coming. He saw the flicker of doubt in the other man's eyes, quickly masked by his rant. It wasn't enough—loyalty needed to hold when the swords were drawn.

Later, under the gnarled trees by the dry creek, the torches came. Flames bobbed like malevolent eyes through the olive grove. Heavy footsteps crunched on gravel. The metallic scent of oiled leather and sweat cut through the night air. Temple guards, looking like a Prefect's legion in their rough tunics and grim expressions, pushed through the trees. Their leader held a lantern high. Judas stepped out from behind them, his face a mask in the flickering light. He moved straight to Jesus, embraced him stiffly. "Teacher," he said, the word loud in the sudden silence and kissed him n the cheek—the signal.

Chaos erupted—Jesus' men scrambled awake, their confusion turning to panic. Peter reacted first—he lunged forward, a short skinning knife flashing in his hand. It caught the lantern light. He slashed wildly. A guard yelled, clutching his ear, blood welling dark between his fingers. The blade had sliced the lobe clean off.

"Peter!" Jesus' voice cracked like a whip. He grabbed Peter's wrist, stopping the next wild swing. The anger Jesus felt earlier surged back, hot and immediate. This wasn't courage; it was reckless stupidity. It complicated everything. "Put the blade away!" Jesus commanded, his eyes blazing. "You think I need your bloodshed? You think this changes anything?" He shoved Peter's hand down, the knife clattering onto the stones. The wounded guard cursed, pressing a cloth to his bleeding ear. The other guards surged forward, grabbing Jesus roughly. Peter stood frozen, breathing hard, the fight draining out of him as quickly as it had flared. He looked from the blood on the stones to the men seizing his teacher. His face was pale.

Jesus met Peter's shocked eyes. The disappointment was a physical ache. This was the rock? This panicked, knife-wielding fool? The guards shoved Jesus towards the path back to town. The other disciples melted into the shadows of the olive grove, disappearing into the night like smoke. Only Peter followed, hanging back, his steps hesitant, trailing the grim procession towards Jerusalem's gates like a lost dog.

The town felt different at night. The narrow streets became dark canyons between looming adobe and stone buildings. The air smelled of smoke, dung, and fear. The guards marched Jesus towards the high priest's compound, a sprawling place with high walls. Peter followed at a distance, his heart hammering against his ribs. He kept to the deeper shadows, his eyes fixed on the torches surrounding Jesus. He needed to know what happened—he needed to be close. He told himself he was waiting for a chance, a sign, something he could do.

He stopped near a low stone wall bordering a small courtyard attached to the high priest's place. Inside, a fire burned in a brazier, casting flickering light on the faces of guards and servants huddled around it for warmth against the desert night's chill—the night air was sharp. Peter edged closer to the arched gateway, drawn to the fire's heat and the need to hear. He pulled his cloak tighter, trying to look like just another bystander, another tired soul drawn by the commotion.

A servant girl approached the fire. Her eyes, sharp in the firelight, scanned the faces—they landed on Peter. She tilted her head, studying him. Peter shifted, looking away, suddenly very aware of his dusty clothes, his Galilean accent. The girl pointed a finger. Her voice cut through the murmur. "Hey. You. You were with that Nazarene. The troublemaker they just dragged in. I saw you out by the creek beds."

Peter froze—ice flooded his veins. He could see the guards near the fire turn their heads. He felt their eyes on him. His mouth went dry. "Woman," he stammered, forcing a dismissive tone. "I don't know what you're talking about. Never heard of him." He took a step back towards the gateway, towards the dark street.

The girl frowned—she didn't look convinced. "Sure looked like you," she muttered, but turned back to the fire. Peter slipped out into the street, his breath coming in short gasps. He leaned against the cold stone wall outside, trying to calm the frantic pounding in his chest. It was just a servant girl—nothing happened—he was safe. He just needed to be more careful. He moved further down the street, finding a deeper alcove in the shadow of a building. He could still see the gateway. He could still wait.

Time crawled by, it seemed to slow down and almost stop. The sounds of the town faded to a low hum—distant dogs barked. Peter's nerves were like frayed wire. He jumped at every sound, he needed to see. He crept back towards the courtyard entrance, staying in the darkness just outside the ring of firelight. He peered in.

A different man, a servant of the high priest, was warming his hands. He glanced out towards the gateway, his gaze sharpening as he spotted Peter lurking in the shadows. The man nudged the person beside him. "This one," he said loudly, stepping towards the archway. "I recognize him too. He's definitely one of that man's followers. Galilean accent, same rough look."

Peter felt the blood drain from his face as panic seized him. "Man," he protested, his voice louder than he intended and tinged with desperation. "I am not! I swear it! I don't know the man!" He backed away, hands raised slightly, palms out. Deny—just deny—make them believe.

The servant eyed him suspiciously but shrugged, turning back to the fire. "Suit yourself. Looked like you, is all." Peter retreated again, melting back into the alleyway. His hands trembled—he leaned his forehead against the cool stone of a building. Twice—he'd denied him twice. He hadn't meant to, it just came out when he was put on the spot. The words of Jesus came back to him in that moment—*Before the rooster greets the dawn, you'll deny me. Not once. Three times*—the rooster hadn't crowed yet. The night was long. Shame burned his cheeks, and the fear was cold in his belly. He should leave—right now—get out of this cursed town. But he couldn't make his feet move. He had to know. He had to see it through. He drifted back towards the courtyard, drawn by a terrible need.

An hour passed—the fire burned lower. The guards changed, some drifted off while others stayed. Peter hovered near the gateway again, like a silent shadow. He was arguing with himself, the fear a constant drumbeat. Then a man stood up from near the fire. He was a relative of the guard whose ear Peter had cut. He'd been staring at Peter for a long while, a hard, calculating look on his face. He walked slowly towards the archway.

"Wait a minute," the man said, his voice cold and certain. He stopped right in front of Peter, blocking the dim light from the fire. He looked Peter up and down, his gaze lingering on Peter's hands, then his face. "I know you. I saw you clear as day out in that grove. Near the dry creek. You're Galilean, no doubt about it. That accent gives you away." He took a step closer. "And you were with him. You're the one who pulled the knife. You're the one who cut Malchus' ear." His voice rose, accusing. "You're one of his gang!"

The accusation hung in the air—the few guards still awake near the fire looked over. Peter felt trapped—the man's eyes bored into him. The weight of the night, the fear, the shame, it all crashed down. Desperation choked him, he couldn't think. He had to escape this—now.

"Damn you!" Peter exploded, his voice cracking with panic and fury. He flung his hands up, his face contorted. "I don't know the man! I swear on my life, I don't know what you're talking about! Leave me alone!" His Galilean accent thickened, unmistakable, ringing loud in the sudden quiet of the courtyard. He spat on the ground near the man's feet. "I never laid eyes on him!"

At that precise moment, clear and piercing in the pre-dawn stillness, a rooster crowed. The sound cut through the night air like a knife. It echoed off the stone walls. The word of Jesus came again—*Deny me. Three times*—The words echoed in his head as he realized what he had done.

Peter froze—the blood seemed to stop in his veins. The curses died on his lips. His eyes, wide with shock and dawning horror, snapped towards the inner courtyard. A door had opened. Guards were leading Jesus out, likely to another hearing. Jesus stood framed in the doorway. He wasn't looking at the guards. He was looking straight at Peter.

Their eyes locked across the smoky courtyard. Jesus' face was drawn, exhausted, bruised from the initial blows. But his eyes...his eyes held a devastation that went beyond physical pain. It was a look of utter betrayal, of a deep, personal wound. It was the look of a man who had expected a rock and found only shifting sand. He didn't speak—he didn't need to. The rooster's cry still hung in the air, as a brutal punctuation to Peter's third denial. Jesus held Peter's gaze for one long, agonizing heartbeat. The disappointment, the crushing hurt, the bitter anger—it was all there, raw and exposed.

Peter saw it all—the world seemed off balance. The blood roared in his ears, drowning out the murmur of the guards, the crackle of the dying fire. He saw the man he'd sworn to die for. He saw the wreckage of his own promises lying shattered at his feet. The shame hit him hard, like a fist to the gut, a crushing weight that stole his breath. He stumbled back, away from the accusing relative, away from the firelight, away from the unbearable sight of Jesus' eyes.

He turned and bolted—he ran blindly into the dark alleyway, his feet pounding on the hard-packed earth. He didn't know where he was going—he just ran, fleeing the courtyard, the rooster's crow and the terrible judgment in his teacher's eyes. He ran until his lungs burned and his legs gave way, collapsing against a rough wall in the darkest corner he could find. The first gray light of dawn began to bleed into the eastern sky, cold and indifferent. He buried his face in his hands, his body wracked with silent, heaving sobs—the rock had crumbled.

Inside the courtyard, the guards jerked Jesus forward roughly. "Move along," one grunted, shoving him towards the door leading deeper into the high priest's domain. Jesus stumbled slightly but caught himself. He took one last look towards the empty archway where Peter had vanished. The raw pain was still etched deep on his face, mixed now with a weary, bitter comprehension. The greater betrayal by Judas was coming, a necessary step on the grim path. But this...Peter's denial...this was a different kind of death. It was the death of trust, the death of a hope he hadn't realized he'd clung to so fiercely.

As the guards pushed him through the doorway, into the shadows of the building, Jesus spoke, his voice low and ragged, not meant for the guards but echoing in the sudden stillness of the courtyard. It was a single word, heavy with the weight of his despair, his exhaustion, his blinding hurt. He didn't see Judas lurking further back in the shadows, watching his own moment approach.

"Judas," Jesus said, the name a broken whisper, a tragic mistake born of shattered faith. The guards paid no mind, shoving him onward into the dark corridor. Outside, the first rays of the sun touched the highest roofs of Jerusalem, illuminating the dust particles dancing in the air like the fragile, broken remnants of hope.

The Scribe's Verdict

Malachi dipped his pen—the ink was expensive—the parchment even more so. His task was copying a section from Leviticus detailing the precise punishments for blasphemy. Stone the offender—stone them without pity. He traced the angular Hebrew letters. His fingers knew the shapes, but the words felt heavy today. Distant shouts filtered through the high Temple windows. The name repeated, twisting through the air like smoke: Jesus—Jesus of Nazareth—the so-called Messiah.

Malachi was a Levite, assigned to the Temple archives. He handled sacred texts, copied legal rulings, recorded Temple transactions. He knew prophecies—he knew the signs expected of the Anointed One. This carpenter's son from Galilee didn't fit. The reports were chaotic—he healed the sick, they said. He spoke against the priests—he claimed authority over the Sabbath. Some people whispered that he called God his Father—blasphemy—that was blasphemy pure and simple, if true. Yet the crowds followed him but Malachi needed facts, not rumors. Was this man the deliverer Israel craved, or another dangerous pretender? He had to know—his duty demanded it.

He sought out pilgrims from Galilee. Their stories were inconsistent. One man claimed Jesus turned water into wine at a wedding—a nice trick for a party. Another spoke of a miraculous catch of fish—useful for fishermen, Malachi thought. Neither proved divinity. A woman, her face alight, described Jesus forgiving her sins—Malachi stiffened. Only God forgives sins. This was arrogance, or madness. He pressed her. Did she see anything tangible? Any sign only God could perform? She faltered—she felt forgiven. Feeling wasn't proof. Malachi recorded the accounts, his notes dry and factual. He underlined "Forgave sins?" and added "Uncorroborated. Subjective."

The next report disturbed him the most. Jesus entered the Temple courtyard, overturned the tables of the money-changers, drove out the animals. Malachi rushed to the scene—chaos remained. Coins littered the stone floor, a broken cage lay on its side. Priests clustered, their faces tight with anger. "He called it a den of thieves!" one spat. "He claimed authority over God's house!" Malachi examined the debris—zeal, yes—righteous fury, perhaps—but the Messiah? The prophets spoke of a king restoring David's throne, purifying worship, yes, but also establishing peace. This act felt like provocation. It invited Roman retaliation—Malachi saw reckless anger, not divine strategy. He thought of the Leviticus passage—stone the blasphemer. The priests likely thought the same.

Malachi heard Jesus taught on the Mount of Olives so he went, blending into the edge of the crowd. The man's voice carried, clear but strained. He spoke of loving enemies—of turning the other cheek. Noble, but difficult ideals. Then his tone shifted. He spoke of the Law, not abolishing it, but fulfilling it. He deepened the commandments—anger akin to murder, lust akin to adultery. The burden felt immense and crushing. Malachi listened, seeking the ring of divine authority, the unshakeable certainty of a prophet like Isaiah. Instead, he heard intensity, a fierce, almost desperate insistence. Jesus spoke of a Father in Heaven who knew every sparrow's fall. Malachi thought of the Leviticus God, demanding flawless sacrifices, striking down Nadab and Abihu for offering unauthorized fire. That God felt like a strict and terrifying judge, not a knowing Father. The disconnect jarred him. Was this man deluded about God's nature?

Later, Jesus spoke of the Temple's destruction. "Not one stone left upon another." Malachi recoiled. This was sacrilege—it invited God's wrath. He watched Jesus' face, deep lines etched around his eyes and a tightness in his jaw. He looked weary. Bitter? Resigned? Malachi couldn't be sure. He didn't radiate the triumphant confidence Malachi expected from God's chosen vessel. He looked like a man pushing against an immense weight, alone. Malachi thought of Elijah fleeing Jezebel, feeling abandoned. Did Jesus feel abandoned too? The idea unsettled him.

Pressure mounted in Jerusalem—the chief priests wanted action. Malachi was summoned before Caiaphas. The High Priest's chamber was cool, and scented with incense. Caiaphas sat, his robes immaculate. "Malachi. You record. You listen. What do you make of this Galilean?" Malachi kept his voice neutral. "He gathers crowds. His teachings challenge tradition. He performs unusual acts, healing mainly." Caiaphas leaned forward. "He claims equality with the Holy One, blessed be He. He threatens the Temple. Rome watches. What do your records say about such a man?" Malachi knew the answer. "The Law is clear, High Priest. Blasphemy demands death." Caiaphas nodded slowly. "Precisely. Your diligence is noted. Continue your observations. Report anything... definitive." The unspoken threat hung in the air—Malachi understood. Find proof of blasphemy or messiahship, but the expectation leaned heavily towards the former. His own search felt perilous now.

He sought out Judas Iscariot. The man was one of Jesus' inner circle, yet he seemed restless, often apart. Malachi found him near the Gihon spring. Judas eyed him warily. "What do you want, Levite?" "Understanding," Malachi said. "Your master. Does he truly believe he is the Son of God?" Judas looked away. "He says it." "But do *you* believe it?" Malachi pressed. Judas hesitated. "He speaks like no other man. He heals...but..." He trailed off. "But?" Malachi prompted. "He speaks of betrayal. Of suffering. He says he will be killed." Judas' voice dropped. "He says it is necessary. Part of God's plan. What kind of plan is that? What kind of God plans the death of his own son? If he *is* his son." Malachi saw confusion, and doubt mirroring his own. "And God? Does Jesus feel God's support?" Judas gave a harsh laugh. "He prays all night sometimes. He comes back looking...hollow. Like he wrestled a demon and lost. He talks about a cup he must drink. He doesn't want it." This matched Malachi's observation—not a triumphant Messiah, but a man facing a terrible fate, perhaps feeling forsaken by the very God he claimed as Father. The vengeful God of Malachi's scriptures seemed capable of demanding such a sacrifice.

Rumors exploded and Jesus was arrested in Gethsemane. Malachi pushed through the agitated crowds towards the High Priest's residence. He gained entry as a scribe. The scene was chaotic, the witnesses gave conflicting testimonies. Jesus stood silent, then he finally spoke when directly asked by Caiaphas if he was the Messiah, the Son of God. "You have said so," Jesus replied, his voice low but clear. Then, more damningly, "But I tell you, from now on you will see the Son of Man seated at the right hand of Power and coming on the clouds of heaven." Malachi took a deep breath. He was claiming the divine throne by directly quoting Daniel's vision of the Son of Man given dominion by the Ancient of Days. This was unequivocal blasphemy to the priests. To Malachi, it was the claim laid bare. Now the test: would God intervene? Would the clouds part? Nothing happened, only Caiaphas tearing his robes and the cry of "Blasphemy!" ringing in the hall. Malachi recorded the words, his hand steady. The claim was made but no sign followed and no heavenly host appeared—just a tired man condemned.

In Pilate's courtyard at dawn, Malachi watched the Roman governor struggle. He saw no guilt deserving death in this provincial preacher but the crowd, whipped into a frenzy by the priests, demanded crucifixion. Malachi saw Jesus then. He was beaten, robed in purple mockery, and a crown of thorns pressed into his scalp. Blood streaked his face. Pilate presented him: "Behold your King!" The priests shouted, "Crucify him!" Jesus looked out over the crowd. His eyes held no defiance, only a profound exhaustion, a deep well of sorrow. Was it bitterness? Acceptance? Malachi searched for any flicker of divine power, any hidden strength. He saw only a broken man. Pilate gave in—the sentence was pronounced.

Malachi followed the grim procession to Golgotha. The sky darkened unnaturally as the soldiers nailed Jesus to the crossbeam. Malachi stood at a distance, near some women who wept. He watched the soldiers cast lots for Jesus' clothing. He heard the mocking priests, the thieves crucified beside him adding their taunts. Hours passed—the sky grew black as night. Then, a raw cry tore from Jesus, shattering the unnatural gloom: "Eli, Eli, lama sabachthani?" *My God, my God, why have you forsaken me?* The words struck Malachi like a physical blow. This wasn't a prayer of communion. This was a cry of utter desolation, a scream into a terrifying void. This man, who claimed unity with God, felt completely abandoned. The vindictive God of Malachi's scriptures, the God who demanded absolute obedience and exacted brutal punishment, seemed present in that cry. This was not a beloved Son fulfilling a glorious plan. This was a man crushed by the weight of his own claims and the silence of Heaven. Malachi saw no loving Father. He only saw the terrifying Judge, absent at the moment of greatest need.

Jesus called out again, weaker this time. "It is finished." Then his head slumped. A soldier confirmed it—he was dead. Malachi waited, he watched the sky and listened for the earth to shake in vindication—nothing happened. The unnatural darkness lifted slowly, revealing only three corpses on grim hillside crosses. There was no earthquake, no angels and no celestial proclamation. Just the sound of weeping women and the indifferent shuffle of departing soldiers. The priests looked satisfied—the Romans looked bored. It was just another day.

Malachi walked back towards the city, the dust settling on the road. He passed the imposing Temple walls. He thought of the prophecies—the suffering servant, the pierced one. Some would try to fit this horror into that mold but Malachi saw only failure. Jesus was only a man who claimed divinity, who promised the Kingdom of God, and was executed as a common criminal. His followers scattered, his movement crushed—his last words were a scream of abandonment. Where was the proof? Where was the power? Where was the Father?

He thought of the God Jesus seemed to serve—a God demanding a torturous death, offering no comfort, no rescue. A God who felt like the ultimate tyrant, demanding blood sacrifice even of his own son. Malachi's quest for understanding reached its end. He had sought evidence for the extraordinary claim. He found only a tragic human story. The teachings, some noble, were overshadowed by the bitter end. The miracles, if real, proved nothing lasting. The claim to be God's Son died on that cross, unanswered and unsupported.

Malachi reached the archive room. The Leviticus scroll lay open where he had left it. The words about stoning blasphemers seemed stark and final. Crucifixion wasn't stoning but it served the same purpose—the end result was the same. Crucifixion was perhaps a more terrifying warning to any future blasphemers. He rolled the scroll carefully. He didn't need to copy more today. He had seen enough, the proof wasn't there. Jesus of Nazareth was not the Messiah, his claims were likely untrue. Malachi felt no triumph, only a heavy certainty and a chilling vision of a universe governed by a distant, vengeful power. He extinguished the lamp and the room plunged into darkness. He left the Temple, walking away from the heart of a faith that suddenly felt hollow, built on a foundation of unproven words and a God whose love seemed indistinguishable from wrath. He didn't know where he would go. He only knew Jerusalem held nothing for him now.

The Unseen Ghost

Dust hung thick in the cramped upstairs room. The door, splintered near the latch from the night of the arrest, stood slightly ajar despite Thomas' efforts to wedge it shut. He leaned his weight against the rough wood, testing it. It was solid enough for now. The other ten huddled near the single, shuttered window, the late afternoon light slicing thin lines across their faces. Their voices were low, urgent whispers, a current of desperate hope running beneath the fear.

"He said three days," Peter insisted, his voice hoarse. His knuckles were white where he gripped the windowsill. "He promised."

Thomas pushed away from the door. "He promised many things, Peter. Death has a way of silencing promises." He picked up a discarded water skin and shook it. It was empty, like their prospects. "We saw the nails. We saw the spear. We saw the stone rolled shut. Dead men don't keep schedules."

John turned, his young face drawn. "He wasn't just a man, Thomas. You know that."

Thomas met his gaze. "I know he was my friend. I know he's gone. Grief twists the mind. Makes us hear promises in the wind."

A heavy silence fell, broken only by the distant clatter of Jerusalem outside. Hope felt like a dangerous luxury. Thomas saw it in their eyes—a fragile, clinging thing. He saw the exhaustion and the terror that still flinched at loud noises in the street. He saw the hollow look of men whose world had ended on a Roman cross. Wishing wouldn't change that—death was the final word. The door he'd just fixed wouldn't keep out that truth.

The sound of running feet pounded on the stairs below, frantic. Everyone froze—hands reached for hidden knives, for anything that could be used as a weapon. Thomas positioned himself beside the door, a length of firewood gripped tight. The latch rattled violently—a voice, gasping, ragged.

"Open! It's me! Mary!"

Peter yanked the door open and Mary Magdalene stumbled in, her hair wild, her robe coated in dust, her eyes wide with something beyond fear. She clutched her chest, struggling for breath.

"They're gone!" she gasped.

"Who?" Peter demanded, grabbing her shoulders. "The guards? Did they find us?"

"The stone!" Mary choked out. "The tomb! The great stone...rolled away!"

There was a collective intake of breath. Thomas kept his grip on the wood, his eyes scanning the stairwell behind her. It was empty.

"His body," Mary stammered, tears streaking the grime on her face. "Gone! The tomb was empty!"

John stepped forward, hope flaring bright in his eyes. "The Romans? Did they take him?"

Mary shook her head violently. "No! No, I looked inside. Two men...they weren't men. They shone! Like lightning! Sitting where his body lay!" She trembled, remembering. "They said...Why seek the living among the dead? He is not here. He is risen." She looked around at their stunned faces, her own filling with a desperate certainty. "He's alive! I felt it! He's risen, just as he said!"

A wave of murmurs swept through the room. Peter's face lit up. John let out a choked sob of relief. Nathanael clapped his hands together. "Praise God!"

Thomas lowered the piece of firewood. He didn't move towards Mary. He watched her, he saw the tremor in her hands, the wildness in her eyes, and the dust of the garden tomb on her clothes. He saw something in her that he recognized. He saw grief, exhaustion and hysteria. "Mary," he said, his voice flat, cutting through the rising excitement. "Think. You went alone, at dawn, to a guarded tomb?"

"It was barely light," she whispered. "The guards...they were gone. Like sleep had taken them."

"Guards don't sleep on duty," Thomas stated. "Not Roman guards. Not with a prisoner like him. They move bodies. They hide evidence. They prevent exactly what people like us might try—stealing a body to fake a resurrection." He looked around at the others. "Her grief is deep. The shock...it plays tricks. She saw an empty tomb. That's all. She imagined the rest. Wanted it so badly she made it real in her mind."

Mary flinched as if struck. "I saw them! They spoke!"

"You saw what your broken heart needed to see," Thomas said, not unkindly, but firmly. "Death is final, Mary. We all saw it. Wishing won't change that stone-cold fact. The Romans moved him. To a common pit, probably. To rot. To be forgotten." His words landed like stones in the sudden quiet. The fragile hope in the room flickered and dimmed by his stark pragmatism. Mary buried her face in her hands, her shoulders shaking. The others looked away, the brief flare of joy extinguished, leaving only the familiar ache of loss and the unsettling echo of Thomas's doubt.

Days went by slow as Jerusalem simmered. Rumors flew like desert sand—talk of stolen bodies, of ghostly sightings near the garden. The disciples kept to the upper room, venturing out only in pairs for food and water, moving like shadows. The atmosphere grew strained. Mary's story became a fragile banner some clung to, while Thomas's skepticism hung like a shroud over others. Their arguments flared in hushed tones.

"He appeared to Simon!" James insisted one evening, his eyes feverish. "Peter saw him! On the road!"

Thomas sat sharpening his knife on a whetstone. The rhythmic scrape filled the tense silence. "Peter saw a stranger. Peter sees hope in every shadow. His guilt drives him."

"Then Cleopas!" John burst out. "On the road to Emmaus! He and his companion walked with him! Broke bread with him! They knew him when he vanished!"

Thomas tested the knife's edge. It was sharp—ready. "Exhaustion. Hunger. Shared grief. They talked themselves into seeing what they desperately needed. A shared dream. Nothing more." He looked up, meeting their frustrated stares. "You want proof? Real proof? Not hearsay from grieving men and women? I need to see him. Not a ghost, not a vision. Him.

The man I followed. The man I saw die. I need to see the holes the nails made in his hands. I need to put my hand into the wound the spear tore in his side. Until then, I won't believe death has lost its grip. I won't believe in ghosts."

A week passed, the strain was a physical thing in the room. Their eyes were shadowed and tempers short. They ate little—slept less. The door remained barred, day and night. Thomas kept watch often, his back against the wood, listening to the city sounds, the whetstone always near. Hope had curdled into a tense, silent dread for most but a grim certainty for him.

Then it happened—one evening, as the last light bled from the sky and the oil lamp cast long, dancing shadows, the air changed. It wasn't a sound—it was a pressure—a sudden, profound stillness. The hair on Thomas's arms stood up and tingled. He was on his feet instantly, knife in hand, scanning the dim corners. The others felt it too—they froze, mid-movement, mid-sentence. Peter dropped a cup and it rolled unheeded across the floorboards.

A figure stood among them.

No door had opened. No window unshuttered. He was simply *there*, near the center of the room. He was dressed in simple, clean robes—calm and unmarked by the grave.

There was a collective gasp in the room. John fell to his knees. Peter cried out, "Lord!"

Thomas stared, his mind screamed—*illusion. Trick. Shared madness*. The figure before them looked...solid and real, yet its suddenness defied sense. He saw the faces of the others—awe, joy, tears streaming down cheeks, mouths agape in wordless worship. They saw him—they *knew* him.

"Peace be with you," the figure said. Its voice was familiar, achingly so, yet it resonated with a depth that vibrated in Thomas' bones. Not loud, but filling the room.

The disciples surged forward, falling at the figure's feet, reaching out trembling hands. "Master!" "You live!" "We knew!" Their voices overlapped, a chorus of ecstatic relief. They touched his robe, his hands. They looked up at his face with utter devotion.

Peter turned, tears cutting tracks through the grime on his face, a triumphant, almost accusatory look fixed on Thomas. "See! Thomas! Look! Here is your proof! He lives!"

Thomas didn't move. He kept his back against the door, the knife held low but ready. He watched the figure. It moved among the kneeling men, placing a hand on a bowed head here, meeting a tearful gaze there. It spoke words Thomas couldn't hear—he saw lips move and the rapt attention of the others. He heard their muffled sobs of joy, but the sound itself didn't reach him. It was like watching a scene through thick, warped glass.

"Thomas!" James called, pointing. "Look at his hands! See the wounds!"

Thomas focused—trying desperately to see what they saw. The figure raised a hand in blessing towards Matthew. Thomas squinted—the lamplight flickered. He saw skin, unbroken skin. He saw no wounds—he saw only the hands of a man.

"Where? Thomas asked, his voice loud and harsh in the charged silence. "I see nothing. I see *him* talking, but I hear nothing. I see you all weeping and touching... what? Air? A dream?"

The figure turned its head. Its eyes met Thomas'. There was a depth in them, an unsettling calm. It took a step towards him. Thomas tensed, gripping the knife tighter. He saw no recognition in those eyes directed at him. Only a profound, alien stillness.

"Don't you see him?" Nathanael pleaded, scrambling to his feet. "He's right here! He's looking at you!"

Thomas kept his gaze locked on the figure. "I see a shadow. I see your grief made flesh. I see nothing real." He took a step forward, his voice rising, challenging the room, challenging the vision. "Death is final! He died! We buried him! You saw the blood, the spear thrust! You saw the life leave him! This...this is madness! Your sorrow has broken you!"

As Thomas spoke, his words sharp and desperate, the figure near him seemed to waver. Like heat haze off desert stone. A faint shimmer traced its outline. The disciples closest to it gasped, pulling back slightly.

"Lord?" Peter whispered, uncertainty creeping into his voice for the first time.

The figure didn't respond to Peter. Its gaze remained fixed on Thomas, but its form flickered again, more pronounced this time. The solidity bled away for a fraction of a second, revealing a transparency, a glimpse of the wall behind it. The warm lamplight seemed to pass *through* it momentarily.

"Thomas is right!" Bartholomew cried out, sudden terror in his eyes as he stared at the flickering form. "Look! He...he shimmers!"

Doubt, cold and sharp, pierced the ecstasy. They stopped reaching out. They stopped weeping with joy. They stared, their faces shifting from adoration to confusion, then to dawning horror. The figure was changing— the calm face began to lose definition. The wounds they thought they saw on the hands vanished entirely. The robes seemed less like cloth, more like swirling dust caught in the lamplight.

"He's fading!" John shrieked, scrambling backward.

Thomas pressed his advantage, his voice raw. "He's gone! He's dead! This is your grief! Your fear! Your desperate hope conjuring a ghost! Look at it! It's failing because *you* are starting to see the truth! Death won!"

The figure flickered violently now, like a faltering candle flame. Its edges dissolved into beams of light. The familiar features blurred and became indistinct, then melted away entirely. The depth in the eyes vanished, replaced by empty, shimmering points of light that held no thought, no recognition. For a moment, it was just a pillar of unstable radiance in the center of the room. Then, with a final, silent sigh of light, it winked out.

Utter darkness plunged down, deeper than the night outside. The oil lamp hadn't gone out, but the absence left by the vanished light felt absolute. The silence was suffocating, broken only by ragged breathing and a low moan of utter desolation that came from Peter.

Thomas lowered the knife—his hand shook. He hadn't realized how hard he'd been gripping it. He felt no triumph—only a hollow, chilling certainty and fear. The fear of being right in this terrible way.

John was weeping openly now, great, heaving sobs of loss renewed, tenfold worse. Nathanael sat slumped against the wall, face buried in his hands. Matthew stared blankly at the empty space where the vision had stood. The shared dream had shattered, leaving only the jagged edges of reality.

Peter finally moved—he walked slowly to the spot where the figure had stood. He reached out a trembling hand into the empty air. His fingers closed on nothing. He sank to his knees, a broken man. "Gone," he whispered, the word a death knell. "Truly gone."

The fragile resurrection faith evaporated like mist under a harsh sun. The certainty of the empty tomb, the angelic messengers, the appearances— all collapsed under the weight of Thomas' stubborn doubt and the terrifying dissolution of their shared vision. The hope that had sustained them through days of terror was exposed as a collective delusion, a beautiful, desperate lie spun from unbearable grief. Death had won—the tomb wasn't empty because of resurrection; it was empty because of Roman efficiency, or grave robbers, or some mundane horror they couldn't fathom. Their leader was rotting in a pit somewhere, or burned, or simply gone. The figure they saw was a phantom of their shattered minds.

Thomas leaned back against the cool wood of the door. The whetstone lay near his foot. The city sounds outside seemed louder now, harsher. Jerusalem hadn't changed. The Romans still ruled—the world was still dark and they were just eleven frightened men in a locked room. They had nothing left but the bitter taste of finality and the cold, hard work of survival. Peter slowly pushed himself up, he didn't look at Thomas—he looked at the others, his face aged and empty. He walked to the corner where their few belongings lay piled. He picked up a discarded fishing net, torn and soiled with old seaweed. He sat down heavily and began, with slow, deliberate movements, to mend it. The scrape of the needle through the rough cord was the only sound in the room. One by one, the others followed. They picked up their tools, their tasks. They didn't speak—they didn't look at the empty center of the room. They just mended nets. They would go back to the sea, the dream was over. Only the long, hard shore of reality remained. Thomas watched them work, the dust particles caught in the lamplight where the ghost had been. He closed his eyes—the silence of that moment was the loudest thing he'd ever heard.

Herod's Reckoning

The sun beat down on the stone walls of Machaerus. Inside the dim cell, John the Baptist pressed his back against the cool rock, a narrow shaft of light piercing the high window. Outside, the sounds of preparation grew louder—shouts, the clang of metal, the nervous whinny of horses. Herod Antipas, Tetrarch of Galilee and Perea, was throwing a party.

Herod paced his chamber overlooking the courtyard. He ran a hand over his close-cropped beard. The preacher's words still echoed, sharp as flint. *"It is not lawful for you to have your brother's wife."* Herodias—her ambition filled the fortress like perfume, thick and sweet. He admired John's courage, even craved his strange, fiery wisdom but Herodias' eyes held a cold promise. She wanted John silenced—permanently. The arrest felt like surrender. He gave the order and his guards dragged John away, the cell door clanged shut. Herod poured himself wine, the cup trembling slightly in his hand. He tried to forget the preacher's steady gaze.

The feast hall roared with hearty laughter and conversation. Oil lamps cast flickering shadows on their sweating faces. Herod sat at the head table, flanked by his officers and the nobles of Perea. Platters of roasted meat, bowls of fruit and goblets of wine crowded the tables. The laughter was loud and forced. Herodias watched him, her expression unreadable while her daughter, Salome, moved with restless energy beside her.

Herod raised his cup again. Wine sloshed over the rim. "More wine! Music!" The musicians struck up a faster tune. Herod's gaze fixed on Salome. "Dance for us, Salome! Dance for your king!" His voice boomed, slurred.

Salome glanced at her mother and Herodias gave her an almost imperceptible nod. Salome stepped into the cleared space, her movements started slow and sinuous, then grew faster and wilder. Her feet stamped the stone floor. Her veils swirled like desert dust devils. The men roared their approval, pounding the tables. Herod leaned forward, mesmerized. The preacher, the guilt, the heat—it all blurred under the wine and the girl's fierce grace. She finished, breathless, bowing before him—the hall erupted.

Herod surged to his feet, swaying—drunk. "Magnificent!" He swept his arm wide. "Ask! Anything! I swear it before all these witnesses. Up to half my kingdom!" The oath hung heavy in the smoky air. A hush fell across the hall. Eyes darted between Herod and Salome—awaiting her response.

Salome's eyes sought her mother's—Herodias beckoned her close, whispering urgently into her ear. Salome's face tightened as she turned back to Herod, her voice clear and cold in the sudden quiet. "I want the head of John the Baptist. Bring it to me. Now. On a platter."

The words hit Herod hard—the one thing he wasn't expecting. He expected that she would want wealth or land. But this? This was never even a consideration. The wine haze shattered as a cold dread washed over him. He saw John's face again, heard the truth in his words. This was Herodias' doing—this was murder. He opened his mouth to refuse, to take back the drunken oath but every eye in the hall was on him—his officers, his nobles, the men whose respect he needed. Weakness now would be fatal. Fear of their judgment clamped his throat shut. His shoulders slumped and he gave a curt, almost invisible nod to the captain of his guard standing rigid nearby. "Do it," he rasped. "See to it."

The captain's face was like stone. He saluted, turned on his heel, and marched out. The heavy door thudded shut behind him. The hall remained silent, waiting. Herod sank back into his chair, the wine sour in his mouth. He couldn't meet anyone's eyes. Time slowed down, marked only by the sputtering lamps. The scrape of the door opening made everyone jump.

The captain returned and walked steadily to the center of the floor. In his hands, a large, plain serving platter and on it, resting on a bed of coarse cloth, lay John's head. The eyes were closed, the beard was matted and blood darkened the cloth beneath. The captain stopped before Salome and offered her the platter without a word.

Salome stared for a heartbeat, her face was pale but determined. She took the platter. It seemed heavy in her hands—she turned and carried it, carefully, steadily, to her mother. Herodias looked at the head, a flicker of triumph in her eyes. She took the platter from her daughter. The hall remained frozen, the festive mood was extinguished. Herod looked away, fixing his gaze on the froth in his cup—he felt sick.

Later, under the cover of night, two figures approached the fortress gates. They were dusty, travel-worn—John's disciples. They had heard the whispers spreading like wildfire from the feast, they demanded their master's body. The guards, perhaps uneasy themselves, perhaps under orders to be rid of the evidence, led them to where the headless corpse had been discarded. The disciples wrapped the body in clean linen with rough, reverent hands. They carried it away into the darkness, towards the lonely hills. They buried him in a secret place, their grief a raw, silent thing under the vast desert stars.

News traveled fast on the dry wind—it reached Jesus as he taught near the Sea of Galilee. A disciple, face ashen, pushed through the crowd, whispering urgently. Jesus stopped speaking and a profound stillness settled over him. He looked towards the south, towards the fortress prison and he understood. He dismissed the crowd. "Come," he said to his closest followers, his voice low. "We need to go. To a desolate place. Alone." They boarded a boat, pushing off from the shore. The usual lively chatter was absent. Jesus sat at the bow, looking out over the water, a deep sorrow etched on his face. He needed the solitude to mourn the prophet, his cousin, the voice crying in the wilderness.

Back in Tiberias, Herod's palace felt like a cage. Sleep abandoned him, when he did drift off, nightmares seized him. He saw John's head on the platter, the eyes snapping open, accusing. He saw Salome dancing, her movements turning predatory. He heard the preacher's voice condemning him, louder, clearer than ever before. He stared at the shadows—a servant dropping a plate made him lunge for the dagger at his belt. The guilt gnawed at him, it was a constant companion sharper than any hunger.

Then reports began filtering in—a man in Galilee, preaching with power, drawing huge crowds, and performing healings. They spoke of authority, of words that cut like John's had. Herod's blood ran cold—he summoned his advisors. "Who is this?" he demanded, pacing his chamber. "I beheaded John! But this man…they say he does the same things. More!" His eyes darted around the room. "It's him! John! I know it! He's come back. Back from the dead. That's why these powers work through him!" His voice rose, tinged with hysteria.

His advisors exchanged worried glances. The chief steward, a man used to managing Herod's moods, spoke cautiously. "Lord, some say it is Elijah returned. Others say one of the ancient prophets risen again." He paused. "John is dead, my lord. You saw it done."

Herod slammed his fist on a table. "You didn't see his eyes! You didn't hear him! It's John! I cut off his head, and now he walks! He's working miracles to prove it! To mock me!" Spittle flew from his lips. "He's coming. He'll want revenge. He'll take everything!" He began muttering to himself, staring wildly at the corners of the room. The advisors withdrew, whispering. The word spread through the palace: the Tetrarch was losing his mind. Guards stood a little straighter, their expressions wary.

Herod's paranoia festered—he doubled the palace guard. He ordered spies into Galilee. Every report of Jesus' movements sent him into fresh panic. He saw John's face in every stranger. He raged at servants for imagined slights, convinced they were agents of the resurrected prophet. Herodias watched his unraveling with cold calculation, but even she began to feel a tingle of unease—a mad ruler was unpredictable.

Jesus continued his work. He taught in villages and synagogues, fed multitudes with scraps, healed the sick. His message was of a different kingdom, not Herod's fragile tetrarchy. But Herod's spies brought back stories that only fueled the Tetrarch's terror. "He commands spirits!" "He walks on water!" "Thousands follow him!" To Herod, each feat was a direct challenge, a sign of John's supernatural vengeance.

A confrontation became inevitable. Jesus' path led him towards Jerusalem, skirting the edges of Herod's territory. Pharisees, seeking to trap Jesus, came with a warning disguised as concern: "Get away from here! Herod wants to kill you!"

Jesus' response was sharp, unflinching. "Go tell that fox: 'Look, I cast out demons and perform healings today and tomorrow, and on the third day I reach my goal.' I must press on today, tomorrow, and the next day. No prophet can die outside Jerusalem." The message was defiance—he wouldn't be cowed by Herod's threats. He wouldn't be hurried off his path. He had work to do, a journey to complete. His time would come, but on his terms, not Herod's.

The message reached Herod. "*That fox.*" The insult stung. But worse was the certainty: this man knew Herod's murderous intent and didn't flee. Only John would be so bold, so unafraid. Only the man he'd wronged would call him a fox. Herod's fear curdled into rage. He *had* to see this man. He *had* to know if it was John's ghost wearing flesh. He issued orders: *find Jesus. Bring him. Alive.* He wanted to look into those eyes himself.

The opportunity came not long after—Jesus was brought before Herod in Jerusalem. Pilate, the Roman governor, hoping to avoid a decision about the Galilean, sent him to Herod, who happened to be in the city for Passover. Herod's palace guard led Jesus into the audience chamber where Herod sat on a raised throne, flanked by his soldiers. Herodias watched from the shadows of a side chamber. The room buzzed with tension.

Herod's eyes widened as Jesus entered. He leaned forward, scrutinizing the figure before him. The same intensity? A similar build? Was it *him*? This man looked different, yet...the presence—the silence. It unnerved him, he felt a cold sweat on his neck. He needed proof—he needed to break that silence.

"So!" Herod's voice boomed, trying to sound confident. "The mighty prophet! The worker of wonders!" He gestured dismissively. "Perform for us! Show us a sign! Show us the power they say you possess!" He sneered, hoping to provoke a reaction, to see the familiar fire of John's condemnation. His soldiers chuckled uneasily.

Jesus stood perfectly still—he looked directly at Herod, his gaze steady and penetrating but he said nothing—not a word. The silence stretched, thick and heavy as Herod shifted in his seat. The man's calm was unnerving. Where was the fiery denunciation? Where was the fear? Where was the recognition?

Herod pressed on, his voice rising. "Cat got your tongue? Or are the stories lies? Can you do nothing?" He turned to his soldiers. "See? He's nothing! Just a peasant rabble-rouser! Or..." His voice dropped and became conspiratorial, tinged with the familiar paranoia. "Or is this part of it? The trick? The revenge?" He stared hard at Jesus. "John? Is it you? Have you come back to torment me?"

Still, Jesus remained silent. His eyes held Herod's, but they revealed nothing of the thoughts behind them. The utter lack of response and the refusal to engage, was more unsettling than any curse. Herod felt his control slipping. This wasn't fear or anger in the prisoner. It was...pity? Judgment? He couldn't bear it.

"Answer me!" Herod screamed, lurching to his feet. His chair scraped loudly on the stone. Spittle flew from his lips. "Are you John? Admit it! Admit you've come back from the dead to destroy me!" He drew his dagger halfway from its sheath, a tremor visible in his hand. The soldiers tensed, hands on their own weapons.

Jesus simply looked at him. The silence was absolute now—deafening—Herod's ragged breathing was the only sound. He searched that face desperately for any sign, any flicker of the man he'd murdered. He saw only calm depth, and an unnerving stillness that felt like an abyss. The pressure in his head built, the guilt and terror merging into a single, crushing weight. This wasn't defiance—it was condemnation. It was silent, absolute, and far worse than any shout.

Herod's nerve broke—the dagger clattered back into its sheath. A strangled sound escaped his throat, half-sob, half-laugh, he waved a frantic, dismissive hand. "Take him away!" he shrieked, his voice cracking. "Take him back to Pilate! He's nothing! A fool! See how he mocks us with his silence?" He slumped back onto his chair, trembling violently, avoiding the eyes of his soldiers, his wife in the shadows, and the silent, watching man being led away.

The soldiers, confused and relieved, roughly escorted Jesus out as Herod buried his face in his hands. The silence in the chamber was worse than before, it pressed in on him, filled with the phantom echo of John's voice and the unbearable quiet of the man he couldn't name. He knew, deep in his fractured soul, he knew the judgment wasn't over. It had just begun, and it lived inside his own crumbling mind, a silence more terrifying than any accusation. He was alone with the ghost he had made, and it would never leave.

Desert Visions

The sun hammered the stones—heat rose in visible waves, warping the distant hills. Jesus knelt on the hard ground, his head bowed. Forty days—forty nights—he had no food and little water—his body was a hollow ache of his former self. His stomach had stopped demanding and settled into a grinding void. The Spirit had led him here, into this desert wilderness, this emptiness east of the Jordan. The purpose felt distant now, buried under the weight of sun and thirst. To be tested? Or broken? The voice in his head, the one that drove him here, was relentless. *Prove yourself. Suffer. Obey.* It sounded like the desert wind, harsh and unforgiving. He saw his Father's face in the blinding glare—not loving, but demanding, a judge waiting for failure.

A shadow fell across him. He didn't lift his head. The shadow moved stealthily and a figure stood beside him, outlined against the white sky. It wore a traveller's dusty robe, face hidden beneath a deep hood. The voice was smooth, a cool current in the furnace air. "Hungry?" The question scraped against his raw throat. The hooded figure nudged a nearby stone with his sandal. It looked like a rough loaf of bread. "You have power. Use it. Command this stone. Make it bread. Feed yourself." The image was sharp, the smell of warm bread impossibly real. His stomach clenched violently. *Just one word.* The traveller's voice was persuasive. "The Father starves you. He demands this pain. Why serve such a master? Take control. Save yourself." The hollow inside Jesus screamed *yes.* He licked his dry, cracked lips—the desert heat was intense. The Law echoed, a counterpoint to the hunger. *Man lives not by bread alone…* The words felt heavy and ancient. They anchored him. "No," Jesus rasped. "It stands written. Man lives by every word from God's mouth." The hooded figure paused. The stone remained a stone.

The desert vanished—he stood on a dizzying height as the wind tore at his robe. Below, the Temple courts in Jerusalem swarmed with tiny figures. He recognized the pinnacle, the drop was sheer and terrifying. The traveller stood beside him, hood thrown back now. The face was ordinary, kind even. "Impressive view," the man said. "He put you here. Testing your trust? Seems cruel." He gestured downwards. "Throw yourself off. Prove He cares. Prove He'll save you. The Scriptures promise it, don't they? *He commands His angels concerning you…they will lift you up.*" The wind howled. The promise felt like a dare. *Make Him act. Force His hand.* The thought was seductive. End the test—force the vindictive Judge to show mercy or be exposed. The ground far below pulled at him. *Jump.* The Law's words surfaced again, a shield against the void. "It also stands written," Jesus forced out, his voice thin against the wind. "Do not test the Lord your God." The ordinary face flickered, a moment of cold irritation. Then the desert heat slammed back and he was on his knees again, gasping.

He was moving—or the world was. The ground tilted, became a mountainside, not the familiar hills of Judea. This peak scraped the sky, cold and immense. The air was thin, hard to breathe. The hooded traveller pointed—the world unfolded below like a vast, shimmering map. Cities glittered like scattered jewels. Armies marched as tiny, disciplined ants. Forests spread wide like green carpets. Oceans flashed under distant suns. Power radiated from the scene, as tangible as the heat. "Look," the traveller breathed, his voice resonant with ownership. "All of it. Every kingdom. Every throne. The glory. The power. It's mine to give. I offer it. To you." He turned, his eyes holding Jesus'. "Forget the desert. Forget the hunger. Forget the demanding voice that starves you. Worship me. Just once. Kneel. That's all. And it's yours. No more tests. No more suffering. Rule it now." The vision was overwhelming—the ache for sustenance, for purpose beyond this desolation, and the image of dominion—Jesus shook his head, tying to clear his mind. He could escape the Father's harsh demands, take the crown and serve the one who offered relief. The traveller waited, expectant. The hollow inside Jesus wasn't just hunger now—it was the vastness of the offer. *Rule...* The ancient words rose, a final, desperate anchor. They cut through the dazzling vision like a knife. "Away!" Jesus shouted, the force surprising him. His voice cracked, but it held command. "Satan! It stands written: Worship the Lord your God. Serve Him alone!" The command hung in the thin air. The glittering kingdoms wavered and the cold mountain dissolved around them.

He was back in the furnace—the sun still beat down—hot—impossibly hot—the stones still burned. He was alone—utterly alone, the traveller was gone. The visions had drained his last reserves of energy, he collapsed onto the hot sand. He faded in and out of consciousness—the voice of the demanding Father was silent. Only the wind spoke now, a dry whisper. He felt himself slipping—the hollow was winning. *He left me...* The thought was final as the darkness crept in.

Coolness touched his brow and he flinched as gentle hands lifted his head. A soft cloth wiped the grit and sweat from his face. The scent of water filled his nostrils. A cup touched his lips—a cool liquid, impossibly sweet, trickled onto his tongue. He swallowed convulsively. Strength, tiny but real, seeped into his limbs. He saw figures, indistinct in the glare. They were radiant shapes, moving with silent efficiency. One offered a piece of moistened bread and he ate. The simple food was life itself. They held him, gave him water and tended to his cracked skin. Were they real? Or the final, merciful illusion of a dying mind? He didn't know. He couldn't care. The terrible pressure in his head eased. The hollow ache lessened, replaced by a fragile calm. The angels, real or imagined, ministered to him. The desert remained but the test was over—for now. He had obeyed the harsh command. He had not broken—he had survived the desert, the hunger, the visions, and the voice of his demanding God. He slept, deeply, under the watchful eyes of the radiant figures, or under the indifferent, burning sky.

The Desert Crossing

The sun beat down like a hammer on an anvil. Jesus pulled his dusty cloak tighter around his shoulders and squinted across the barren wasteland. Behind him, twelve men struggled through the sand, their faces cracked and weathered like old leather. They had been walking for three days without finding water.

"Teacher," Peter called out, his voice hoarse. "The men are dying. We need to turn back."

Jesus stopped walking, his jaw clenched tight. "Turn back to what? To the crowds who want to make me king? To the Romans who want to crucify me?" He spat into the sand. "God led us into this desert. Let God lead us out."

The disciples exchanged worried glances. They had never heard such bitterness in their master's voice.

"Perhaps we misunderstood," Matthew said carefully. "Perhaps we should pray for guidance."

Jesus laughed, but there was no joy in it. "Pray? I have been praying for thirty years. God speaks only in riddles and demands only suffering." He kicked at a bleached animal skull. "Look around you. This is God's creation. Death and emptiness."

Thunder rumbled overhead despite the cloudless sky. The ground trembled beneath their feet.

"Teacher," John whispered, fear creeping into his voice. "Something is wrong."

A dust devil formed in the distance, spinning faster than nature allowed. It moved toward them with purpose, growing larger with each passing moment. Inside the swirling sand, shapes flickered—Faces—Angry faces with burning eyes.

"He questions us," a voice boomed from the whirlwind. "He doubts our plan."

Jesus stood his ground while his disciples fell to their knees. "Your plan?" he shouted at the sky. "Your plan is madness. You ask me to die for people who stone prophets and worship golden calves."

The thunder grew louder. Lightning cracked without rain.

"You gave me power to heal, but the sick keep dying. You gave me words of love, but men still hate. You promise salvation, but deliver only judgment." Jesus raised his fist toward heaven. "I am tired of being your puppet."

The dust devil reached them. Sand stung their eyes and filled their mouths. Through the chaos, they heard laughter. It was a cold and merciless laughter.

"You think you can bargain with us?" The voice came from everywhere at once. "You think you understand suffering? We will show you suffering."

The wind stopped suddenly. The silence felt heavier than the noise had been.

Andrew pointed with a shaking finger. "Look."

On the horizon, riders approached. They were Roman soldiers on horseback, their armor glinting in the brutal sun. Behind them came more figures on foot. They were the Temple guards—Pharisees—All armed—All hunting.

"They have found us," Thomas breathed.

Jesus felt something cold settle in his chest—a feeling he didn't like. He had led his followers into a trap. The desert had no hiding places, no escape routes—just open sand in every direction.

"We can fight," Peter said, drawing a short blade from his robes.

"With what?" Jesus gestured at their small band. "Twelve fishermen and tax collectors against a hundred trained killers?"

The riders drew closer. Dust clouds marked their approach like smoke signals announcing death.

"You wanted to test my faith," Jesus called out to the empty sky. "You wanted to see if I would break. Congratulations. You win."

He turned to his disciples. Their faces showed confusion, fear, and something worse—doubt—not in God, but in him.

"I led you here," he said quietly. "I told you to follow me into the wilderness. I promised you would see the kingdom of heaven." He gestured at the approaching soldiers. "This is what my promises are worth."

The sound of hoofbeats grew louder. They were getting closer.

Judas stepped forward. His hand rested on a small leather pouch tied to his belt. Coins clinked inside.

"Teacher," he said, his voice steady for the first time in days. "There is still time to surrender. They want you, not us."

Jesus looked at each of his disciples in turn. These men had left everything to follow him, their families, trades and comfortable lives. Now they would die in the desert because he had believed God's voice in his head.

"Do what you must," he told Judas.

The soldiers were close enough now to see individual faces. They were grim men who killed for wages. They carried ropes and chains along with their swords.

"We could have had everything," Jesus said to the sky. "Peace. Love. A kingdom built on mercy instead of fear." He laughed bitterly. "But you prefer blood, don't you? You always have."

The first rider reached them. A centurion with scars across his cheek and hate in his eyes.

"Are you the one they call the Nazarene?" he demanded.

Jesus looked at his disciples one final time. Peter's hand still gripped his knife. John had tears streaming down his face. The others just stared at the ground.

"Yes," Jesus said. "I am."

The centurion smiled. It was not a pleasant expression.

"Good. We have been looking for you."

As the soldiers dismounted and approached with their chains, Jesus felt the last of his faith crumble like sand through his fingers. God had led him into the desert to die. Not as a savior, but as a failed prophet whose own followers would watch him fall.

The chains felt cold against his wrists.

Behind him, Judas counted thirty pieces of silver.

The Cana Standoff

Dust hung thick over Cana. It coated the low stone buildings, the scraggly olive trees and the dry road leading into town. The wedding feast pulsed inside a large, crowded courtyard. Laughter and music fought the heat, but a sharper tension cut through the merriment. Jesus stood near the edge, watching. His new wife, Mary, moved among the guests, her smile was strained. Her dark hair was braided simply, her dress clean but plain. The wedding itself had been quiet, almost furtive. His mother's quiet insistence had overridden his own hesitation. The Father's silent disapproval felt like a physical weight, a constant pressure behind his eyes.

He felt eyes on him—not just the curious glances of townsfolk, but the heavy, judging gaze from above. Every joyful shout, every touch Mary gave him, felt like a challenge thrown at a distant, furious throne. *You defy me*, the silence seemed to scream. *You choose flesh over spirit.* The familiar dread coiled in his stomach. He knew the cost of displeasure. The desert test had nearly broken him. His knuckles were white where he gripped the edge of a rough-hewn table too tight.

His mother approached, her face was tight with worry, not joy. "They have no wine," she said, her voice low. She didn't look at Mary, but the implication was clear—running out so early was a disaster. It was a disaster, it was shame for the groom nd ruin for the bride's family—a social death sentence in this small town.

Jesus flinched—the demand in her eyes mirrored the greater demand he felt crushing him. "Woman," he said, the word sharp, pushing her away. "What do you want from me? My hour hasn't come." He meant the hour of confrontation, the hour the Father would inevitably demand, the hour of reckoning for this act of defiance—his marriage. Performing a sign *now*, at *his* wedding feast? It felt like waving a red flag before a bull. He saw the Father's rage, a storm gathering on the horizon of his mind. *Draw attention. Invite wrath.*

His mother didn't argue. She turned to the servants hovering nearby, their faces pale with the crisis. "Do whatever he tells you," she instructed, her voice firm, ignoring his protest. It was a gamble, her belief against his fear.

Six large stone jars stood against the courtyard wall. They were for the purification rites, holding gallons of water each. They were empty now. They were symbols of the rigid Law that felt like a cage now. Jesus looked at them, then at the expectant servants. The pressure built—the shame threatening Mary, his mother's quiet command, the crushing weight of the watching sky. The risk was immense. Drawing the Father's focused anger here, now, upon Mary, upon his mother, upon everyone...it could mean fire from heaven, swift and terrible punishment. He'd seen the Father's vengeance before, in whispers of history and the cold dread in his own soul. Yet, the alternative was Mary's disgrace.

A decision hardened within him, born of defiance and desperation. "Fill the jars with water," he ordered the servants. His voice was flat. "Fill them to the brim." The servants exchanged nervous glances but moved quickly. They hauled buckets from the well, sweating under the sun. Water sloshed into the massive stone containers. Jesus watched, his gaze fixed on the clear liquid, not seeing it. He saw the Father's face, stern and unforgiving. He felt the old terror—*This will provoke Him.*

When the jars were full, the water shimmering just below the rim, Jesus pointed. "Draw some out now. Take it to the steward." The servants hesitated. Taking plain water to the master of the feast? It was madness. It invited immediate ridicule, confirming the disaster. But they remembered the mother's command. One dipped a pitcher into the jar and drew it out. The liquid swirled, clear. He exchanged another look with his companions, his face etched with dread of the steward's reaction. They carried the pitcher towards the head table where the steward, a respected elder, held court.

Jesus didn't watch them go. He stood rigid, braced and waited for the sky to darken, for the earth to shake, for the sudden, searing judgment to fall. Mary moved closer to him, sensing his tension. She touched his arm. He didn't look at her. His focus was upward, waiting for the blow. The laughter and music continued, oblivious. The steward, flushed from the meager wine already consumed, took the offered pitcher. He poured a cup, grumbling about the delay. He raised it to his lips, expecting stale water or thin vinegar.

His eyes widened—he took a slow sip, then another, a deeper one. He stared into the cup, then at the servant. "Where did this come from?" he demanded, his voice thick with surprise. The servant just gestured vaguely towards the courtyard wall, towards Jesus. The steward pushed back his chair. He scanned the crowd, his gaze settling on the groom, and Mary's father, who was sweating nervously nearby. The steward strode over, grabbing the groom's arm. He thrust the cup at him. "Taste this!"

The groom, expecting the worst, took a hesitant sip. His expression shifted from fear to utter confusion. The steward laughed, a loud, relieved sound that cut through the courtyard chatter. People turned to look. "Every man serves the good wine first!" the steward boomed, clapping the bewildered groom on the shoulder. "And when people are drunk, the worse. But you!" He pointed the cup at Jesus. "You saved the best wine until now!" The crowd murmured, then cheered. Relief washed over the groom's face. Laughter returned, louder, fueled by the unexpected bounty.

Jesus felt no relief—the servants, who knew the water's origin, stared at him with a mix of awe and fear. His disciples nearby exchanged significant looks; they saw the power, the defiance. Mary squeezed his arm, her eyes searching his face but Jesus only felt the oppressive gaze intensify. The miracle worked—the disaster was averted but the act was done. The flag had been waved, he had used the power bestowed upon him, not in quiet obedience, but in an act of open defiance, to shield his own choice, his own wife. The best wine flowed, a symbol not of divine blessing, but of a son's dangerous gamble. He looked up at the harsh blue sky—the Father's silence now felt heavier, and more threatening than any storm. The wrath hadn't fallen here, not today but it would come. The standoff in Cana was over. The real confrontation was just beginning. He could feel it in the stillness, a promise of a future fury.

The Prophet's Burden

The sun beat hard on the dusty trail winding up from Jericho. Jesus walked ahead, his stride long, the worn leather of his sandals scraping stone. Sweat plastered his tunic to his back. His disciples followed, kicking up puffs of pale dust that hung in the still air.

"Remember Micah," Jesus said, his voice rough. He didn't turn. "From you, Bethlehem Ephrathah, shall come the ruler in Israel. Bethlehem. My birth town. A sign."

Peter wiped grit from his eyes. "We know, Rabbi. We believe you are the one."

Jesus stopped abruptly, facing them. The lines around his eyes seemed deeper, etched by sun and something heavier. "Do you? Truly? Isaiah spoke it clear. 'Behold, your God will come...he will come and save you.' Salvation. That's the promise. Does this feel like salvation?" He gestured vaguely at the harsh landscape, the distant haze marking Jerusalem. His jaw tightened. "Sometimes...sometimes I wonder if He even listens anymore. Or if He just demands."

Thomas shifted uncomfortably. "The signs, Master. The healings. Lazarus...rising. They prove it."

"Prove it to whom?" Jesus snapped, a flash of bitterness breaking through. "To the priests? To Rome? Or just to us, walking this damned road?" He started walking again, faster now. "Zechariah. 'Rejoice greatly... your king comes to you...humble, riding on a donkey.' A donkey. Not a warhorse. Not what they expect. Not what *I*..." He trailed off, clenching his fists. He muttered, low and harsh, "Why must it be this way? Why the suffering?"

John, walking closest, touched his arm briefly. "We follow you, Master. Wherever it leads."

They reached Bethany as the sun dipped low, casting long, distorted shadows. Word had flown ahead of them. People pressed into the narrow street, their faces eager and desperate. Jesus paused, his exhaustion momentarily replaced by a fierce intensity. He spoke of the Kingdom, a realm not of swords and crowns, but of justice and mercy. He spoke of himself as the door, the shepherd, the long-awaited branch from Jesse's stump. His voice, though tired, carried conviction. "The time is fulfilled! The kingdom is near! Repent, and believe the good news!" But his eyes held a hollow look, scanning the hopeful crowd as if searching for an escape he knew he wouldn't find.

Mary Magdalene stood at the edge, her gaze fixed on him. There was a quiet understanding in her eyes, a shared weight. She moved through the crowd to meet him as he finished speaking. Their hands brushed, a brief, electric contact that lingered a moment too long. No words passed between them, only a look filled with unspoken grief and a fierce, protective loyalty.

They stayed at the house of Mary, Martha, and Lazarus. The air inside was thick with unspoken tension, despite Martha's bustling hospitality and Lazarus' quiet presence, a walking reminder of impossible things. The meal was eaten mostly in silence. Jesus pushed food around his plate—contemplating what has led him to this moment—and what is pushing him towards the next. Later, Mary Magdalene brought him water. Their fingers touched again on the clay cup. He held her gaze, a silent plea for comfort in his own eyes before he looked away, retreating into his thoughts. That night, sleep was fitful.

Before dawn, Jesus was awake. He found Peter and John. "Go into Bethphage," he ordered, his voice low and urgent. "You'll find a donkey tied, and her colt with her. Untie them and bring them to me."

Peter stared. "Master...take them? Just like that? That's stealing."

Jesus' eyes flashed, cold and hard. "Where is your faith? Have you heard nothing? Zechariah spoke the word: 'Behold, your king is coming to you...mounted on a donkey, and on a colt, the foal of a beast of burden.' It *must* happen. Exactly as written. If anyone questions you, say only, 'The Lord needs them.' He will understand."

Peter hesitated, exchanging a worried glance with John. "The Lord? Which lord?"

"The Lord who demands obedience!" Jesus hissed, a tremor of suppressed rage in his voice. "The Lord whose plan leaves no room for questions! Go!"

They went, the early morning air chilling their skin. Bethphage was quiet. They saw the animals tied near a low stone wall—a sturdy gray donkey and a smaller, skittish brown colt. As they fumbled with the knots, the door of the nearby house burst open and a burly man stormed out, his face flushed with anger.

"Thieves!" he roared, striding towards them. "What do you think you're doing with my animals? In broad daylight!"

Peter stepped forward, his heart pounding. "The Lord needs them," he stammered, repeating the words.

"The Lord?" The man spat. "What lord? Caesar? Herod? Pilate? Some bandit chief hiding in the hills?"

"The Messiah," John blurted out. "Jesus of Nazareth. The prophecies...Zechariah...he must ride them into Jerusalem."

The man's anger faltered, replaced by confusion and a flicker of fear. "The Nazarene? The one they say raised a man?" He looked from the animals to the disciples, then back towards Bethany. He muttered something under his breath, a curse or a prayer. Finally, he waved a dismissive, almost fearful hand. "Take them. Just...go."

They led the animals back to Bethany, the colt pulling nervously against the rope. Jesus was waiting outside, his face grimly set. The disciples draped their heavy cloaks over the backs of the donkey and the colt, as makeshift saddles. They stood back, unsure of how this was going to work.

Jesus approached them and placed one hand on the donkey's back, the other on the colt. He took a breath, then swung a leg over the donkey. He shifted, trying to position his other leg over the colt. The donkey stood calmly, but the colt shied, stepping sideways. Jesus wobbled, grabbing mane and rope. He urged them forward slowly, the donkey plodded; the colt resisted, pulling against the rope tethering it to the larger animal. Jesus lurched forward, struggling to keep his balance atop the two mismatched animals moving out of sync.

Peter couldn't contain himself. "Master! Why not just ride the donkey or the colt? The prophecy...surely it means one animal?"

Jesus' face contorted as he wrestled the animals to a halt. "Fulfillment requires precision!" he snapped, his voice tight with strain and frustration. "Every word! 'on a donkey, *and* on a colt'! Do you question the scripture? Do you question *Him*?" His glare silenced them. They saw the raw edge of fear beneath the anger. He kicked the animals forward again, clinging precariously.

The news spread—by the time they reached the road towards Jerusalem, a crowd had gathered—people from Bethany, travelers, and the curious. They saw Jesus struggling atop the two animals—a murmur went through the crowd. Then, spurred by some unseen signal, they surged forward. People ripped off their dusty cloaks and threw them onto the rocky path in front of the stumbling animals. Others scrambled up the slopes, hacking at palm branches with knives, laying down a rough green carpet. The path became a chaotic sea of cloaks and foliage.

The crowd thickened—those ahead turned back, joining those pressing behind. A roar built, swelling into a chant that echoed off the hillsides: "Hosanna to the Son of David! Blessed is he who comes in the name of the Lord! Hosanna in the highest!"

The noise was deafening—Jesus rode through it, his face pale, jaw clenched. He wasn't smiling. He just looked straight ahead, towards the looming walls of Jerusalem, his knuckles white where he gripped the donkey's mane and the colt's rope too tight. The hosannas washed over him like waves, but his eyes held the bleak acceptance of a man walking towards a crucifixion. The crowd saw triumph—his disciples, close behind, saw only a man utterly alone, caught in the grinding gears of a prophecy dictated by a distant, demanding God. The golden city shimmered ahead, it was beautiful and treacherous. The shouts of acclamation filled the air, a stark counterpoint to the cold dread settling in their hearts. The road dipped, Jerusalem rising before them, its gates like the jaws of a trap—just waiting to snap shut.

The Bandit's Freedom

The knife slid between the Roman merchant's ribs like butter through bread. Barabbas watched the man's eyes widen in surprise before the life drained out of them. Blood pooled in the desert sand, already turning black under the scorching sun.

"Clean work," Gestas said, wiping his own blade on the dead man's robes. "Quick and quiet."

Barabbas rolled the corpse over and cut the purse from the merchant's belt. It was heavy with gold coins, enough to feed his band of outcasts for months. The Romans taxed everything that moved through Judea, leaving the people to starve while their overlords grew fat. Taking back what belonged to the land seemed like justice to him.

"Search the wagon," he commanded his men. "Take everything useful. Leave nothing for the vultures in uniform."

They had been hitting Roman supply caravans for two years now, ever since the centurions had burned his village and killed his family for refusing to pay tribute to Caesar. The official charge had been sedition, but the real crime had been poverty. His father had worked the same plot of ground for forty years, but the Roman taxes had bled them dry.

Barabbas remembered standing in the ashes of his home, watching his mother's body burn while Roman soldiers laughed and passed around jugs of wine. That night, he had sworn an oath to the God of his fathers. Every Roman death would be payment on the debt they owed his people.

The wagon held grain, olive oil, and wine intended for the garrison at Jerusalem but now it would fill the bellies of refugees hiding in the hills. Barabbas had built a network of caves and hideouts throughout the wilderness, sheltering families driven from their homes by Roman greed.

"Boss," called Dysmas from his position watching the road. "Riders coming. Roman patrol."

Barabbas counted six mounted soldiers approaching at a gallop. They had found the merchant's body sooner than expected. He drew his sword and whistled sharply. His men emerged from behind rocks and scrub brush, surrounding the approaching Romans in a circle of steel.

The patrol leader, a grizzled centurion with battle scars crossing his face, raised his hand to halt his men. He looked around at the trap they had ridden into and smiled grimly.

"Barabbas the Bandit," he said. "Rome has put a fine price on your head."

"Rome can collect it when I am dead," Barabbas replied. "Until then, you trespass on free land."

"Free land?" The centurion laughed. "This is Roman territory, purchased with Roman blood. Your people are subjects of Caesar, nothing more."

"My people were here when Rome was still a village of mud huts," Barabbas snarled. "We will be here when your empire crumbles to dust."

The centurion's smile faded. "Surrender now and I promise you a quick death. Resist and we will crucify you slowly, as an example to other rebels."

Barabbas raised his sword. "Come and try."

The battle was brief but vicious. The Romans fought with discipline and training, but Barabbas and his men fought with the fury of the dispossessed. When the dust settled, five Romans lay dead in the sand. Only the centurion remained, bleeding from a dozen wounds but still breathing.

"Finish him," Gestas urged, but Barabbas shook his head.

"Let him live. Let him crawl back to his masters and tell them what happens to those who steal from the people."

The centurion spat blood and glared at him with hatred. "This is not over, bandit. Rome has a long memory."

"So do I," Barabbas replied.

They took the Roman horses and weapons, then disappeared into the maze of canyons and hidden paths that only the locals knew. By nightfall, they were safe in their mountain stronghold, a series of caves connected by narrow passages carved into the living rock.

Barabbas distributed the gold among his followers, keeping only enough to buy information and supplies. His network of informants in Jerusalem kept him informed of Roman movements, troop strengths, and valuable targets. The widow Rachel, whose husband had died in Roman chains, sold him details about merchant caravans. Young Timothy, who cleaned stables for the garrison, reported on patrol schedules.

For three years, Barabbas waged his private war against the occupation. He never attacked civilians, only soldiers and officials who profited from oppression. The common people called him a hero. The Romans called him a zealot. He called himself a free man in a world of slaves.

But freedom, he learned, came with a price that compounded like debt.

The Romans responded to his raids with increasing brutality. For every soldier killed, they executed ten civilians. For every caravan robbed, they burned a village. Barabbas watched from the hills as innocent families paid for his victories with their blood.

"We are making it worse," Dysmas said one night as they watched smoke rise from yet another burning settlement. "The Romans blame the people for our actions."

"The people were already suffering," Barabbas replied, but his voice lacked conviction. "At least now they know someone fights for them."

"Do they?" Gestas challenged. "Or do they curse our names as they bury their children?"

Barabbas had no answer—the God of his fathers remained silent on the matter of justice and revenge. If the Almighty cared about Roman oppression, He showed no sign of it. The rains still fell on Roman fields. The sun still warmed Roman faces. Divine justice, it seemed, was a luxury for the afterlife.

The trap came on a cold morning in early spring. Barabbas and twelve of his best men were riding to intercept a gold shipment bound for Caesarea when Roman cavalry surrounded them in a narrow valley. Someone had betrayed them, sold their location for Roman silver.

They fought like cornered wolves, but lacked numbers and position—one by one, his men fell. Dysmas took a spear through the chest and Gestas died with a sword in his hand and a curse on his lips. When the last of his followers lay still, Barabbas threw down his weapons and raised his bloody hands.

"I surrender," he called out.

The Romans bound him with chains and dragged him to Jerusalem for trial. The charges were murder, robbery, sedition, and inciting rebellion against Caesar. The penalty was death by crucifixion, the slow agony reserved for enemies of the state.

They threw him into a cell beneath the Antonia Fortress, a stone box barely large enough to lie down in. Rats scurried across his feet in the darkness. Water dripped from somewhere above, marking time like a funeral drum.

For weeks, he waited for death—hoped for it—prayed for it. The Romans seemed in no hurry to execute him. Prison guards brought moldy bread and sour wine, keeping him alive but weak. Sometimes he heard screaming from other cells, the sound of interrogations and torture. He wondered which of his people were being questioned, which names would be dragged from their lips by Roman blades.

Then came the morning when everything changed.

"Get up, bandit," the guard commanded, unlocking his cell. "You have an appointment with justice."

They dragged him into the courtyard of the fortress, blinking in the sudden sunlight. A crowd had gathered, hundreds of people packed into the space between the walls. Roman soldiers held them back with spears and shields, but barely. The air resonated with the tension and barely controlled violence.

At the center of the courtyard stood a raised platform where Pontius Pilate, the Roman governor, waited in his purple robes. Beside him stood another prisoner, a thin man with long hair and hollow eyes. Blood streaked his face from a crown of thorns pressed into his scalp.

"Citizens of Jerusalem," Pilate called out, his voice carrying across the crowd. "It is the custom at Passover for the governor to release one prisoner chosen by the people. Today you must choose between two men."

He gestured first to Barabbas. "This man stands accused of murder and rebellion against Rome. He has killed soldiers and stolen from the empire."

A rumble of approval ran through the crowd. Many had heard his name, some had benefited from his raids on Roman supplies.

"And this man," Pilate continued, pointing to the other prisoner, "stands accused of claiming to be King of the Jews, of preaching sedition against Caesar."

Barabbas looked at his fellow condemned man with curiosity. He had heard stories about this Jesus of Nazareth, a traveling preacher who spoke of love and forgiveness. Those were strange teachings for a rebel, but the Romans crucified men for less.

The crowd grew restless—voices called out from different sections, some shouting "Barabbas!" others yelling "Jesus!" The noise built like a storm gathering strength.

"Choose!" Pilate commanded. "Which prisoner shall I release?"

"Give us Barabbas!" The chant started somewhere in the back and spread through the crowd like wildfire. "Barabbas! Barabbas! Barabbas!"

Barabbas felt a surge of elation—the people had chosen him, had demanded his freedom. But as he looked at the other prisoner, he saw something that chilled him. The man called Jesus was staring directly at him, and his eyes held no hope, no peace, only bitter resignation.

"What shall I do with Jesus of Nazareth?" Pilate asked.

"Crucify him!" the crowd roared. "Crucify him!"

Jesus continued to stare at Barabbas, and now the bandit could see madness flickering behind those dark eyes. This was not the serene teacher described in the stories. This was a broken man who had expected salvation and found only betrayal.

"My Father," Jesus whispered, his voice barely audible above the shouting crowd, "why have You forsaken me already?"

The guards released Barabbas from his chains, the metal fell away like shed skin, and he was free. Around him, the crowd celebrated his release while demanding the death of the preacher. He should have felt triumph, but instead he felt hollow.

"Go," Pilate told him. "You have been judged and found worthy of mercy by your people."

As Barabbas walked through the crowd, hands slapped his back and voices praised his name. But behind him, he could hear the other prisoner being led away to his death. The man who had preached love was dying while the man who had killed for revenge walked free.

Barabbas left Jerusalem that same day, walking the roads he had once traveled as an outlaw but the countryside had changed during his imprisonment. Roman patrols moved freely through areas he had once controlled. His network of supporters had scattered or been arrested and the caves that had sheltered refugees now stood empty.

He made his way to the ruins of his childhood village, now nothing but broken stones and weeds. Standing in what had once been his family's house, he tried to feel something—grief—anger—purpose. Instead, he felt only the weight of years and the futility of his war against Rome.

"Barabbas."

He turned to find Rachel the widow standing behind him. She looked older, worn down by years of struggle and loss.

"I thought you were dead," she said.

"I should be. Another man died in my place."

She nodded. "I heard about the choice. The people freed you and condemned the Nazarene."

"Do you think they chose correctly?"

Rachel was quiet for a long moment. "The Nazarene preached that we should love our enemies. You showed them how to kill their oppressors. Which message do you think they needed to hear?"

Barabbas had no answer. Around them, the wind whistled through broken walls where children had once played and families had once laughed. The Romans had won not through superior virtue but through superior violence. Love had proven weaker than hate, mercy less practical than revenge.

"Where will you go now?" Rachel asked.

"I do not know. My war is over. My men are dead. The cause I fought for died with them."

"Then find a new cause. Find a new way to fight."

But Barabbas knew there was no new way. Violence only bred violence in an endless cycle. The Romans would continue to oppress because that was their nature. The people would continue to suffer because that was their fate. The God of his fathers would continue His silence because that, apparently, was His will.

He left Rachel standing in the ruins and walked north, toward Galilee. Perhaps there he could disappear, become just another face in the crowd, another broken man trying to forget the weight of his choices.

For months, he wandered the countryside, taking odd jobs and avoiding cities where Roman soldiers might recognize him. He worked as a laborer, a guard for merchant caravans, a hunter of wild animals that threatened livestock. The work was honest but meaningless, a way to pass time until time passed him.

Then came the night when his past caught up with him.

He was sleeping rough in a grove of olive trees when armed men surrounded his camp. They were not Romans this time, but Jews. Men he recognized from his days as an outlaw.

"Barabbas the Bandit," their leader said. It was Judas Iscariot, one of the Nazarene's former disciples. "We have been looking for you."

"I am no longer a bandit," Barabbas replied, keeping his hands visible and away from his weapons. "I am nobody now."

"That can change," Judas said. "We need your skills. Your knowledge of Roman weaknesses."

"The Romans have no weaknesses. They have only strength and the will to use it."

"The Nazarene thought differently," Judas spat. "He preached love and forgiveness right up until the nails went through his hands. Much good it did him."

Barabbas studied the men surrounding him. He could see desperation in their faces, the look of people who had lost everything and were ready to lose more.

"What do you want from me?" he asked.

"Lead us," Judas said. "The people still remember your name. They still believe you can hurt Rome."

"I cannot. My time is finished."

"Your time will never be finished as long as Rome stands on our necks," Judas insisted. "The Nazarene failed because he was weak. You can succeed because you are strong."

"The Nazarene failed because you sold him out. Betrayed him. For what? Thirty pieces of silver?" Barabbas retorted. "Am I to suffer the same fate?"

"It was prophecy," Judas said. "Jesus was big on prophecy being fulfilled. I was just doing my part, someone had to. Jesus revealed that I would be the one to betray him at our Last Supper. I just needed to find a scripture that could be claimed as a prophecy to justify it. Zechariah's thirty pieces of silver was a perfect fit."

Barabbas thought of the broken man with the crown of thorns, staring at him with eyes full of bitter defeat. Had Jesus been weak, or had he simply understood something that the rest of them missed?

"The Nazarene died for his beliefs," Barabbas said. "Are you prepared to do the same?"

"We are already dead," Judas replied. "The Romans killed us when they killed our teacher. We just have not stopped breathing yet."

That night, around a fire built from dead olive branches, they planned their war. Not the careful, strategic campaign Barabbas had once waged, but a desperate final strike meant to wound Rome's pride if not its power. They would attack the tax collection point at Jericho, kill the Roman officials, and distribute the money to the poor.

It was suicide disguised as heroism, but Barabbas found himself agreeing to lead them. Not because he believed they could win, but because he could not bear to see them die without purpose.

The attack came at dawn, just as the tax collectors opened their strongboxes to count the previous day's tribute. Barabbas and his new followers struck like lightning, overwhelming the guards before they could raise an alarm. The Roman officials died quickly, their blood mixing with scattered gold coins on the stone floor.

But even as they divided the treasure among themselves, Barabbas could hear horns blowing in the distance. A Roman cavalry was coming, summoned by riders who had escaped the initial assault.

"We knew this was the end," Judas said, hefting a bag of gold that would never reach the poor. "At least we struck one last blow."

They made their stand in the ruins of an ancient watchtower, using the crumbling stones as cover while Roman arrows whistled overhead. One by one, Judas and his men fell. Each death was meaningless, a waste of life that would change nothing and help no one.

When only Barabbas remained alive, he threw down his sword and walked out to face the Roman commander. The officer was young, perhaps twenty-five, with the soft look of someone born to privilege.

"Barabbas the Bandit," the young man said. "You are far from home."

"This is my home," Barabbas replied. "All of Judea is my home."

"Not anymore. Caesar claims this land by right of conquest."

"And I claim it by right of birth."

The Roman smiled. "Rights are determined by strength. Caesar is stronger than you."

"Caesar is dead," Barabbas pointed out. "Murdered by his own senators. Where was his strength then?"

The Roman's smile faded. "Caesar is eternal. The man dies, but the empire endures."

"Everything dies," Barabbas said. "Even empires."

They bound him again with the same chains he had worn years before. The cell in Jerusalem looked exactly as he had left it, down to the same stains on the walls. But this time, there would be no reprieve, no crowd to demand his freedom.

On the morning of his execution, they dragged him to Golgotha, the place of skulls. Two crosses waited, his and one for a common thief who had been caught stealing bread. The Romans crucified criminals in pairs when possible, believing that shared suffering increased the agony.

As they nailed his hands to the crossbeam, Barabbas looked out over Jerusalem. The city sprawled beneath him, unchanged by all his years of fighting. The same Roman standards flew from the same towers. The same tax collectors squeezed coins from the same suffering people. His war had accomplished nothing except to add more names to the lists of the dead.

The thief on the neighboring cross was weeping, calling out for mercy from a God who gave no sign of listening. Barabbas wanted to tell him that mercy was a luxury the divine could not afford, but his throat was too dry for speech.

Hours passed—the sun climbed toward its peak and began its descent. Vultures circled overhead, waiting for death to release their feast. In the distance, Barabbas could see smoke rising from cooking fires, the ordinary business of life continuing while extraordinary suffering played out on the hill.

As darkness began to gather around the edges of his vision, Barabbas thought he heard laughter. It was not the cruel mockery of Roman soldiers, but something warmer and sadder. The laughter of a broken teacher who had finally learned the punchline to God's cosmic joke.

Love was weakness, mercy was folly and justice was whatever the strongest decided it should be. The meek would inherit nothing but graves, and the peacemakers would find only pieces of their shattered dreams.

The laughter grew louder, or perhaps he was simply dying and hearing things that were not there. Either way, it followed him into the darkness, the sound of divine madness echoing across a world where freedom was just another word for choosing how to die.

His last thought was of the crowd that had chosen him over the Nazarene, demanding the release of a killer while condemning a teacher of love. They had chosen correctly after all. In a world ruled by monsters, monsters were the only ones who could survive.

But survival, he realized too late, was not the same thing as living.

The Woman at the Well

The sun hammered the cracked earth. Heat waves shimmered above the sand dunes, turning the distant hills into liquid ghosts. Jesus leaned against the rough stone rim of Jacob's Well, a deep, dark hole punched into the desert floor. Sweat tracked lines through the dust on his face. His throat felt like old leather. The disciples had ridden ahead to Sychar for supplies, leaving him alone in this parched stretch of contested land. The well sat squarely in Samaritan territory, a place where a lone Jew invited trouble.

Hoofbeats disturbed the heavy silence. It was not the steady rhythm of his disciples returning, that he expected. A single rider approached, leading a weary pack mule. Dust caked the rider's clothes and the animal's flanks. As the figure neared, the wide-brimmed hat pulled low couldn't hide the sharp angles of a woman's face. Her eyes, when they flickered towards him, held a guarded hardness. She dismounted smoothly, her hand resting near the worn handle of a knife sheathed on her belt. She ignored him, looping her mule's reins over a sun-bleached post. Her movements were efficient and practiced.

She grabbed a clay jar from the mule's pack and walked towards the well. The rope and bucket lay coiled nearby. She didn't look at him again, but her posture stayed tight, ready.

"Give me a drink," Jesus said. His voice cut through the dry air.

The woman froze, halfway to lowering the bucket. She turned slowly, her gaze swept over him, taking in his dusty robes and his travel-worn sandals. Suspicion hardened her features. "You're a Jew. I'm a Samaritan. Why ask me for water?" Her voice was flat and challenging. It was more than just custom; it was law in this borderland. Samaritans and Jews shared nothing, especially not water—trouble brewed easy here.

Jesus met her stare. "You don't know God's gift. You don't know who asks you for water. If you did, you'd ask him. He'd give you living water."

A harsh laugh escaped her and she gestured at the deep well. "Mister, you got no bucket. This well is deep. Where's your 'living water'? You greater than Jacob? He dug this well. He drank from it. His sons drank.

His herds drank." She shook her head, dismissing him, and began lowering the bucket. The rope scraped against the stone.

"Everyone drinking this water gets thirsty again," Jesus said. His words stopped the scraping rope. "Whoever drinks the water I give won't ever thirst. The water I give becomes a spring inside. It bubbles up into lasting life."

The woman straightened up, leaving the bucket dangling. She studied him anew, the hardness in her eyes mixed with something else—a flicker of desperate hope, quickly masked. "Give me this water," she said, her voice losing some of its edge. "Then I won't get thirsty. I won't need to keep hauling water out here." Her gaze drifted towards the distant cluster of Sychar's low buildings. The chore was heavy, but the stares in town were heavier.

"Go," Jesus said. "Get your husband. Come back here."

Her head snapped back towards him. A flush crept up her neck, visible beneath the dust. Her hand tightened on the rope. "I don't have a husband," she stated, the words clipped and final.

"You spoke truth," Jesus replied. His eyes held hers, steady and knowing. "You had five husbands. The man you live with now isn't your husband."

The color drained from her face and she took a step back, bumping against the mule, it snorted softly. Her knuckles were white where she gripped the rope—fear replaced the hardness. He knew—this stranger, this Jew sitting at the well, knew her whole broken story. The five men, buried or gone. The current arrangement, a matter of grim survival in a town that whispered her name like a curse. How could he know?

"Mister," she breathed, her voice barely above a whisper. "I see you're a prophet." She scrambled for solid ground, shifting the focus. "Our ancestors worshipped on this mountain. You Jews say Jerusalem's the place to worship." She gestured towards the rugged peak looming over Sychar. It was an old argument, a safe argument.

Jesus leaned forward slightly. "Believe me, woman. A time comes when worshipping the Father won't be about this mountain or Jerusalem.

You worship what you don't know. We worship what we know. Salvation comes from the Jews. But a time is here. True worshippers will worship the Father in spirit and truth. That's what the Father wants."

She absorbed his words, the tension easing slightly, replaced by a dawning wonder. The familiar walls of division—Samaritan, Jew, mountain, city—seemed to blur. "I know Messiah's coming," she said slowly, testing the words. "The one called Christ. When he comes, he'll explain everything."

"I am he," Jesus said. "The one speaking to you now."

The clay jar slipped from her fingers and hit the hard ground with a dull thud but didn't break. She didn't seem to notice. Her eyes were wide and fixed on him. The dusty outlaw woman, the outcast, stood face-to-face with the promised deliverer. The knowledge hit her like a punch in the stomach, stealing her breath. The harsh lines of her face softened—a light sparked in her eyes, something untouched by the desert or the town's scorn.

Hoofbeats could be heard in the distance. They were loud, many riders, coming fast—not from Sychar—from the east, the open desert. Dust plumed on the horizon, resolving into a tight group of riders—ten, maybe twelve—hard men on hard horses. Sun glinted off sword blades and scabbards. Their clothes were rough and mismatched, not town clothes. Their faces were obscured by bandanas pulled high against the dust.

Jesus turned his head, watching their approach. The woman followed his gaze. The new light in her eyes flickered, replaced by the old wariness and sharpened by fear. She recognized the type. They were raiders—border trash—men who took what they wanted.

The riders reined in hard, their horses skidding in the loose dirt. They formed a loose half-circle around the well, cutting off escape towards Sychar and the open desert. Their leader, a broad man with cold eyes above his bandana, spat near the woman's dropped jar. His eyes swept over Jesus, then lingered on the woman with a predatory interest.

"Well now," the leader drawled, his voice muffled by the cloth. "What we got here? A Jew preacher man and Sychar's favorite sinner." He chuckled, a dry, humorless sound. His men shifted in their saddles, hands resting near weapons. "Heard tell there was a stranger asking questions 'bout water. Didn't hear he was fraternizing with the local scandal."

The woman stood very still, her back pressed against the mule. Her hand drifted towards her knife.

The leader's eyes tracked the movement. "Easy there, darlin'. We ain't lookin' for trouble with you. Yet." He turned his attention back to Jesus. "We got a problem, preacher. Your kind ain't welcome here. Stirrin' up the locals. Talkin' crazy about water and worship." He nudged his horse a step closer. "We keep things quiet 'round these parts. Don't need no trouble-makers."

Jesus stood up and faced the riders. His expression was calm, but his eyes held the leader's gaze. "I only offered water," he said. His voice was clear, carrying over the restless snorts of the horses.

"Water?" The leader barked a laugh. "We got all the water we need. What we don't need is you. Or your talk." He looked past Jesus, at the woman. "He tell you sweet lies, girl? Promise you somethin' better?" His voice dropped, turning ugly. "Nothin' better out here for the likes of you. Or him."

One of the other riders, younger, twitchy, gripped the handle of his knife. "Heard he knew things. Private things. That true, preacher? You spyin' for someone?"

The tension tightened like a drawn bowstring. The desert air crackled with it. The woman saw the twitchy rider's grip tighten. She saw the leader's hand drop casually to the sword scabbard on his saddle. She saw Jesus, standing exposed. The words he'd spoken—*living water, lasting life*—echoed in her mind, a fragile, impossible hope against the brutal reality surrounding them.

"No!" The cry tore from her throat, raw and desperate. She lunged forward, not towards her knife, but towards Jesus, as if to shield him or pull him back. Her movement was sudden and instinctive.

It was the spark.

The twitchy rider flinched, his hand jerked. The knife pulled free from its sheath, his grip loosened and the knife soared through the still air. The woman stumbled, a dark stain blooming high on her chest, spreading fast across her dusty shirt, the knife embedded deep. Her eyes met Jesus', wide with surprise, then confusion, then nothing. She crumpled to the ground beside her unbroken jar.

Silence slammed down, heavier than before. Even the horses seemed stunned. Dust particles danced in the harsh sunlight.

The twitchy rider stared at his knife in the woman's flesh, his face pale beneath the bandana. The leader swore violently, his cold eyes flicking from the dead woman to Jesus, then to his own man. "Fool!" he snarled. He turned his horse, gesturing sharply. "Ride! Now!"

The riders spun their mounts, kicking up a fresh cloud of choking dust. They galloped back the way they came, leaving only the sound of fading hoofbeats and the buzzing of flies already finding the dark stain on the ground.

Jesus stood alone by the well. He looked down at the woman. Her eyes stared blankly at the unforgiving blue sky. The jar lay beside her, empty. The desert stretched out, vast and indifferent. The disciples would return soon, talking of bread. The water in the deep well below waited, untouched. The only sound was the dry wind, scouring the stones.

The Gerasene Silence

The canyon walls baked under the midday sun. Scraggly mesquite clung to cracks in the sun-baked rock. Below, in the deep shadow of the eastern gorge, lay the tombs. They were not grand sepulchers, but caves gouged into the cliff face, places where the town of Gerasa dumped its dead and its unwanted. The air hung heavy, thick with the smell of dust and something else—decay, maybe, or madness.

Jude felt the familiar pressure building behind his eyes. It started as a low hum, a vibration in his bones. Then the voices came—not one, but many—Legion. They filled his skull, screaming arguments, laughing at him, whispering dark promises. He clawed at his temples, his nails scraping skin raw. He'd broken free of the ropes again. They always tied him, the townspeople. Tied him to the iron rings hammered into the rock near the caves but the strength the voices gave him snapped rope like thread.

He staggered from the cave mouth, blinking against the harsh light. His clothes hung in filthy rags. Sunlight gleamed on the heavy chains dragging from his wrists and ankles, links worn smooth by constant friction against the canyon floor. He saw the pack mule first, a cloud of dust approaching along the dry desert trail. Then the figure walking beside it—a stranger. He was lean, dressed in simple trail clothes, but carrying an unsettling stillness.

The voices inside Jude roared—Fear—Hatred—Recognition. *Him. It's Him. The One. The Nazarene.* The cacophony swelled, a tidal wave crashing against the inside of his skull. He stumbled forward, chains clanking, driven by the force possessing him, yet fighting it with every shred of his own trapped will. He fell to his knees in the dust before the approaching man, the pack mule pulling up short, the stranger looking deep within his eyes.

"What do you want with me, Jesus, son of the highest God!?" The voice that ripped from Jude's throat wasn't his own. It was a guttural chorus, layered and grating. "Swear by God you won't torture me!" The man, Jesus, stopped. His gaze fixed on Jude—it wasn't fear Jude saw there—it was something deeper, older. A terrible calm.

"Come out of this man!" Jesus commanded. His voice cut through the demonic clamor like a knife.

Jude convulsed and slammed his forehead into the hard ground. The voices shrieked in protest, a sound that scraped the air. "What is your name!?" Jesus asked, his tone level, relentless.

The answer came, forced out through Jude's clenched teeth. "Legion. My name is Legion. There are many of us." The voices gibbered, pleading now. "Don't send us away from this region! Don't send us into the abyss! Let us go into the swine. Let us go into the herd!"

Jude's eyes, wide and bloodshot, flickered towards the western ridge. On the plateau above, a vast herd of pigs belonging to the Gerasa miners rooted in the sparse scrub. There were hundreds of them—a major investment. Food for the miners, collateral for loans. Jesus followed his gaze, then back at Jude and the writhing terror within him. A flicker of sorrow touched his eyes. Then he spoke a single word. "Go!"

The effect was immediate, Jude felt the pressure inside his head explode outward. It wasn't pain, but a terrifying release, a vacuum forming where the screaming crowd had been. A profound silence descended—he gasped, drawing clean air into lungs that felt new. The constant ache in his muscles, the gnawing terror, the alien thoughts—gone. He looked down at his hands. They were his own hands—trembling, but his.

A low rumble pulled his attention upwards. On the plateau, the pig herd exploded into frantic motion. A wave of panicked animals surged, squealing with an unnatural, high-pitched terror. They weren't running aimlessly. They stampeded directly towards the western edge of the plateau, where it dropped sharply into the deep, churning waters of the Sea of Galilee below. The herders yelled, cracking whips uselessly. The pigs ignored them, driven by a terror beyond instinct. They plunged over the cliff edge in a squealing, tumbling cascade, hundreds of bodies hitting the water with sickening thuds. The sound echoed off the canyon walls—the frantic squeals cut short, replaced by the heavy splash and then the churning water as the entire herd drowned.

Silence fell again, deeper and heavier than before. The herders stood frozen on the plateau, staring at the empty space where their livelihood had just vanished. Down in the canyon, Jesus clutched the reins of his pack mule, his face pale. Jude remained on his knees, breathing hard, touching his own face as if confirming it was real.

The herders scrambled down the steep path, their faces masks of shock and dawning horror. They ran past Jude and Jesus without stopping, heading straight for Gerasa, shouting the news. Word spread like wildfire through the mining town. Men dropped their picks, women gathered children close. The miner's faces turned purple when they heard—the pigs—all the pigs—gone. Driven into the sea by...by what? By the demoniac? By this stranger?

Fear, colder than the canyon shadows, gripped Gerasa. They knew the power that had held Jude. They'd seen it—Feared it—Contained it. Now this stranger had commanded it. He commanded it into their pigs. What else could he command? What else would he destroy? The miracle wasn't welcome—it was a catastrophe. It was power they couldn't control. It was a power, they feared—a power they wanted out of their town.

They came armed, swords drawn. It wasn't a mob, exactly, but a grim delegation. Men with swords, knives, picks and whatever they could find to arm themselves, their faces set hard. A big, burly man led them, flanked by hard-eyed miners and the shaken pig herders. They found Jesus near the tombs. Jude sat beside him, washed and wearing borrowed clothes that hung loose on his frame, his face was peaceful but watchful taking in the silence. The big burly man spat into the dust.

"That your doing?" he asked Jesus, jerking his head towards the distant sea.

Jesus met his gaze. "The unclean spirits left the man. They went into the swine."

A murmur ran through the men. They shifted their weight, their swords angled slightly, but the tension didn't ease. "Unclean spirits," the big burly man scoffed, but there was fear underneath the bravado. "Call 'em what you want. You cost this town. Cost the miners. Cost every man here his stake." He gestured at the watching miners. "That herd was our future. Food. Security. Gone. Because you played preacher with the madman."

"We want you gone," a miner spoke up, his voice tight. "This ain't your territory, Nazarene. Take your...your power...somewhere else."

"Leave," the big burly man stated flatly. "Leave now. And don't come back. Ever." The men behind him nodded, a wall of fearful resolve. Their swords were raised again, not quite pointing, but the threat was clear. "Take that pack mule of yours and leave. Head east. Keep going."

Jesus looked at them—he looked at the fear etched on every face. He looked at Jude, sitting quietly, a man reborn. He didn't argue, he didn't plead, he simply stood and walked towards the waiting pack mule.

As Jesus walked away, he turned back. His eyes found Jude. "Go home," he said, his voice carrying clearly in the still air. "Go home to your own people. Tell them everything. Tell them what the Lord did for you. Tell them how he showed you mercy."

Jude met his gaze and nodded. A spark of purpose ignited within him. He would tell them—he would make them understand the power and the mercy he had seen.

The pack mule slowly walked away from Gerasa, kicking up dust. Jesus walked beside the animal, Jude watched them go until they disappeared around a bend in the canyon.

He walked back towards Gerasa alone. The weight of the chains was gone, but a new weight settled on him. The town gates were open, but men stood watching. He saw their faces as he approached. The looks were not relief, not welcome. It was suspicion—anger—fear. The big burly man stood near the gatehouse, arms crossed. The miners who had chased Jesus away clustered nearby, their expressions were hard.

Jude stopped a few yards from the gate. He drew a deep breath. He opened his mouth. "Listen," he began, his voice rusty but clear. "Listen to what happened. The man, Jesus…"

"Shut it, Jude!" a miner barked. "We know what happened. He wrecked the herd. He brought trouble."

"Trouble?" Jude pressed, taking a step forward. "He freed me! The voices…Legion…they're gone! He commanded them out! He showed me mercy!"

The big burly man stepped forward. "Mercy?" His voice was low and dangerous. "Mercy cost us two thousand head of prime swine. Mercy scared this town half to death. Mercy will bring armed men to our gates demanding answers we ain't got." He jabbed a thick finger at Jude. "You. You were contained. We handled you. Tied you. Kept you out there. Wasn't pretty, but it worked. Then *he* comes. Stirs things up. Wrecks our livelihood." He leaned closer. "You want mercy? Here's mercy. Keep your mouth shut. Bury that story deep. We don't want it here. We don't need reminding of what he did, or what you were. You speak one word about that Nazarene, about demons, about pigs in the sea…" He let the threat hang, lifting his sword, slightly pointing in Jude's direction—sunlight gleaming off the blade.

Jude looked from the big burly man's cold eyes to the faces of the miners. He saw no opening, no crack for his testimony—only fear, hardened into hostility. The purpose Jesus had ignited flickered and died under the weight of their collective dread. Telling them wouldn't bring understanding. It would just bring rage—it might bring the sword.

He lowered his head. The chains were gone, but new bonds snapped tight around his heart. He turned away from the gate, away from the town. He didn't go home—there was no home for him here anymore. He walked back towards the tombs, towards the caves. The silence inside his head was complete now—Blessed, terrifying silence. He sat down on a sun-warmed rock near the caves, the empty iron rings beside him glinting dully. He stared out at the canyon, the dust settling where the pack mule had vanished. He had the greatest story ever told burning inside him. A story of power and mercy—a story that could change everything and he knew, with a certainty colder than the tomb caves, that he would never tell a soul. The silence of Gerasa had swallowed him whole.

Lazarus Undone

The sun beat down hard on the cracked earth near the Jordan. Dust hung in the air, thick and choking. A rider came hard, his horse lathered, kicking up a plume behind him like a dirty banner. He slid to a stop near Jesus, who sat on a flat rock, staring west. The rider's words were gasped, urgent. "Teacher...Lazarus...Bethany...sick. Bad sick. Martha and Mary sent me. They beg you come. He needs your hand."

Jesus looked at the man, his eyes were dark and hollowed. He said nothing for a long moment. The silence stretched, broken only by the horse's ragged breathing and the buzz of flies. Finally, he nodded once, a curt gesture. "Tell them the sickness won't end in death." The rider stared, confused, he was expecting movement or command but Jesus just looked away, back towards the empty horizon. "Go. Tell them." The rider kicked his weary horse back towards the trail, leaving Jesus alone with the oppressive heat and his own thoughts.

Two days passed and Jesus stayed put. The disciples watched him, uneasy. They knew Lazarus was a friend, someone Jesus cared for. Thomas voiced it, low. "He loved that man. Why sit here while he suffers?" But Jesus remained unmoved, a statue carved from sorrow and something harder. On the morning of the third day, he stood abruptly. "We go to Judea."

A ripple went through them. "Teacher," Philip protested, "just days ago they tried to stone you there! And you want to go back?"

Jesus turned, his face was grim. "Are there not twelve hours of daylight? A man who walks by day doesn't stumble. Lazarus sleeps. I go to wake him."

Confusion mixed with relief. "Lord, if he sleeps, he'll get better," Peter said, hopeful.

Jesus met his eyes, the words fell like stones. "Lazarus is dead." He let the silence hang, heavy. "And for your sake, I'm glad I wasn't there. Now you will see. And you will believe. Let's go." He started walking, heading west towards the hills and the danger.

The journey was harsh. The trail wound through bleached canyons and across vast, waterless deserts shimmering with heat. Thorny scrub clawed at their robes. The disciples followed, the news of Lazarus' death settling like dust in their throats. They walked close to Jesus, seeking shade near rock faces when they could.

Thomas walked beside Jesus. "Lord," he started, hesitant, "we know Lazarus was your friend. Close. Why wait? Why let him...?" He couldn't finish.

Jesus kept walking, his gaze fixed on the distant, hazy outline of the hills. The sun beat on his back. "You think the Almighty cares about friendship?" His voice was rough, devoid of its usual warmth. "He sees the pattern. The threads. He pulls them tight, snaps them when it suits His purpose. Lazarus...Lazarus served a point." He spat the word. "Like everything."

Andrew pushed forward. "But Teacher, what point? A good man dies in pain, his sisters grieve...what point justifies that?"

Jesus stopped and looked at the small group, their faces etched with sun and confusion. "You struggle to see beyond the dirt under your nails. Death isn't the end He decrees. It's just...relocation. The Boss decides the neighborhood." A bitter twist touched his lips. "Let me tell you a story. Helps pass the miles."

They walked on as he spoke, his voice cutting through the dry air.

"There was a rich man. Lived large. Purple robes, fine linen every day. Feasted like a king, table groaning. Right outside his gate, dumped like refuse, lay a beggar named Lazarus. Covered in sores. Dogs licked his wounds. He'd have given anything for the scraps falling off the rich man's table. Nothing. Not a crumb. Not a glance."

Jesus painted the scene starkly. The opulence—the filth—the indifference. The disciples pictured Herod Antipas in his fancy palace, ignoring the starving wretch in the alley.

"Time came. The beggar died. Carried away by angels, straight to Abraham's side." Jesus gestured vaguely upwards. "The rich man died too. Buried. Found himself in torment. Flames licking him. He looked up, saw Abraham far off, and Lazarus right there, comfortable beside him."

The disciples shuffled, the image was stark in the desert heat.

"The rich man cried out. 'Father Abraham! Mercy! Send Lazarus! Just let him dip his fingertip in water, cool my tongue! This fire is agony!'"

Jesus paused, letting the plea hang. "Abraham answered. 'Son, remember? You had your good things in life. Lazarus got the bad. Now he finds comfort here. You find agony. Besides...' Abraham pointed down, then up...a great chasm is fixed. No crossing. Either way.'"

Judas frowned. "So...the beggar got rewarded? The rich man punished? For...ignoring him?"

"For ignoring him," Jesus confirmed, his voice flat. "For seeing need, right at his gate, every day, and turning his face. For loving his fine linen more than his neighbor's pain. The Boss notices that. Hates indifference more than outright sin, maybe. The rich man had Moses, the prophets. He ignored them too. Ignored the cries outside his door. Now...he burns. And there's no exit." Jesus stared hard at them. "Neglect has consequences. Eternal ones. The Boss keeps score. Settles accounts. Painfully."

He resumed walking, faster now. "That Lazarus," he added, jerking his head back towards the direction they'd come, "the one rotting outside the gate? He mattered. His suffering mattered. The Boss saw it. The Boss sees everything. And He remembers who looked away." He didn't elaborate on the connection to their friend. He didn't need to. The parable hung heavy, a dark promise of divine reckoning.

Bethany looked like a settlement clinging to the hillside, baked brown under the relentless sun. News of their approach traveled faster than they did. Martha met them on the edge of the cluster of stone houses. Her face was drawn, etched with grief and something hotter—anger—rage, maybe. Dust coated her mourning clothes.

"Lord," she said, her voice tight and controlled. "If you had been here, my brother wouldn't have died." The accusation was clear, sharp as flint. "Even now...I know God will give you whatever you ask." It was faith, but faith strained thin by anger.

Jesus looked at her, the lines around his eyes deep. "Your brother will rise again."

Martha nodded, weary. "I know he will rise in the resurrection on the last day."

Jesus stepped closer and the sun glinted off the sweat on his brow. "I am the resurrection. I am the life. Anyone believing in me, even though he dies, will live. Everyone living and believing in me will never die. Do you believe this?"

Martha met his gaze—the bitterness in his eyes startled her, but the words were undeniable. "Yes, Lord. I believe you are the Messiah, the Son of God, the one coming into the world." She turned. "Mary is home. I'll get her."

Martha hurried away. Jesus stood still, a solitary figure on the dusty path. The disciples shifted, uncomfortable. They heard whispers from the houses, saw faces peering from doorways. The town felt watchful and hostile.

Soon, Mary came. She ran, stumbling in her grief, her friends trailing behind her, wailing. She fell at Jesus' feet. "Lord! If you had been here, my brother wouldn't have died!" Her voice broke, raw with a pain Martha had kept locked down. The sound of her weeping, joined by the other women, filled the dry air.

Jesus looked down at Mary, then at the weeping women, then at the silent, accusing faces of the townspeople gathering. His jaw tightened, a muscle flickered in his cheek. He closed his eyes for a moment. When he opened them, the dark fury was replaced by a profound weariness. "Where did you put him?" His voice was thick.

"Come and see, Lord," Martha whispered.

Jesus started walking, they followed—the disciples, the sisters, the mourners, a grim procession moving out of the settlement, up the rocky slope towards the burial caves. The air smelled of dust and decay.

Jesus stopped and looked towards the hills, then back at the tomb—a cave mouth sealed with a heavy stone. His shoulders slumped, just for an instant. He took a deep, shuddering breath. The disciples saw his eyes were red. He wiped his face roughly with his sleeve. Some in the crowd muttered.

"See how he loved him!" Others were harsher. "He opened the blind man's eyes! Couldn't he have kept this man from dying?"

Jesus turned to face the tomb, his hands clenched at his sides. He looked up, not towards heaven, but towards the harsh, unforgiving blue of the sky. His voice, when it came, was low, guttural, carrying over the sudden silence. "Why?" It wasn't a prayer. It was a demand, flung at the empty expanse. "Why did You make me wait? Why this?" He stood rigid, breathing hard, as if waiting for an answer that wouldn't come. The bitterness he carried seemed to radiate from him, colder than the desert night. He lowered his head. "Fine," he rasped, the word barely audible. "Fine. You win. Again." He took another breath, deeper this time, forcing control. When he spoke again, it was louder, directed at the crowd, at the sisters, at the silent rock sealing the cave. "Take away the stone."

Martha, practical even in despair, recoiled. "Lord, by this time there's a stench! He's been dead four days!" The blunt reality hung in the air like decay and finality.

Jesus turned his head slowly to look at her. His eyes held no comfort, only a terrible certainty. "Didn't I tell you? If you believed, you would see the Boss' ugly handiwork?" He gestured sharply at the stone. "Move it."

Men stepped forward—grunting, straining against the weight, they rolled the stone aside. A dark opening yawned and a foul, sweet-sick smell drifted out, making people cover their noses and step back. Jesus didn't flinch, he walked right up to the entrance. The darkness inside was absolute. He raised his voice, a raw command that echoed off the rock face.

"Lazarus! Come out!"

Silence—absolute silence followed the echo. The crowd held its breath. The disciples leaned forward, straining to see into the blackness. Martha clutched Mary's arm. There was nothing—seconds stretched into minutes—a fly buzzed. Doubt flickered across their faces—had the Master failed? Was this the final, cruel joke?

Then, a sound—a shuffling, scraping sound from deep within the cave. A shape emerged from the gloom, stumbling into the harsh afternoon light. It was Lazarus, but death had marked him. His burial wrappings clung to him, strips of linen stained with grave-spices and corruption. A cloth covered his face. He moved stiffly, unnaturally, like a puppet with tangled strings. He stood there, swaying slightly, shrouded and silent.

A collective gasp went up, people recoiled. Mary buried her face in Martha's shoulder. Even the disciples took a step back, their faces pale with awe and horror. This wasn't the joyful reunion they'd half-imagined. This was something wrong.

Jesus looked at the figure, his expression was unreadable, like stone. He spoke again, his voice flat, devoid of triumph. "Unbind him. Let him go."

People hesitated—Martha, trembling, moved first. She approached her brother, her hands shaking as she reached for the cloth covering his face. Slowly, she peeled it back.

The eyes that stared out were Lazarus' eyes, but empty—lifeless—like dull stones. They didn't blink against the blinding sun. They didn't focus on Martha. They stared straight ahead, seeing nothing. The face beneath was pale, waxy and slack. No breath stirred the linen across his chest.

Jesus watched—he saw the emptiness in those eyes. He saw the horror dawning on Martha's face, on Mary's, on the faces of the crowd. He saw the disciples staring, not at a miracle, but at an abomination.

A terrible understanding washed over him, cold and final. This wasn't life restored. This was a puppet show—a grotesque display orchestrated by the vengeful tyrant above to prove a point, to settle some cosmic score outlined in that damned parable. Lazarus was back, but whatever made him *Lazarus*—the soul, the spirit, the spark—was gone. Trapped? Obliterated? Jesus didn't know. He only knew the chasm Abraham spoke of was real, and it had swallowed his friend whole. The Boss didn't restore—he only punished. Even in apparent victory, He dealt only in torment. Lazarus was condemned to walk the earth bound, a walking accusation, a hollow testament to divine cruelty.

Jesus turned away from the silent, staring figure of his friend. He didn't look at the horrified sisters. He didn't look at the sky. He looked down at the dry, cracked earth beneath his feet. A single, harsh laugh escaped him, a sound like breaking stone. He had played his part perfectly. The show was over. The trail ahead stretched long, leading only to another tomb, another stone—next time, maybe his own. He started walking, alone, back towards the desert. The crowd parted before him, silent now, not with awe, but with dread. Behind him, Lazarus stood, motionless, a monument not to life, but to the terrible, vindictive silence of heaven.

The Silence After the Sermon

Part 1

The sun hammered the bleached rock as Jesus climbed, the rough stone scraping his sandals. His small band of merry-men followed—Peter, Andrew, John, James, Matthew and the others. Their faces were tight, etched with dust and the strain of constant movement. Below, a trickle of people snaked up the slope: fishermen mending nets left tangled, tax collectors abandoning their tables, women carrying sick children. Word travelled fast out here. The man who silenced the storm and touched lepers was speaking.

He stopped on a broad ledge overlooking the gray-green scrub stretching to the Dead Sea's bitter edge. The air shimmered in the heat. More people arrived, a slow flood converging on the mountainside. They spread out on the rocky ground, a restless sea of worn tunics and anxious eyes, staring up at Jesus. Jesus sat. His disciples gathered close, forming a rough half-circle. The crowd hushed, the only sound was the dry rasp of wind over stone.

He looked at his followers, then out at the multitude. His voice cut through the stillness, clear and hard as flint. "Blessed are the poor in spirit. The kingdom of heaven is theirs." Murmurs rippled. *Poor in spirit?* That meant the broken, the desperate. Like most of the people gathered here under the punishing sky. "Blessed are those who mourn. They will be comforted." A woman clutching a thin child wept silently. "Blessed are the meek. They will inherit the earth." Skepticism hardened some faces, meekness got you nothing but dust out here.

He spoke of the persecuted, the hungry for righteousness, the pure in heart. Each pronouncement felt like a promise scraped raw against the harsh reality of Roman boots and empty bellies. "You are the salt of the earth," he stated, his gaze sweeping the crowd. "But if salt loses its taste, it's useless. Trodden underfoot." His eyes held a warning. "You are the light of the world. A city set on a hill." He paused, letting the image settle over the barren landscape. "Don't hide it. Let your light shine before others. So they see your good works. So they give glory to your Father in heaven."

Peter shifted. "Master," he began, his voice rough, "The Law...Moses taught us strict justice. Eye for an eye, tooth for a tooth." It was the way of survival in this hard land, the only code many knew.

Jesus turned his head slowly. The lines around his eyes seemed deeper in the relentless light. "You heard it said. But I tell you this: Don't resist the one who is evil." A gasp went up. "If someone strikes you on the right cheek, turn the other also." Disbelief mixed with shock on the disciples' faces. "If anyone forces you to go one mile, go two. Give to the one who begs. Don't refuse the one who wants to borrow."

"Love your enemies," Jesus continued, his tone flat and devoid of warmth. "Pray for those who persecute you." He stared out towards Jerusalem, unseen beyond the hills. "That you may be sons of your Father. He makes his sun rise on the evil and the good. He sends rain on the just and the unjust." A bitter twist touched his lips, fleeting. "If you love those who love you, what reward do you have? Even tax collectors do that. Be perfect, therefore, as your heavenly Father is perfect." The word 'perfect' hung heavy, impossible, like the unyielding rock beneath them. The silence was broken only by the wind. Perfection demanded by a Father whose justice felt as remote and unforgiving as the desert sky.

Part 2

The crowd had swelled—thousands now packed the mountainside, a vast, thirsty herd seeking water in a dry place. Jesus watched them, his expression unreadable. The disciples sat closer, sensing a shift. The initial shock of his blessings and commands settled into a deeper, more uneasy anticipation.

"Beware practicing your righteousness before other people," Jesus announced, his voice carrying easily over the multitude. "Don't do it to be seen by them. If you do, you will have no reward from your Father." He fixed his eyes on a group of Pharisees near the front, their fine robes stark against the dust. "When you give to the needy, sound no trumpet. Like the hypocrites do in the synagogues and streets. They have their reward. Truly, I tell you." His voice held no condemnation, only a cold certainty. "When you give, don't let your left hand know what your right hand is doing. So your giving may be in secret. And your Father who sees in secret will reward you."

John leaned towards Andrew, whispering, "Reward? What reward? When has the Father shown anything but demands?" Andrew shook his head, troubled.

"And when you pray," Jesus continued, his gaze sweeping past the Pharisees, "Don't heap up empty phrases like the Gentiles do. They think they'll be heard for their many words." He paused, his eyes seeming to look through the crowd, towards something vast and terrible. "Your Father knows what you need before you ask him. Pray then like this: Our Father in heaven, hallowed be your name." The title felt heavy, formal. "Your kingdom come. Your will be done. On earth as it is in heaven." He spoke the words, but a weariness clung to them. "Give us this day our daily bread. And forgive us our debts, as we also have forgiven our debtors." His voice hardened slightly. "And lead us not into temptation. But deliver us from evil." He stopped. The simple prayer hung in the air, a stark contrast to the elaborate public prayers common in the temple courts.

"Your Father knows," Jesus repeated, his voice dropping lower. "If you forgive others their trespasses, your heavenly Father will also forgive you. But if you do not forgive others, neither will your Father forgive your trespasses." It sounded less like grace and more like a grim transaction enforced by a distant, implacable power.

"When you fast," he said, shifting focus, "Don't look gloomy like the hypocrites. They disfigure their faces so others see they're fasting. Truly, I tell you, they have their reward. When you fast, anoint your head and wash your face. So it won't be obvious to others. Only to your Father who is in secret. And your Father who sees in secret will reward you."

Matthew, the former tax collector, spoke up, his voice hesitant. "Master…rewards, treasures…where should our heart be? We see men storing grain, hoarding silver…"

Jesus' eyes snapped to him. "Don't lay up treasures on earth. Moth and rust destroy. Thieves break in and steal." He gestured vaguely towards the distant, fortified estates of the wealthy. "Lay up treasures in heaven. Where moth and rust don't destroy. Thieves don't break in and steal. For where your treasure is, there your heart will be also." He paused, a flicker of something bleak in his eyes. "The eye is the lamp of the body. If your eye is healthy, your whole body is full of light. But if your eye is bad, your whole body is full of darkness. If the light in you is darkness, how great is that darkness!"

Thomas frowned. "But Master, how can we serve? A man cannot serve two masters. He will hate one and love the other. Devotion to God or devotion to money?" It was the constant struggle of every poor man under Roman rule.

"Exactly," Jesus said, the word sharp. "You cannot serve God and money. Therefore I tell you, don't be anxious about your life. What you will eat. What you will drink. About your body, what you will put on. Isn't life more than food? The body more than clothing?" He pointed towards the sky where hawks circled. "Look at the birds. They don't sow or reap. They don't gather into barns. Your heavenly Father feeds them. Aren't you more valuable than they?" He paused, his jaw tightening. "Which of you by being anxious can add a single hour to his span of life? Why be anxious about clothing? Consider the lilies…how they grow. They don't toil or spin. Yet I tell you, even Solomon in all his glory wasn't arrayed like one of these." He gestured towards the sparse, hardy desert flowers clinging to cracks in the rock. "If God so clothes the grass, here today and tomorrow thrown into the oven, will he not much more clothe you? Men of little faith?"

The question hung—was it reassurance, or an indictment?—no one knew—His tone held little comfort. "Don't be anxious, saying, 'What shall we eat?' or 'What shall we drink?' or 'What shall we wear?' The Gentiles seek all these things. Your heavenly Father knows you need them all." He looked out at the multitude, their faces etched with the very anxieties he named. "Seek first his kingdom and his righteousness. And all these things will be added to you." He paused, a long, heavy silence. "Therefore don't be anxious about tomorrow. Tomorrow will be anxious for itself. Sufficient for the day is its own trouble." It felt less like a promise of provision and more like a command to endure the relentless grind under a watchful, demanding eye.

Part 3

The sun was lower now, casting long, distorted shadows across the multitude. The air cooled slightly, but the tension hadn't eased. Jesus stood. The vast crowd watched with a collective held breath. His disciples braced themselves—the hardest words seemed yet to come.

"Judge not," Jesus began, his voice flat, "That you be not judged. For with the judgment you pronounce you will be judged. With the measure you use it will be measured to you." He stared at them, his eyes dark. "Why do you see the speck in your brother's eye, but don't notice the log in your own eye? How can you say to your brother, 'Let me take the speck out of your eye,' when there is a log in your own? You hypocrite. First take the log out of your own eye. Then you will see clearly to take the speck out of your brother's eye."

James, the brother of John, spoke, frustration edging his voice. "Master, how do we know truth? Some speak smooth words, others shout warnings. Who do we trust?"

"Beware false prophets," Jesus answered immediately, his voice cold. "They come to you in sheep's clothing. Inside they are ravenous wolves." He scanned the crowd as if searching for hidden threats. "You will recognize them by their fruits. Are grapes gathered from thornbushes? Figs from thistles? So, every healthy tree bears good fruit. The diseased tree bears bad fruit. A healthy tree cannot bear bad fruit. A diseased tree cannot bear good fruit." His gaze was piercing. "Every tree not bearing good fruit is cut down. Thrown into the fire." He paused, letting the image of consuming flames settle. "Thus you will recognize them by their fruits."

Philip raised a hand. "Master, doing the Father's will...it feels impossible. Like shouting into the wind. Does it matter? Does He even hear?"

Jesus turned his head sharply. "Not everyone who says to me, 'Lord, Lord,' will enter the kingdom of heaven. Only the one who does the will of my Father. On that day many will say to me, 'Lord, Lord, did we not prophesy in your name? Cast out demons? Do mighty works?'" His voice rose slightly, a harsh edge cutting through. "Then I will declare to them, 'I never knew you. Depart from me, you workers of lawlessness.'"

A collective shudder seemed to pass through the crowd. The threat was naked and brutal. "Everyone then who hears these words of mine and does them," Jesus continued, his tone shifting to something almost mechanical, "Will be like a wise man who built his house on the rock. Rain fell. Floods came. Winds blew and beat on that house. It did not fall. It had a foundation on the rock." He paused, his eyes distant. "Everyone who hears these words and does not do them will be like a foolish man who built his house on the sand. Rain fell. Floods came. Winds blew and beat against that house. It fell. Great was its fall."

Silence, absolute and crushing, descended. The stark image of utter ruin hung over them, amplified by the surrounding desert's indifference. The disciples exchanged troubled glances. The words were clear, but the foundation felt like shifting sand itself. Trusting a Father whose character seemed defined by vengeance? Doing His will under such a shadow?

Jesus looked out over the sea of faces one last time. The initial trickle had become a multitude drawn by hope, but his words had offered only impossible demands and dire warnings under the fist of a celestial tyrant. He saw the confusion, the fear and the flicker of disillusionment already taking root. He had come to fulfill, but the Law felt like chains forged in heaven's cold fire. He felt the familiar, bitter ache of abandonment, the crushing weight of a fate accepted only because resistance was futile against such overwhelming power.

He turned away abruptly, without blessing, without farewell. He began walking down the mountainside, away from the crowd, away from his stunned disciples. The people watched him go, the silence broken only by the crunch of his sandals on the gravel. The magnificent sermon, a blueprint for a kingdom built on shifting sands, ended not with amens, but with the hollow sound of retreat. The sun dipped below the horizon, plunging the stark landscape into twilight. The multitude sat in the gathering gloom, the hard, unforgiving words echoing in the sudden chill, the promised kingdom feeling further away than ever, swallowed by the vast, indifferent desert and the shadow of a vengeful God. The only thing built was a deeper sense of dread.

Meeting Nicodemus

The desert wind carried grit, not relief. Nicodemus pulled his hood lower, the rough wool scratching his cheek. Jerusalem's lights were distant smudges behind him. He followed the faint path worn by desperate men to the shack near the ravine. Lamplight bled through cracks in the warped wood. He knocked, the sound swallowed by the vast night.

The door opened and Jesus stood there, framed by the weak yellow light. He looked older than Nicodemus remembered from the temple debates, harder. Dust coated his sandals, deep lines etched his face, carved by sun and something heavier. His eyes held no welcome, only a cold assessment. "Rabbi," Nicodemus said, his voice tight.

"Nicodemus." Jesus stepped back, granting silent entry. The room held little: a rough table, a stool, a cot. The air smelled of dust and lamp oil. Jesus gestured to the stool. Nicodemus sat, feeling the eyes of this man upon him. "You came at night," Jesus observed. His voice was flat and devoid of inflection.

"The council watches," Nicodemus admitted. "They speak against you. Open association is...unwise." He hesitated. "We know you are a teacher sent by God. No one performs these signs unless God is with him." The words felt inadequate in the cramped silence.

Jesus gave a short, harsh sound. Not a laugh. "God is with me?" He moved to the window, staring out at the black expanse. "God demands. God punishes. God uses a rod of iron." He turned back, his face shadowed. "No one sees God's kingdom unless born again." The statement hung, stark and strange.

Nicodemus frowned. "Born again? A grown man cannot re-enter his mother's womb." The desert logic felt solid.

Jesus leaned against the table, the lamp casting his features into sharp relief. "Flesh gives birth to flesh. Spirit gives birth to spirit. Do not marvel I said you must be born again." His gaze fixed on Nicodemus. "The wind blows where it wills. You hear its sound, but you don't know where it comes from or where it goes. So it is with everyone born of the Spirit." Nicodemus felt a chill, unrelated to the night air. This wasn't the hopeful teacher of the crowds. This man spoke of forces beyond control.

"How can these things be?" Nicodemus pressed, confusion mixing with the need to understand this dangerous figure.

"You are Israel's teacher," Jesus stated, a hint of that old bitterness surfacing, "and you do not understand these things? I speak of earthly things and you disbelieve. How will you believe if I speak of heavenly things?" He pushed away from the table. "No one ascends to heaven except the one who descended from heaven—the Son of Man." He paused, the title heavy. "Just as Moses lifted the serpent in the wilderness, so the Son of Man must be lifted up, that whoever believes in him may have eternal life."

Nicodemus seized on the familiar reference. "Eternal life? This is the hope?"

"For God so loved the world," Jesus began, the words sounding mechanical and rehearsed, "that he gave his only Son, that whoever believes in him should not perish but have eternal life." He stopped, his jaw tightening. He looked past Nicodemus, through the wall, into the desert night. "For God did not send his Son into the world to condemn the world..." His voice trailed off. He seemed to wrestle with the next words. When he spoke again, it was lower, harsher. "...but that the world through him might be condemned."

Nicodemus stiffened. "Condemned?"

Jesus turned back, his eyes burning now with a cold, resigned fire. "Yes. Condemned. The light came, Nicodemus. The true light. But men loved darkness. They chose it. They *prefer* it. Their deeds are evil. They hate the light." He gestured vaguely towards Jerusalem. "They hate me. Because I expose them. To the great Judge."

"The Judge?" Nicodemus whispered.

"The one who sits enthroned," Jesus said, his voice dropping to a near whisper, thick with a terrible certainty. "The one who demands absolute obedience. The one who crushes rebellion. He sent me as the final proof. The final test. They fail. They always fail. I am the sign of their condemnation. My presence seals their fate." He looked directly at Nicodemus, no trace of comfort in his expression. "Whoever believes faces the Judge with my name. The Judge sees only his own demand met. Or not." He shrugged, a gesture of utter weariness. "The verdict is written before the testimony is given."

Nicodemus felt the hope drain from him, replaced by cold dread. This wasn't salvation offered; it was condemnation confirmed. "But...the signs...the healings..."

"Proof," Jesus interrupted, his voice flat once more. "Proof of the power behind the sentence. Proof they ignored. Proof that damns them further." He walked to the door and opened it. The desert wind rushed in, carrying the scent of dry earth and despair. "Go back, Nicodemus. Go back to your council. Tell them the Son of Man walks the desert, waiting for the appointed hour. Tell them the axe is laid to the root. The Judge requires his due." He offered no blessing and no comfort, only the dark, open door.

Nicodemus stood, his legs unsteady. He stepped out into the biting wind. He looked back—Jesus stood silhouetted in the lamplight, not watching him leave, but staring out into the endless, indifferent night. The door closed with a final thud, leaving Nicodemus alone in the vast, dark emptiness, the words echoing: *condemned...the Judge...the axe...*The path back to Jerusalem felt longer and bleaker, leading only towards a wrath he now understood was inescapable. The meeting hadn't brought answers—it had extinguished the last flicker of hope. The light hadn't come to save—it had come to judge.

Nicodemus' Last Stand

The sun hammered Jericho flat. Heat shimmered and rose over the cracked earth beyond the town's low walls. Dust coated everything—the rough wooden beams of the structures, the worn robes of the people, the sparse leaves of the struggling acacia trees. It felt less like ancient Judea and more like some forgotten outpost at the edge of a vast, merciless desert. A lone hawk circled high overhead, a dark speck against the bleached sky.

Inside a dim room attached to a merchant's courtyard, the air hung thick and still. Sunlight sliced through a high window, illuminating swirling dust particles. Nicodemus ben Azariah smoothed the fine linen of his sleeve, a stark contrast to the rough-spun tunic of the man seated opposite. Nicodemus represented the Sadducees: wealthy, powerful, guardians of the Temple, strict interpreters of the written Law. They acknowledged no resurrection, no angels, no spirit beyond this life. They saw only the harsh reality ordained by a demanding God.

The man facing him was Jesus of Nazareth, lines etched his face deeper than his years warranted. His eyes held a weary bitterness, the look of a man who had walked too long under a punishing sun. He accepted a clay cup of water from a silent follower, his hand steady but his gaze distant.

"Nazarene," Nicodemus began, his voice cool and precise. "Your words travel far. Too far. They reach ears they shouldn't. You speak of forgiveness freely given. You eat with tax collectors, with sinners. You heal on the Sabbath. These acts disregard the Law. The Law given by God." He leaned forward slightly. "You claim authority. Some even whisper 'Messiah'. Do you claim this title? Do you set yourself above Moses?"

Jesus took a slow drink and set the cup down with deliberate care. The sound echoed in the quiet room. "The Law stands," he said, his voice low, gravelly with dust and fatigue. "But it points beyond itself. It points to a justice deeper than ritual. To a mercy harder than stone."

"Mercy?" Nicodemus' lip curled. "God demands obedience. Sacrifice. Blood pays for sin. That is the covenant. That is the justice you undermine with your easy blessings. Your God sounds weak."

A flicker of something raw crossed Jesus' face. He looked past Nicodemus, through the wall, towards the blinding whiteness outside. "My Father..." He paused, the word heavy. "He is not weak. He demands everything. He demands the final payment." His voice dropped, almost to a whisper. "He demands *me*."

Nicodemus frowned. This wasn't the fiery prophet or gentle teacher reported in the marketplaces. This man seemed hollowed out—resigned. "You speak of sacrifice? The Temple sacrifices suffice. God accepts the blood of bulls and goats. He does not demand the blood of men claiming to be His anointed."

Jesus met Nicodemus' eyes then. The bitterness was plain. "You think you know God's demands? You think you measure His wrath?" A harsh, dry sound escaped him, almost a laugh. "He is a jealous God. A consuming fire. He will have His due. He will have *all* the debt paid. Not with the blood of animals. With mine." He spread his hands, calloused palms upward. "He appointed me for this. The Lamb. Led to slaughter because He demands it. Because nothing less satisfies His...justice."

The word 'justice' hung in the air like the dust—it felt like vengeance. Nicodemus shifted, unsettled. This despairing acceptance was unexpected. It lacked the defiance he anticipated. "So you admit it? You claim Messiahship only to become a sacrifice? A dead Messiah saves no one, Nazarene. It mocks the prophecies. It mocks God's promise. You lead people astray with false hope."

"Hope?" Jesus echoed. The weariness deepened. "There is only the cup. The cup He filled. I must drink it. There is no other path." He looked down at his hands again. "He has turned His face away. I walk this road alone. To satisfy the hunger of His Law."

The starkness of the admission shocked Nicodemus. This wasn't a man building a kingdom; this was a man marching towards his own execution, believing a vengeful God required it. It was madness. Dangerous madness. His own anger flared, hot and sudden. This broken man threatened everything—the Temple order, the Sadducee authority, the very understanding of God's covenant. It was an affront that couldn't stand.

"Blasphemer!" Nicodemus hissed, the controlled façade cracking. He surged to his feet, the chair scraping harshly on the stone floor. "You twist the Holy One into a monster! You make yourself a martyr for a lie! Your death won't satisfy God. It will only prove your deception!"

Jesus didn't flinch, he didn't rise. He simply looked up at the furious Sadducee, his expression bleak, accepting. "It is finished," he murmured, not to Nicodemus, but to the empty air and the uncaring walls.

The unexpected stillness and the utter lack of resistance, seemed to snap something in Nicodemus. Reason fled before a wave of outrage. This passive acceptance felt like a deeper insult than any defiance. His hand shot to the dagger concealed within his robe—a finely crafted weapon, a symbol of status, never intended for this.

The movement was swift, born of blinding fury. The polished blade flashed once in the shaft of sunlight. Nicodemus lunged, not with the precision of a ritual knife, but with the desperate, clumsy violence of a man pushed too far. The blade plunged deep, just below the ribs.

Jesus gasped—a sound of pure shock, then pain. His eyes widened, locking onto Nicodemus' for a fractured second—not with accusation, but with a terrible, dawning realization. His hand clutched weakly at the hilt protruding from his side. Blood, shockingly red, spread across the dusty brown fabric.

He slumped forward, his forehead hitting the rough wood of the table with a dull thud. His body shuddered once, then went still. The cup he'd drunk from rocked slightly, spilling the last drops of water onto the thirsty stone floor, mingling with the darkening pool spreading beneath the table.

Nicodemus staggered back, the dagger still gripped in his hand, now slick and red. He stared at the crumpled form, at the blood soaking into the dust. The silence in the room was absolute, broken only by the frantic buzzing of a fly drawn to the scent. The hawk outside screamed once, a sharp, lonely sound cutting through the desert heat. The follower who had brought the water stood frozen in the doorway, his face a mask of utter disbelief and horror.

Nicodemus looked from the body to the bloody knife, then to the empty, sun-blasted sky visible through the window. He had silenced the blasphemer. He had defended the Law. He had appeased God's justice. So why did the desert air suddenly feel so cold? Why did the vengeful God he served feel like a vast, indifferent void, staring back at him? The deed was done. The Nazarene was dead. Not on a cross, as prophecy might whisper, but on a dusty floor in Jericho, killed by a priest's rage. The tragedy wasn't the death itself, but the brutal, meaningless stupidity of it. Nicodemus ben Azariah stood in the sudden, terrible quiet, the architect of an ending no one had foreseen, least of all himself.

Thirty Pieces of Silver

Judas Iscariot kicked dust from his boots outside the stable. Inside, the air tasted thick with old hay and animal heat. Jesus sat on a feed sack, his back against the rough planks. Sweat tracked lines through the dirt on his face. He looked drained and hollow. The coins felt like lead in Judas' pouch.

"He demands blood," Judas stated flatly. "The Lord. Payment for their sins. Your blood." He watched Jesus' face.

Jesus lifted his head—his eyes held no surprise, only a deep, dry bitterness. "The Father turned away. He demands the debt paid." His voice cracked. "Judas. Do what you came to do."

Judas pulled the rope from his saddlebag, coarse hemp. He secured one end to a thick beam overhead, dust choking the air. He fashioned the noose, his hands steady. He looked back. Jesus hadn't moved, his gaze fixed on the dirt floor.

Judas stepped onto an overturned bucket. He looped the rope around his own neck. The rough scratch felt final. He thought of the coins, the priests, the vengeful God requiring sacrifice. He kicked the bucket hard.

The rope snapped tight. A strangled gasp escaped him. His legs jerked, then stilled. Jesus finally looked up at the hanging man—a flicker of something ancient and tired crossed his face. Jesus murmured to the empty stable. "Judas did what was required." He closed his eyes.

Hour of Darkness

Part 1

Chapter 1

The upper room held the smell of dust and roasted lamb. Smoke from the oil lamps curled towards the ceiling beams. Jesus sat at the head of the low table, the worn wood smooth under his palms. He felt the pressure in the air, thick as the desert heat. Death walked close tonight. He could almost hear its dry footsteps on the stone floor.

His followers filled the space around the table. Thirteen men, their faces shadowed and uncertain in the lamplight. Their usual chatter had died down hours ago. Now they watched him, waiting. Mary sat near him, closer than the others. Her presence was a quiet warmth against the chill growing inside him. The lamplight caught the deep red of her hair.

A servant brought the Passover meal. Platters of bitter herbs, bowls of charoset, the brown paste sweet with dates and nuts. The roasted lamb sat steaming at the center. The men ate. The sound of chewing filled the silence. Jesus picked at the herbs. The sharp taste stung his tongue—it felt like a mockery.

He reached for the flatbread, a simple round loaf. He broke it with a sharp crack. Every head lifted, their eyes fixed on his hands.

"Take," he said. His voice sounded strange to him, flat. "Eat. This is my body." He passed the pieces down. The disciples took them, their faces confused. They chewed slowly. He saw Peter frown, looking at the bread in his hand. John leaned forward, his young face tight with worry. They were waiting for meaning, for the fire he usually brought. It wasn't there.

Jesus poured wine into a shared cup. The dark liquid swirled. "Drink," he commanded, the word harsher than he intended. "This is my blood." He drank first. The wine was sour. He passed the cup, it went around the table. Each man drank—their lips touched the rim where his had been. Judas took his turn near the end. He kept his eyes fixed on the cup, his knuckles white as he gripped it. He drank quickly, passed it on without looking up.

Under the table, Jesus felt movement as Mary's hand brushed against his leg. Her fingers found his, they tangled together, hidden by the long tablecloth. Her touch was firm, real. For a moment, the crushing weight lifted. He squeezed back—it was the only comfort he had. The only thing that felt true. He thought of quiet moments away from the crowds, her voice low and steady. He needed that steadiness now—he needed her.

The weight returned, heavier—it wasn't just death—it was absence. A vast, hollow silence where God's presence should be. It was like standing in an empty temple and he felt it pressing down on his shoulders, a physical ache in his chest. Where was the Father? Where was the plan's certainty? He felt only cold distance between them—a tyrant demanding tribute. A blood tribute. '*My* blood.' He thought. The bitterness of the herbs flooded his mouth again.

He looked around the table. These men, his friends, his betrayer. The knowledge was a stone in his gut. He had to say it. The silence demanded it.

"Listen," Jesus said. The word cut through the quiet. "One of you sitting here will betray me. Tonight."

The silence shattered. The disciples stared, first at him, then at each other. Shock turned to disbelief, then to rising panic.

"What?" Peter's voice boomed, rough. He slammed a fist on the table. Platters jumped. "No! Not possible! Who? Tell us who!" His face flushed red.

James leaned forward, eyes narrow. "Master, surely you don't mean..." He trailed off, scanning the faces opposite.

John looked stricken. "Lord? Who is it?"

Voices overlapped, sharp and anxious.

"Not me!"

"Could it be...?"

"Master, point him out!"

"Let me at him!"

They leaned away from each other. Suspicion flickered in their eyes. Peter glared across the table. Matthew watched Thomas. Philip studied Bartholomew. The camaraderie of moments before vanished, replaced by fear and accusation. The room felt smaller and hotter.

Jesus watched the chaos. He saw Judas shrink back. The man kept his head down, staring fixedly at his empty plate. His shoulders hunched forward as if trying to disappear. He offered no denial, he asked no question—he just sat, rigid, radiating guilt like heat from a stone. The silence around Judas was louder than the shouting.

"Is it me, Rabbi?" Andrew asked, his voice thin.

"Surely not I?" James the Less pleaded.

"Master, say it isn't so," John whispered.

Jesus looked from face to face. He saw the the fear, the confusion and the desperate need for reassurance. He felt the vast emptiness above him, the absence of any guiding hand. This was the plan? This chaos? This loneliness? He was the sacrifice chosen by a distant, vengeful power. The thought choked him. He didn't want this cup—he didn't want the nails—he didn't want the darkness. A wave of pure, cold terror washed over him. He wanted to run—he wanted to hide—he wanted to take Mary's hand and vanish into the Galilean hills.

He looked at Judas again. The man flinched, finally meeting his gaze for a split second. There was fear there, yes, and shame but also a terrible resolve. It was done. The wheels were turning. There was no stopping it now—God's machinery demanded its fuel.

The arguing petered out. The disciples fell quiet, watching him, waiting for an answer he wouldn't give. The accusation hung in the air, unanswered. The only sound was the sputtering of the oil lamps and someone's ragged breath.

Jesus pushed his plate away. The food was untouched. The sour taste of wine and dread filled his mouth. He looked at the faces around the table—friends, followers, betrayer. He felt Mary's hand still gripping his under the cloth. It felt like the only anchor in a churning sea. He felt utterly alone—abandoned—the silence was overwhelming.

"Finish the meal," he said. His voice was a dry rasp.

No one moved—No one spoke. They sat frozen in the lamplight. The uneaten lamb cooled on its platter. The bitter herbs lay wilted. The silence pressed in, thick and suffocating. It was the silence before the storm. The silence of a trap about to spring.

Jesus stared at the rough wood grain of the table. The weight on his chest was immense. God's absence was a presence itself, cold and demanding. The plan—his death—it was coming—faster now. He felt its approach like a shadow falling across the room. He didn't want it, he feared it but the choice felt like it had been ripped from him long ago. The taste of betrayal was more bitter than the herbs. The silence was complete. The meal was over.

Outside, the city slept. Torches flickered on distant walls. Jerusalem lay quiet under the stars, unaware of the silent dread filling a small upper room. The night air was cool, smelling of stone and distant desert. It offered no comfort. The next hours would bring soldiers, chains, and pain. The path was set. Jesus felt the cold certainty of it settle in his bones, heavy as the silence in the room. He looked towards the window, towards the sleeping city, and the dark hills beyond.

Chapter 2

The silence from the upper room clung to them like dust as they walked. Jerusalem's streets were empty, the stones cold underfoot. Moonlight cast sharp shadows. Jesus led the way, his steps were heavy. Peter, James, and John followed close, their breathing loud in the quiet. The rest had scattered earlier, melting into the night like ghosts. Only Mary had trailed them, a silent figure keeping well back, her presence a flicker of warmth in the cold dread settling over Jesus.

They left the city through a small gate. The path sloped down into the Kidron Valley. The air smelled of damp earth and crushed herbs. Across the valley, the Mount of Olives rose, a dark hump against the star-filled sky. The gnarled shapes of ancient olive trees stood sentinel. Gethsemane—the oil press.

Jesus stopped near a cluster of the oldest trees. Their twisted trunks looked like frozen agony in the moonlight. He turned to the three men, their faces were pale, etched with the fear and confusion from the meal. Peter gripped the hilt of the short sword tucked into his belt. James kept glancing back toward the city. John just looked young and scared.

"Wait here," Jesus said. His voice sounded raw, scraped thin. "Keep watch. Pray you don't fall into testing." He didn't wait for their reply. He walked deeper into the grove, leaving the small circle of moonlight near the path. The darkness swallowed him.

He found a small clearing, bare earth surrounded by thick, knotted roots. He sank to his knees. The ground was cold and hard. He pressed his forehead against the rough bark of the largest tree. The weight he'd carried since the meal crushed down, harder now. It was more than fear—it was a cold, yawning emptiness where God's presence should be—a vast silence. The silence of a throne room where the king had turned his back.

Father. The word felt like ash in his mind. *You can do anything. Take this cup from me.* The image rose from his mind: the rough wood of the cross, the bite of iron nails, the slow suffocation. His stomach clenched. He didn't want it. The terror was a physical thing, cold sweat breaking out across his skin, soaking through his tunic. *Please. Not this. Anything but this.* He dug his fingers into the dirt. *Is there no other way? No price smaller than my blood?* He thought of Mary, her hand gripping his under the table. He wanted that life—Simple—Quiet—Human.

He strained, listening. There was nothing—no answer from the God—the Father demanding his life as a blood sacrifice. There was only the rustle of a night creature in the underbrush, the sigh of wind through the olive leaves and the absolute, oppressive silence. It wasn't the silence of listening. It was the silence of dismissal. The silence of a tyrant who had issued his decree and would not be swayed. Vengeance demanded blood. His blood. The perfect sacrifice. The thought tasted bitter. *Why me? Why this?*

The pressure built inside his skull. Sweat poured down his face, stinging his eyes. It felt thick and heavy, like blood welling from a wound. It dripped onto the dry earth between his knees, dark spots in the moonlight. He gasped for air—the terror wasn't receding. It was growing, a wave threatening to drown him. *Father!* He threw the plea into the void. *If it must be...if there is truly no other path...then let your plan stand.* The words choked him. It was submission that tasted like defeat—like death. The silence remained. There was no comfort, no reassurance, only the cold certainty of the coming dawn—he felt utterly abandoned.

He pushed himself up, his legs trembled and he wiped the sweat-blood from his brow with a shaky hand. The grove suddenly felt colder. He walked slowly back toward where he'd left the others. The moon had shifted, casting longer, stranger shadows. He saw them before he heard them.

Peter, James, and John were sprawled on the ground, backs against tree trunks their heads slumped forward. Peter's mouth hung slightly open, James snored softly and John's face was slack with deep sleep. The sight hit Jesus like a blow—they couldn't even stay awake for one hour? Not for him? Not on this night? The loneliness deepened, like a vast, cold ocean. He was truly alone.

"Still sleeping?" His voice cut through the quiet, sharper than he intended. "Resting? Couldn't you watch with me for one hour?" The three men jerked awake, blinking and scrambling to their feet. Shame flooded their faces. Peter opened his mouth, perhaps to protest, but Jesus cut him off. "Get up. Pray. Your own spirit is eager, ready, but your body... it's weak." He saw the confusion, the lingering sleepiness. They didn't understand the tide rushing in. He turned away, the bitterness rising like bile. He walked back into the darkness, back to his private wrestling match with the silent sky.

The second time was worse. The terror was a living thing, coiling in his gut. He threw himself on the ground, face pressed into the dirt. *Father!* The plea was a silent scream inside his skull. *If there is any way please...let this pass!* He strained until his muscles shook—only the emptiness answered—the vast, uncaring void. The plan was set in stone, carved by a distant, demanding will. His sweat felt cold now, clammy—he shivered. The acceptance he'd forced out before felt hollow, meaningless. He didn't accept, he raged—silently—futilely. He raged against the machine grinding him down. Finally, spent, he whispered the required words again, his voice, broken. *Your plan...not mine.* He pushed himself up, staggering.

He found them asleep again. They didn't even stir as he approached. They looked like dead men. He didn't wake them this time. What was the point? He stood over them, looking down. The moonlight showed the lines of exhaustion on their faces. They were just men, weak and frightened—like him. But they got to sleep, they got to hide. He turned away, a cold fury mixing with the despair. He walked back to his patch of ground.

The third time he prayed, it was different. The terror was still there, a cold knot pulsing in his chest. The dread of the nails, the thirst, and the slow tearing pain but the fight was draining out of him, replaced by a heavy, cold resignation. The silence wasn't just absence anymore—it was a presence. A vast, implacable *No*. The tyrant had spoken, the sacrifice was required and bargaining was over. He knelt, but his spine felt like iron. "Father." The word was flat and final. "Your plan stands." There was no plea left, only acknowledgment. The cup wouldn't pass. He would drink it as he was always meant to. He stood up, his legs felt steadier now but they were cold and numb. He walked back to his followers for the last time.

He didn't need to speak. The sound woke them, not his footsteps, but another sound. It was distant at first, then growing louder as it got closer. The rhythmic tramp of many feet on the path and the clink of metal. The low murmur of men and the torchlight that flickered through the trees, casting dancing, monstrous shadows on the gnarled trunks. An orange light washed over the clearing where Peter, James, and John stood frozen, suddenly wide-eyed, scrambling for their weapons. Fear twisted their faces.

The torchlight grew brighter, pushing back the moonlight. Guards emerged from the trees. They were temple guards, armed with clubs and short swords. Their polished leather armor gleamed dully in the firelight. Their faces were obscured by shadows. Behind them, Roman soldiers stood, disciplined, silent, hands resting on the pommels of their swords. Their presence was a cold reminder of the Empire's reach. The air filled with the smell of pitch smoke and sweat.

And there, at the front, was Judas.

He looked pale, his eyes wide, darting nervously. He took a step forward, away from the guards, his gaze locked onto Jesus. For a second, Jesus saw the conflict there—fear, guilt, maybe even a flicker of regret. But it vanished, replaced by a terrible resolve. Judas walked straight toward him. The guards tensed, their hands tightening on their weapons. The disciples huddled closer to Jesus, Peter stepping slightly in front, his hand on his sword hilt.

"Rabbi," Judas said. The word sounded strange in the tense air. Then he leaned in. It was a quick and awkward movement. His lips brushed Jesus's cheek. A dry, cold touch—a signal. It was over.

Chaos erupted. The guards surged forward. Peter reacted instantly. He roared, a sound of pure fury and fear. He yanked his sword free, the blade flashed in the torchlight. He lunged past Jesus, swinging wildly at the nearest guard, a man stepping forward to grab Jesus' arm. The blade connected, there was a wet, tearing sound and a scream split the night. The guard stumbled back, clutching the side of his head. Blood poured between his fingers. His ear lay on the ground, a small, dark shape in the dirt.

"Enough!" Jesus' voice cut through the noise like a whip. He didn't shout, but the command stopped Peter cold. The big fisherman froze, sword raised, breathing hard. Jesus looked at him, then at the wounded guard writhing on the ground. The man's eyes were wide with pain and terror as the blood soaked his tunic. Jesus felt nothing but a weary disgust. More violence—more pain—pointless. He stepped toward the guard. The other guards flinched, raising their clubs, but Jesus ignored them. He knelt and picked up the severed ear. It was warm and slippery. He placed it against the gushing wound on the guard's head and pressed his hand over it. For a second, there was nothing, then a faint warmth spread from his palm. The guard gasped—the bleeding stopped. The torn flesh knit itself together under Jesus' touch. The guard lowered his hand, trembling, touching his intact ear in disbelief.

Jesus stood up and faced Peter, his eyes were cold. "Put your sword away. All who take the sword die by the sword." He looked around at the ring of torches and weapons. "Do you think I can't call on my Father? He would send more than twelve legions of angels right now. But then…" He paused, the bitterness thick in his throat. "…how would the writings be fulfilled? How would this happen?" He gestured vaguely at the guards, the soldiers, and the night. This was the plan—the tyrant's demand. He spread his hands wide, an empty gesture. "This is your hour. The hour when darkness rules."

The guards hesitated no longer, they rushed him. Their rough hands grabbed his arms, twisted them behind his back. Coarse rope bit into his wrists—he didn't resist. He saw the shock on Peter's face, the dawning horror on James and John's. He saw Judas step back quickly, melting into the crowd of guards, his face averted.

Then the disciples broke—the sight of their Master bound, the mass of armed men, the reality crashing down—it shattered them. Fear won, James turned first, bolting into the dark trees—John followed a heartbeat later—Peter stood for a second longer, his face a mask of anguish, the bloody sword still in his hand. A guard lunged at him, Peter dropped the sword. He turned and ran, crashing through the undergrowth, vanishing into the shadows.

Jesus stood alone, bound, surrounded by the torchlight and armed men. The guards tightened the ropes, one shoved him roughly. He stumbled but stayed upright. They began to move, forming a tight knot around him, pulling him back toward the path, toward the city gates, toward the waiting priests and the machinery of death.

High on the slope above the grove, hidden in the deep shadow of an ancient olive tree, Mary Magdalene watched. She had seen the torches arrive. She had seen Judas step forward—he had seen the kiss. She had seen Peter strike, seen the ear fall, seen the impossible healing. She had seen the disciples flee. She had seen the ropes bite into his wrists. Her own hands were clenched into fists, nails digging into her palms. Her breath came in short, sharp gasps. Tears streamed down her face, but she made no sound. She watched the knot of torchlight move away, taking him with it, back toward the dark walls of Jerusalem. The grove was plunged back into near-darkness, the moon casting long, distorted shadows where moments ago chaos had reigned. She stayed frozen for a long moment, the image of him bound and surrounded burned into her mind. Then, moving with the silent determination of a shadow, she began to follow. She kept to the deeper darkness, staying well back, her eyes fixed on the bobbing torches that marked his passage into the city, into the trap. The path was set—the cup could not be refused.

Chapter 3

The torchlit courtyard of the high priest's house buzzed like a kicked hornets' nest. Guards shoved Jesus through the milling crowd of Temple officials, scribes, and elders. Their faces were sharp with anticipation and anger under the flickering light. Rough hands propelled him forward, the ropes bit deeper into his wrists. He stumbled on the uneven stones, no one offered help, only more shoves. He felt the emptiness above him, colder here, within these walls dedicated to the distant tyrant demanding his blood.

Inside, the air was thick with incense and tension. The chamber was large, stone walls hung with rich tapestries that absorbed the lamplight. The Sanhedrin, or a hasty gathering of its most powerful members, sat on benches arranged in a semicircle. Caiaphas, the high priest, occupied the central seat. His robes were spotless white linen, his expression carefully composed, but his eyes were hard and watchful. He surveyed Jesus as the guards forced him to stand in the center of the open space. The room fell silent, the only sound the crackle of torches and the heavy breathing of the guards flanking Jesus.

Caiaphas leaned forward slightly. "These men," he began, his voice smooth but carrying an edge, "bring serious accusations. They say you spoke against this holy place. They say you claimed power to destroy the Temple and rebuild it in three days. What do you say to this?"

Jesus stood still, he looked at Caiaphas, then at the faces of the men standing against him. He saw no justice here, only a predetermined path leading to the cross. He offered no defense, no explanation. His silence was heavy, and defiant.

Caiaphas exchanged a glance with a man beside him. He raised a hand. "Bring the witnesses."

One by one, men stepped forward. Their stories were vague and contradictory. One mumbled about hearing Jesus threaten the Temple. Another claimed Jesus spoke against the Law. A third swore Jesus called himself king. Their words tangled, tripped over each other. They couldn't agree on the details but Jesus remained silent throughout, his gaze fixed on a point somewhere beyond the high priest's shoulder. He felt the pressure building, the inevitable push toward the question they needed him to answer. The question that would seal his fate under their law.

Frustration etched Caiaphas's face. The witnesses were useless, he stood up, his robes rustling and walked slowly toward Jesus, stopping a few paces away. The room held its breath. "Have you nothing to say?" Caiaphas demanded, his voice louder now. "What is this testimony these men bring against you?" Still, Jesus said nothing. The silence was a wall.

Caiaphas stepped closer, his voice dropping, becoming more intense, trying to pierce the silence. "I charge you under oath by the living God. Tell us if you are the Anointed One, the Son of God."

The air crackled, every eye locked onto Jesus. This was the moment—the trap—to claim it was blasphemy—or to deny it…would it matter? They wanted blood. The distant tyrant wanted blood. He felt the vast, cold indifference of the heavens. No legion of angels waited—no voice of comfort—only the crushing weight of the plan. The bitterness rose, thick and choking. He didn't want this. He wanted to live. He wanted Mary. He wanted the quiet hills of Galilee. He wanted *away*.

He met Caiaphas' demanding stare. A flicker of defiance sparked, cold and bleak. "You say that I am," Jesus replied. His voice was flat, devoid of conviction, yet carrying a strange finality. Then he added, "You will see the Son of Man seated at the right hand of Power. You will see him coming on the clouds of heaven." It was the truth, twisted by the bitterness of knowing what came first. The throne lay beyond the cross. Beyond the abandonment. Beyond the crushing silence of God.

Caiaphas reacted instantly. He tore his own robe at the neckline, a dramatic gesture of outrage. "Blasphemy!" he cried, his voice ringing through the chamber. "Why do we need more witnesses? You have all heard the blasphemy with your own ears!" He turned to the council. "What is your verdict?"

The response was immediate, a low rumble building to a roar. "He deserves death!" voices shouted. "Blasphemer!" "Death!"

The formal vote was a blur of hands raised and nods given—the sentence passed. The machinery of the tyrant's vengeance clicked forward another step. Relief and grim satisfaction replaced the tension in the room. They had what they needed.

The guards needed no further prompting. They surged forward, the first spit struck Jesus' face, warm and wet. He flinched—more followed. Thick globs landed on his cheeks, his forehead, and his tunic. Then the blows started. Fists hammered his chest, his shoulders, his back. Someone shoved a rough cloth sack over his head, blinding him. The world plunged into stifling darkness filled with the smell of sweat and cheap cloth. The blows became harder, more frantic. "Prophesy!" a guard jeered, his voice close, hot breath hitting the sack. "Who hit you, prophet? Tell us!" Another punch, hard to the ribs. Jesus gasped, doubling over. There was more laughter and more blows. He tasted blood in his mouth where his lip had split against his teeth. The sack absorbed the spittle, and muffled the sounds. He felt only the impacts, the jarring pain, the humiliation, and the vast, echoing silence of God. He didn't cry out, he absorbed it. Each blow felt like a nail being hammered through flesh and bone. The path was clear.

In the shadowed archway leading to the courtyard, Judas stood frozen. He had followed the procession, like a ghost drawn to the scene of his betrayal. He saw the guards drag Jesus inside, he heard the muffled sounds of the trial through the high windows. Then he saw the guards bring him back out into the torchlit courtyard, not to freedom, but for punishment. He saw the spitting, the sack pulled down and the first blows land. His stomach clenched. This wasn't what he expected. He thought…he wasn't sure what he thought. A stern rebuke? Imprisonment? Not this raw, ugly violence—not this condemnation. The coins in his purse felt suddenly heavy, burning against his hip. He watched a guard land a vicious punch to Jesus' kidney, saw him stagger. Judas turned away, pressing his forehead against the cold stone of the arch. He felt sick.

Mary Magdalene moved through the shadows near the outer gate of the high priest's compound. The crowd had thinned, but guards still patrolled. Her heart hammered against hard in her chest. She had followed the torches from Gethsemane, keeping her distance, a silent wraith in the night. She saw them take him inside. Then hours passed and the torches burned low. The sky was fading from black to a deep gray in the east, dawn was coming. She needed to know. She spotted a guard leaning against a wall, picking his teeth, looking bored. He was younger than the others, less hardened. She took a breath, gathered her courage, and approached.

The guard straightened, eyeing her suspiciously. "What do you want? Move along."

Mary kept her voice low, steady and calm. She held out her hand. Two silver coins gleamed in the dim light. "News," she said. "Of the man from Nazareth. The one they brought in."

The guard glanced at the coins, then at her face. He hesitated, then snatched the coins, quick, furtive. He leaned closer, his voice a harsh whisper. "Trial's done. Just now. Council found him guilty. Blasphemy." He spat the word. "They're sending him to the Romans at first light. Want him dead." He looked past her, nervous. "Now go. Before someone sees."

Blasphemy. Death. The words hit Mary hard—she swayed. The guard had already turned away, pocketing the coins, resuming his bored posture. She stumbled back into the deeper shadows near the wall. She pressed her back against the cold stone, struggling to breathe, crying. *Guilty. Sent to the Romans. Dead by dawn.* The sky was definitely lighter now. A thin band of pale gray outlined the rooftops to the east. The darkest hour was passing, giving way to the light that would illuminate his death. She slid down the wall, crouching in the dirt, her arms wrapped around herself. She felt hollow, scraped raw. The coins were gone. The news was worse than she feared—he was lost. She buried her face in her knees, silent sobs shaking her shoulders. The city began to stir. The sound of a slamming door echoed nearby. A cock crowed, sharp and clear in the pre-dawn air. The sound cut through Mary's grief. She lifted her head, wiping her face with the back of her hand. Her eyes, red-rimmed but dry now, fixed on the gate. They would take him out soon, to the Roman governor—to death. She wouldn't leave him—not now. She pushed herself up, bracing against the wall. She would follow, she would be there, even if she could do nothing. She would see him—she would bear witness to the tyrant's final demand.

Inside the chamber, the council members stood, stretching and murmuring. The verdict was delivered, the sentence pronounced. Religious law demanded death for blasphemy but only Rome could carry out the execution. Caiaphas smoothed his torn robe, his face set. "Dawn is near," he announced. "We must take him to Pontius Pilate. The Prefect must confirm the sentence. He must see the threat this man poses." He gestured toward Jesus, who stood slumped between guards, the sack removed, his face bruised, blood trickling from his split lip and a cut above his eye. He breathed slowly, deeply, his eyes half-closed. The beating had taken its toll, but a strange stillness had settled over him. The fight was gone, replaced by a cold, hard acceptance. The cup was his, he would drink it—the abandonment was complete. The silence of heaven was absolute—he felt utterly alone—only the bitter man remained.

The guards tightened their grip. "Move," one growled, shoving Jesus toward the door. They led him out of the council chamber, back into the torchlit courtyard, now bathed in the first weak, gray light of dawn. The air was cool and damp. The stars were fading. Caiaphas and several senior council members followed, their expressions grimly satisfied. They had done their part, now Rome would do the rest. They formed a small procession—priests, guards, the condemned man—moving toward the main gate, toward the Praetorium, toward the Roman governor who held the power of life and death.

Judas, still pressed against the archway, saw them come out. He saw Jesus' battered face in the gray dawn light. He saw the official procession forming. He heard Caiaphas say the name: "Pilate." The full weight crashed down. That could only mean one thing, *Death—Roman death—Crucifixion.* He had sold him for thirty pieces of silver, and it had bought this. This broken man walking to an agonizing death. A choked sound escaped him. He turned and fled, pushing past early risers in the street, the coins in his purse jingling like a death knell. He ran, blind with horror, seeking only to escape the sight, the sound, and the crushing guilt.

Mary saw the gate open. She saw the grim procession emerge. There he was, bruised, bleeding and bound but walking. His head was up, his eyes looking straight ahead, not at the priests, not at the guards, but at the growing light in the eastern sky. There was no fear in his face now, only a terrible weariness, and beneath it, a frightening resolve. He looked like a man walking through the valley of the shadow of death who had finally stopped struggling. He looked like a man who had accepted his fate. The priests walked with purpose. The guards marched with professional detachment. Jesus walked with the heavy step of a man fulfilling a contract written in blood long before his birth. The path led uphill now, toward the fortress Antonia, to the Roman governor judgement seat. Mary waited until they passed, then fell into step far behind, a small, determined figure in the dusty street. The sun's first rim breached the horizon, casting long, sharp shadows. The city of Jerusalem awoke to a new day. A day of judgment—a day of execution. The last day for the man from Nazareth and the first day of the tyrant's final victory. The procession moved steadily forward, leaving the hushed sanctity of the Temple precinct behind, heading into the harsh, pragmatic world of Roman power. The sound of their footsteps echoed on the stone pavement. The sky lightened even more. The birds began to sing. The path to the cross stretched before them, paved with silence and sanctioned by a vengeful God. It was finished—the beginning of the end.

Part 2

Chapter 1

The chill in the high priest's courtyard bit deeper than the night air. Peter huddled closer to the charcoal brazier, its meager glow doing little against the creeping dawn cold or the ice forming in his gut. He rubbed his hands over the embers, watching the sparks dance. The smell of smoke couldn't mask the lingering scent of fear and dust. Guards stood watchful nearby. Servants moved quietly. The muffled sounds from inside the house—raised voices, a sharp cry—stopped hours ago. Silence now felt worse.

A servant girl approached the fire, refueling the brazier with chunks of charcoal. She paused, her eyes narrowing as she studied Peter's face in the flickering light. He avoided her gaze, staring hard at the glowing coals. "You," she said, her voice clear in the quiet courtyard. "You were with that man. The Nazarene." Peter stiffened. He kept his eyes down. "Woman," he muttered, his Galilean accent thick despite his effort, "I don't know him." The lie felt heavy, clumsy. He moved away from the fire, deeper into the shadows near the gateway.

Time crawled by. Peter found another fire, smaller, near the entrance to the servants' quarters. He needed the heat—he needed to disappear. He leaned against the cool stone wall, trying to blend in. A different servant, a man this time, joined the group warming themselves. He looked Peter up and down. "You're one of them too," the man stated. It wasn't a question. Peter felt sweat on his neck despite the cold. "Man," he said, louder this time, pushing away from the wall, "I am not!" His denial echoed slightly in the confined space. He saw the knowing look pass between the servants. He walked away again, his heart hammering.

An hour later, maybe less. The light was stronger now, details sharpened. Peter stood near the main gate arch, shivering, watching the street outside for any sign of the others. A relative of the guard whose ear he'd cut off stepped close. The man's face was hard. "Didn't I see you in the garden with him?" he demanded. Peter felt the blood drain from his face. The man pressed. "Your speech betrays you. You're a Galilean. Like him." Panic seized Peter, it clawed at his throat. He threw his hands up, his voice rising to a shout, rough with fear and denial. "I swear! I don't know the man!" He cursed. He invoked things he shouldn't name. The words tasted like sour in his mouth.

As the last syllable left his lips, cutting through the tense courtyard air, it came. It was sharp and clear. The crow of a rooster perched on a nearby wall. *Ku-ku-laok* The sound pierced Peter's skull like a nail. Time froze, he saw Jesus' face in the olive grove, weary, and knowing. *Before the rooster crows, you will deny me three times.* The memory flooded his mind. He hadn't just lied, he'd sworn, he'd cursed and he'd disowned the man he'd called Master, the man he'd promised to die for, while that man faced death inside.

The courtyard seemed to tilt—Peter felt sick, overcome with guilt. The faces of the servants and the guard, blurred. Their low murmurs became a roaring in his ears. He looked down at his hands—the hands that had held a sword, the hands that had gripped fishing nets, the hands that had broken bread with Jesus. They were a betrayer's hands. A strangled sob escaped him. He turned blindly, stumbling over his own feet. He shoved past a startled guard, through the gateway arch, out into the gray street. He ran, he ran without direction, the rooster's crow echoing endlessly in his mind, chased by the sound of his own weeping, loud and raw and full of despair. He ran until his lungs burned, until the city walls were behind him, collapsing finally against a dusty outcrop, retching, weeping into the cold dirt as the sun rose over Jerusalem.

Judas watched Peter flee. He'd been lurking near the outer gate. He saw Peter's frantic denial, heard the rooster, witnessed the collapse. It mirrored his own inner ruin. The thirty silver coins in the leather purse hung at his belt like a millstone, they burned against his hip. The image of Jesus' battered face, the cold acceptance in his eyes as the priests led him away to Pilate, wouldn't leave him.

Revulsion surged. He turned and walked, not running like Peter, but with a heavy, doomed tread back toward the Temple. The city was waking, merchants set up their stalls. People hurried about their morning routines. Judas moved through them unseen, a man already dead. He reached the vast outer courts of the Temple. The morning sacrifices had begun. The smell of incense and burning flesh hung heavy in the air. The sweet aroma from the burnt offering rose into the sky. *God must be pleased with this sacrifice,* Judas thought, *Would he be pleased with Jesus' sacrifice?* Priests in white linen moved with ritual precision. Judas walked straight to the section where the chief priests and elders gathered, conferring, their faces satisfied.

He saw Caiaphas and saw Annas. He pushed through the small crowd of officials. He held out the leather purse, the coins inside clinking faintly. His hand shook. "I have sinned," Judas said, his voice cracking. The words felt inadequate, and hollow. "I betrayed innocent blood." He thrust the purse towards them. "Take it back."

The priests stopped talking and looked at him, not with anger, but with cold disdain. Annas waved a dismissive hand. "What is that to us?" he said, his voice flat. "That's your affair." Caiaphas didn't even look at him, already turning back to his conversation. They had what they wanted, the money was irrelevant. The blood price was paid—the sacrifice was secured—the transaction was complete. They dismissed him like a troublesome beggar.

Judas stood frozen, the purse still extended. The coins felt like hot coals now. It was innocent blood and they didn't care. They wouldn't take it back, they wouldn't absolve him. The weight of what he'd done, the utter finality of it, crashed down. The priests walked away, leaving him standing alone in the vast, sunlit courtyard surrounded by the indifferent hum of Temple business. The innocence he'd betrayed was being led to slaughter, and his payment felt heavy in his purse.

A strangled cry tore from his throat. He looked at the purse in his hand, the symbol of his damnation. Then, with a violent motion, he hurled it. It arced through the air, coins spilling out in a bright, tinkling shower, scattering across the smooth stone floor of the Temple treasury. They rolled and spun, catching the morning sun. He didn't wait to see where they fell. He turned and fled the Temple, not weeping, but silent, his face a mask of utter desolation.

He walked, blind and purposeless, through the city. The sounds of life grated on him. He found himself outside the city walls, in the barren hills to the south, the Hinnom Valley—a place of trash, of waste, of burning. He saw a potter's abandoned field, the furnace cold, clay pits half-filled with stagnant water. A gnarled, twisted fig tree stood near the edge of one pit, a stark silhouette against the brightening sky. He walked towards it. He took the rope he'd carried as a belt and fashioned a noose. He climbed onto a low branch. He looked back once, towards the city, towards the Antonia fortress where Jesus would now stand before Pilate. Then he stepped off. The rope snapped tight. His body jerked, his legs kicked once, twice, then went still. He hung there, swaying slightly in the morning breeze, a dark fruit on a dead tree. Below him, the coins gleamed in the Temple treasury, already being gathered by priests who would later use them to buy this very field—a place to bury strangers. The price of betrayal paid twice over.

The journey from the high priest's house to the Praetorium was short, brutal, and public. Guards flanked Jesus, their grip hard on his arms. Priests walked ahead, robes sweeping the dusty street. The dawn light was harsh, revealing every bruise, every smear of blood and spit on Jesus' face and tunic. The city was stirring, people stopped to stare. Some pointed and some whispered. Some recognized the prisoner and looked away quickly. Jesus walked with his head up, his eyes fixed straight ahead. The physical pain from the beating was a constant throb. The ropes chafed his wrists but deeper than that was the hollow ache of abandonment. The silence of heaven was a physical pressure, heavier than the guards' hands. He had begged for another way. The answer was the fist, the spit, the rope, and the slow walk to Roman judgment. The tyrant demanded payment. He felt no presence, only the vast, cold absence of a Father who had turned his face away. He was the sacrifice, alone.

Mary Magdalene followed. She kept her distance, blending with the early crowds, a shadow trailing the grim procession. She saw the stiffness in Jesus' walk, the way he favored his side. She saw the dried blood. She saw the utter lack of resistance. He moved like a man already dead. Her heart ached, a physical pain in her chest. She remembered his hand gripping hers under the table, the warmth, the fleeting comfort. Now there was only cold stone and Roman justice ahead. She wrapped her arms around herself, shivering despite the growing warmth of the sun. She wouldn't leave him. She would see this through.

They reached the outer courtyard of the Praetorium, the fortress Antonia. Roman soldiers stood watch, impassive in their segmented armor, spears held upright. The Jews stopped at the threshold, entering a Gentile dwelling, especially during Passover, would make them ritually unclean. They couldn't risk it, not for this. Caiaphas spoke to a Roman centurion. The man listened, nodded curtly, and disappeared inside the fortress gate. They waited. The priests stood apart, aloof. The guards shifted, bored now the short walk was over. Jesus stood between them, silent. He looked at the stone pavement beneath his feet. He looked at the high walls of the fortress. He didn't look at the priests, he didn't look for Mary, he just absorbed the reality. This was the path—Pilate held the power of the sword. The final steps were Roman steps. The abandonment was complete, only the mechanics of death remained. He closed his eyes for a moment, drawing a slow breath. The bitterness was still there, a knot of cold iron in his chest, but the frantic terror of Gethsemane was gone, replaced by a heavy, cold resolve. He would walk it—he would drink the cup, not for the tyrant's satisfaction, but because the trap was sprung, the path chosen long before his birth. There was no other way out.

The centurion returned. He gestured. "Bring him in. The Prefect will see him now." The guards tightened their grip. They hauled Jesus forward, across the threshold, into the shadowed archway of the Praetorium. The priests remained outside, watching him go. Mary pressed forward in the crowd outside the courtyard gates, straining to see. The heavy wooden doors of the fortress began to swing shut behind the prisoner and his guards. The last thing she saw was Jesus' back, straight despite the ropes, disappearing into the dark hall of Roman power. The doors boomed shut. The sound echoed in the suddenly quiet courtyard. The priests exchanged glances. The first part was done. Now, the real negotiation began. Inside, in the judgment hall, the Prefect of Judea, Pontius Pilate, waited. The fate of the Nazarene carpenter rested on the whims of Rome. The sun climbed higher, baking the stones. The city held its breath as the final act was beginning.

Chapter 2

The heavy doors of the Praetorium shut behind Jesus, sealing him in a different world. The air inside was cooler, smelling of stone, leather, and authority. Sunlight slanted through high windows, illuminating dust particles dancing above the mosaic floor. Roman soldiers stood rigid along the walls, their segmented armor gleaming dully, faces impassive beneath helmet rims. The contrast to the chaotic Temple courtyard was stark. Here, order reigned. It was cold, efficient, Roman order.

Guards marched Jesus down a wide corridor. Their hobnailed sandals echoed sharply. He walked between them, ropes still biting his wrists, the bruises on his face livid in the clear light. They stopped before a set of tall, carved wooden doors. A centurion knocked once, a voice from within called out and T he doors swung open.

The judgment hall was large, and austere. A raised platform dominated one end. Behind a simple wooden table sat Pontius Pilate, Prefect of Judea. He wore a white tunic with a purple border, the mark of his rank. His face was intelligent, weary, and lined with the strain of governing a troublesome province. He studied the prisoner as the guards pushed him forward into the open space before the platform. Priests crowded near the entrance, Caiaphas at their front, but they stayed back, respecting Roman space. Pilate ignored them for now, his gaze fixed on Jesus.

The Prefect leaned forward slightly, resting his elbows on the table. His voice was calm, measured, carrying easily in the quiet room. "Are you the King of the Jews?"

Jesus looked up at him. His eyes met Pilate's. There was exhaustion there, and pain, but no fear. Only that unsettling stillness. "Do you ask this yourself," Jesus replied, his voice hoarse but clear, "or did others tell you about me?"

Pilate's eyebrow lifted slightly. There was a flicker of annoyance, perhaps interest. "Am I a Jew?" he countered, a dry edge to his voice. "Your own people, your chief priests, handed you over to me. What did you do?"

"My kingdom isn't of this world," Jesus said. The words were simple. "If it were, my followers would fight. They wouldn't let the Jews take me. But my kingdom...it's not from here."

Pilate leaned back. "So you are a king, then?"

"You say I am a king." Jesus met his gaze steadily. "I was born for this. I came into the world for this: to witness to the truth. Everyone who belongs to the truth hears my voice."

"Truth?" Pilate repeated the word, a hint of weary cynicism in his tone. "What is truth?" He didn't wait for an answer. He stood up, turning away from Jesus to address the priests near the door. "I find no basis for a charge against this man."

A murmur rippled through the priests. Caiaphas stepped forward, his voice tight with controlled anger. "He stirs up the people! He teaches throughout Judea, starting from Galilee, all the way here!"

"Galilee?" Pilate seized on the word. A look of calculation crossed his face. "This man is a Galilean?" He didn't wait for confirmation. "Then he falls under Herod's jurisdiction. Herod Antipas is in Jerusalem for the feast." He gestured sharply to the guards. "Take him to Herod. Let the Tetrarch deal with his own." Relief was evident in his posture.

The guards grabbed Jesus again. The priests looked momentarily confused, then exchanged glances. They followed as the prisoner was marched out of the Praetorium, back into the morning sunlight, now brighter and warmer. The small procession wound through the streets toward the old palace of Herod the Great, where his son Antipas resided when in Jerusalem.

Mary Magdalene saw them emerge. She saw the direction they took. She moved through the growing crowds, keeping pace, her heart a cold stone. Why Herod? What new game was this? She pressed closer, risking notice, needing to see.

Herod Antipas' palace was opulent, a stark contrast to the Roman fort's austerity. Tapestries hung on walls, mosaics glittered underfoot and the air smelled of perfumed oil and wine. Herod himself lounged on a cushioned chair, surrounded by courtiers. He was a thin man with restless eyes, dressed in fine silks. He'd heard of Jesus, the miracle worker from Galilee. He'd wanted to see him for a long time, hoping for a sign, a spectacle.

When Jesus was brought in, bound and bruised, Herod's face lit up with curiosity. "So! The prophet!" he exclaimed, clapping his hands softly. "Perform for us! Show us a sign!" He leaned forward eagerly.

Jesus stood before him. He said nothing. He looked at Herod, then through him, his gaze distant, fixed on some point beyond the gilded ceiling. The stillness was absolute.

Herod waited. The silence remained unbroken. His smile faltered, replaced by irritation. He fired questions about John the Baptist, whom he'd beheaded, about the kingdom Jesus preached and about his followers. Jesus remained silent. He didn't react to the questions, the stares, or the growing murmur of the courtiers. He absorbed the hostility like stone absorbs rain.

Herod's irritation turned to anger, then to mocking contempt. "Fine! Silent king!" he sneered. He gestured to his guards. "Dress him! Let's see the King of the Jews!" Laughter rippled through the court. Soldiers roughly stripped off Jesus' own tunic, already torn and stained. They draped a discarded robe of rich purple over his shoulders—a mockery of royalty. Someone made a circular band, not of gold, but of sharp thorns, and jammed it onto his head. Blood welled instantly, trickling down his temples, mingling with the dried blood and sweat. The soldiers shoved a reed into his bound hands like a scepter. They knelt before him in exaggerated, mocking homage. "Hail, King of the Jews!" they jeered, spitting at his feet. Herod laughed, the sound high and unpleasant.

Jesus stood amidst the ridicule, the purple robe hanging awkwardly, the thorns digging into his scalp, the reed clutched in his bound hands. He didn't flinch. He didn't speak. His silence was a wall Herod couldn't breach, an affront that only fueled the Tetrarch's impotent rage. The performance fell flat. The joke grew stale.

"Enough!" Herod snapped, waving a dismissive hand. His face was flushed with frustration. "Take him back! Back to Pilate! He's no threat. Just a fool." He looked at Jesus with contempt. "Pilate can have his troublesome prophet back."

The purple robe was ripped off. The thorn crown torn away, drawing fresh blood. Jesus was shoved back towards the guards. The journey to the Praetorium began again, the prisoner now marked by fresh humiliation, blood dripping onto the dusty street stones. Mary watched, her nails cutting into her palms. The cruelty was casual, vicious. It carved another piece out of her heart.

Back in Pilate's judgment hall, the atmosphere had shifted. The priests were more numerous now, more insistent. A crowd had gathered outside the Praetorium gates, stirred by the priests and their supporters. Their murmur was a low, threatening rumble, audible even inside.

Pilate looked exasperated. He addressed the priests and elders gathered before him. "You brought me this man as one who stirs up the people. I examined him before you. I found no basis for your charges. Herod found nothing either. He sent him back. He's done nothing deserving death. I will punish him and release him." It was a compromise. Scourging, a brutal, public beating, enough to appease the mob, he hoped, without killing an innocent man.

A roar erupted from the priests and the crowd noise outside swelled in response. "No! Not this man! Give us Barabbas!"

Pilate frowned. They wanted Barabbas. He knew the name. He was a known insurrectionist, a murderer, rotting in a cell awaiting execution. The choice was stark, illogical. "Barabbas?" he asked, incredulous. "You want me to release Barabbas to you? What shall I do then with Jesus, called the Anointed One?"

The response was a deafening wave of sound crashing against the stone walls: "Crucify him! Crucify him!"

Pilate raised his hands, trying to regain control. "Why? What crime has he committed? I find no reason for death! I will punish him and release him!"

The roar intensified. "Crucify! Crucify!" It became a chant, rhythmic, and relentless. The priests stood silent, their faces grimly satisfied. They had whipped the crowd into a frenzy. The will of Rome was buckling under the sheer weight of their unified demand.

Pilate saw the danger of a riot on Passover, in Jerusalem, reported to Rome…it could end his career. He looked at Jesus, standing silent, bloodied but unbowed amidst the chaos. He looked at the screaming mob—he felt the trap closing. He called for water, a servant brought a basin and pitcher. Pilate stood before the crowd, visible from the raised platform. He poured water over his hands, washing them in full view. "I am innocent of this man's blood!" he declared, his voice loud but strained. "It's your responsibility!"

The crowd's response was immediate, and savage. "His blood be on us! And on our children!" The cry echoed, a terrible acceptance of guilt shouted in a collective frenzy.

Pilate dried his hands and turned to the centurion waiting nearby. "Do it. Give them Barabbas." He gestured towards Jesus, his face tight with disgust—at the crowd, at the priests, at the whole sordid business. "Scourge him. Then crucify him. The words fell like stones.

The centurion saluted. "Yes, Prefect." He signaled his men.

Guards seized Jesus roughly, they dragged him out of the judgment hall, not back through the main entrance, but down a narrower corridor, away from the crowd's view. The roar of the mob faded, replaced by the harsh clang of an iron door opening.

Mary saw the soldiers bring Jesus out through a side entrance. She saw the grim set of their faces, the purposeful way they hauled him towards a lower part of the fortress. She knew what that meant. She pushed through the edge of the crowd, ignoring the jostling, her eyes fixed on the doorway they disappeared through. She couldn't follow there, so she found a spot near the outer wall, close enough to hear. She pressed her back against the sun-warmed stone, closed her eyes, and prayed she was wrong.

Inside the guardroom, they stripped Jesus naked and pushed him toward a low stone column. They bent him over it, his back exposed. His wrists were tied to rings set low in the stone. His ankles were secured to rings set in the floor. He was stretched tight, vulnerable.

A soldier picked up the whip—the scourge. It was tipped with four thin strips of leather studded with sharpened pieces of bone and metal. The man hefted it, testing the weight. He took position behind the bound man and drew his arm back.

The first blow landed with a sickening crack, leather and metal tore into flesh. Jesus' body jerked against the ropes. A gasp escaped him, quickly stifled. Blood welled instantly from the parallel gashes.

The soldier swung again and again—methodical—professional. Each stroke laid open skin and muscle. Blood sprayed, it ran down his back, his sides, pooling on the stone floor. The sound was wet, rhythmic: the whistle of the whip, the impact, and the choked intake of breath.

Jesus clenched his teeth. He pressed his forehead against the cold stone. He didn't cry out—he endured. Each lash was fire burning through his body. Each tore a piece of him away. The physical agony was immense, a white-hot world of pain. But beneath it, deeper, was the vast, cold silence. The absence—the tyrant watched—the tyrant demanded this. The bitterness rose, a black tide threatening to drown him. He didn't want this, he hadn't chosen this—yet he endured because the path was set—this was his fate. He squeezed his eyes shut. He focused on breathing—In—Out. Surviving the next blow and the next. The soldiers grunted with effort.

Outside, leaning against the wall, Mary heard the sounds. The sharp crack, the muffled impact and the low grunts. She heard no scream but his silence was worse—it told her everything. She slid down the wall, sinking to the ground, her hands pressed over her ears, but she couldn't block it out. Each crack of the whip tore through her. Tears streamed down her face, silent and hot. She rocked slightly, the rough stone scraping her back, the sounds of his destruction echoing in the pit of her stomach. The sun beat down. The crowd outside the main gate still chanted, a distant, mindless roar. Inside, the measured brutality continued. The scourging had begun. The path to the cross was paved with blood and Roman efficiency. The soldiers worked on, the Prefect's order was being carried out. The condemned man endured. The sun climbed higher. Time moved toward noon.

Chapter 3

The scourging stopped. The soldiers untied the ropes and Jesus collapsed, he hit the stone floor hard. He lay there, breathing in shallow gasps. His back was covered in fresh wounds, blood pooled around him. The air stank of sweat and copper.

Rough hands hauled him upright. He swayed, vision blurring. Someone threw his own tunic over his shoulders, the rough fabric scraped the open wounds. He hissed through clenched teeth as the agony shot through him. The purple robe Herod had used was gone, only his own blood-soaked garment remained.

The soldiers weren't done. They shoved a bundle of wood onto his shoulders. It was heavy and unbalanced. It was the crossbeam, rough-hewn timber, thick as a man's thigh, meant to bear his weight later. Its weight slammed down on his torn back. He staggered under the impact, pain exploded, white-hot. He almost fell. A guard laughed, shoving him forward. "Move, King!"

The morning sun hit him as they pushed him out into the courtyard. The crowd was still there, larger now. A sea of faces, some curious, some angry and some indifferent. They saw the blood soaking through the thin tunic, the shredded flesh on his face, and the swollen eye. They saw the heavy wood crushing him. A murmur ran through the crowd.

The procession began. The soldiers cleared a path and Jesus walked or tried to. Each step sent shockwaves up his legs, jarring his broken body. The crossbeam ground into the raw mess of his back. He focused on putting one foot in front of the other but the stones of the street were uneven and he stumbled as he walked. The crossbeam felt like the weight of the world pressing down on his shoulders—he struggled to keep his balance—but he endured. Dust rose, sticking to his sweat, his blood. He tasted grit.

The street sloped upward. The gate out of the city lay ahead and Golgotha—Skull Hill—waited beyond. The weight became impossible, his legs buckled, he stumbled and fell hard onto his knees. The crossbeam slammed down beside him, raising dust. He gasped, unable to breathe for a moment. Pain consumed everything.

A guard kicked him. "Up, dog!" He tried—he pushed with his hands but his arms trembled. He couldn't get his legs under him. The weight was too much and the pain was too great. He slumped forward, forehead pressed to the hot stone. The crowd pressed closer—some jeered and some just watched.

The soldiers looked impatient, they had a schedule to keep—executions by noon. One scanned the crowd, his eyes fixed on a man near the edge, watching with a mix of horror and fascination. The man looked strong with broad shoulders and dusty clothes—a traveler. The soldier pointed. "You! Cyrenian! Come here!"

Simon of Cyrene froze. He'd come to Jerusalem for Passover, he hadn't expected this. He tried to shrink back, but other soldiers moved quickly. They grabbed his arms and hauled him forward. "Help carry this," the first soldier ordered, gesturing to the crossbeam lying beside the fallen man.

Simon protested. "I have nothing to do with this!"

"Now you do," the soldier said flatly. "Pick it up."

Simon looked at Jesus, crumpled on the ground. He looked at the soldiers' hard faces. He saw no choice. He bent down and grabbed the heavy timber. He lifted it but the weight was almost unbearable, he staggered under it. The soldiers hauled Jesus roughly to his feet. "Move!" they barked at Simon.

Simon fell into step beside Jesus, the beam balanced awkwardly on his shoulder. He felt the eyes of the crowd—the shame—the anger—the helplessness. He just wanted it to be over. Jesus walked beside him, leaning heavily, breathing in ragged gasps. He said nothing, his eyes were fixed on the ground, on the next step and the next stone.

They passed a group of women—Jerusalem women standing nearby. They knew the horror of crucifixion. They saw the condemned man's condition. They began to wail. A high, keening sound of grief and pity. "Lord! Lord!" one cried out. "Have mercy!"

Jesus stopped and lifted his head slowly. His face was streaked with dirt and blood, his eyes sunken. He looked at the weeping women. His voice, when it came, was a rasp, but it cut through their wailing. "Daughters of Jerusalem," he said. The women hushed, startled. "Do not weep for me." He paused, drawing a painful breath. His gaze swept over them, over the watching crowd. "Weep for yourselves. Weep for your children. Days are coming…" He stopped, another wave of pain hitting him—he swayed." Simon instinctively shifted the beam, trying to steady him. Jesus continued, his voice low, filled with a terrible certainty. "Days are coming when people will say, 'Blessed are the childless, the wombs that never bore, the breasts that never nursed.' Then they will say to the mountains, 'Fall on us!' and to the hills, 'Cover us!'" He looked at them, his eyes bleak. "For if they do these things when the wood is green…what will happen when it is dry?" He turned away, signaling he was done. The weight of the future he saw crushed him as much as the wood Simon carried. The women stared, silenced and confused, a new dread settling over them.

The procession moved on. The city gate loomed and beyond it, the road climbed toward the barren hill. The crowd thinned slightly. Many wouldn't follow outside the walls. The spectacle was nearly over.

Mary Magdalene pushed her way through the crowd. She used elbows, shoulders, sheer desperation. She had to get closer. She had to see him. She shoved past robed men, ducked under arms, ignored curses. Her eyes were fixed on the stumbling figure beside the Cyrenian. She saw the blood, the way he dragged his feet and the utter exhaustion that consumed him.

She broke through the front edge of the crowd just as they neared the gate. Soldiers marched on either side. She lunged forward, trying to reach the narrow space between the guards and the prisoners. "Jesus!" Her voice tore from her throat.

A soldier saw her—he moved fast, his arm shot out. The butt of his spear caught her hard in the chest. The air exploded from her lungs and she stumbled back, falling against the people behind her. The pain flared inside her. She gasped, struggling to breathe.

Jesus heard her cry—he stopped and turned his head, his eyes searched the crowd. They found her—she was on her knees, clutching her chest, her face contorted with pain and terror. Their eyes locked.

He saw her terror—he saw the love, the desperation and the crushing helplessness—it mirrored his own. A cold fist clenched around his heart. His own fear, momentarily buried under pain and exhaustion, surged back. It tightened his chest like the ropes that had bound him. He remembered the voice in the desert, the promises, the sense of purpose. *You are my beloved Son. With you I am well pleased.* The words echoed in the vast, silent emptiness within him. They felt hollow now—meaningless. They felt like a lie whispered before the trap snapped shut. The promises led here, to this pain, to this abandonment and to leaving her alone.

The soldier shoved him hard. "Move!" Jesus stumbled forward, it broke his eye contact. He looked at the ground again, the dust and his blood mixing with it. The gate was just ahead—the open road—the hill. The bitterness was a cold, empty feeling in his gut—the promise felt just as empty. He remembered the silence in Gethsemane—the silence now, seemed so much worse. The tyrant demanded his due—the path was set—so he walked on.

Simon grunted under the beam's weight. He glanced at the man beside him. He saw the brief connection with the woman, the raw pain in the man's eyes before he looked down. Simon felt a pang of something unexpected. Pity? Horror? He adjusted the heavy wood, his muscles burning. He just wanted to put it down but the tyrant was watching—and the path was set—so he walked on.

They passed through the gate, the city walls fell behind. The road became rougher and steeper. The hill rose before them, its shape vaguely skull-like against the brightening sky. Golgotha—a place of death. There were a few twisted trees, rocks and a flat area near the top.

Roman efficiency awaited. Soldiers had gone ahead and dug holes for the execution stakes. Tools lay ready: hammers, long iron nails and a crude ladder. Another prisoner was already there, guards standing over him. A third was being led up another path. The air was still, expectant. Flies buzzed around the fresh-turned earth.

The soldiers escorting Jesus and Simon reached the flat area. "Here!" the lead soldier called. "This is the place." Simon stopped gratefully. He let the heavy crossbeam slide from his shoulder and it thudded to the dusty ground. He stepped back quickly, wiping sweat from his brow, wanting only to vanish.

Soldiers grabbed Jesus and pulled the tunic off him again, the fabric tore at the wounds on his back. He stood naked in the harsh sunlight, exposed to the soldiers, the other prisoners and the few onlookers who had followed this far. His body was a map of pain: the bruised face, the swollen eye, the lacerated back and dried blood everywhere. He shivered slightly, though the sun was warm. He looked at the holes dug in the ground and the heavy wooden stake already positioned upright in one of them. Then he looked at the iron nails glinting on a rock and the hammers scattered nearby—the tyrant remained silent.

The lead soldier picked up one of the long nails and hefted a heavy mallet. He looked at Jesus, then at the upright stake. "Get him down," he ordered his men, nodding toward the ground. "On his back. Arms out."

Jesus closed his eyes and drew a slow, shuddering breath. The fear became real, it became alive inside him. He didn't want the nails. He didn't want the wood. He didn't want the slow, suffocating agony. He remembered Mary's terror-stricken face. He remembered the silent sky. The promise felt like a mockery. The man inside him was silently screaming—trapped inside his purpose, his fate, his destiny. The soldiers moved, their hands grabbed him and forced him down onto the hard-packed earth beside the waiting stake. The rough ground scraped his torn back. He cried out then, a short, sharp sound of pure agony. They pulled his arms out, straight, along the heavy crossbeam Simon had carried. One soldier knelt on his forearm, pinning it to the wood. The cold iron point of the nail touched the center of his wrist.

The soldier with the mallet raised it. He sighted the nail head. The sun glinted off the iron. The other prisoners watched, wild-eyed. Simon turned away, unable to look. The hill was quiet, waiting for the first blow. Jesus stared up at the empty, indifferent blue sky. The silence of God was louder than any scream. The mallet reached its apex. The soldier took aim. The execution stake waited.

Part 3

Chapter 1

The mallet fell—the sound was a sickening crack as iron met bone. Jesus' body arched off the ground. A guttural cry tore from his throat, raw and terrible. The pain exploded, white-hot, radiating up his arm. The soldier leaned his weight onto the wrist, pinning it. He raised the mallet again. *Crack*. The nail drove deeper. Jesus gasped, his breath ragged. The soldier moved to the other wrist. The same brutal efficiency, he pinned the wrist down with a knee. *Crack*. Another cry, choked this time. Blood welled dark around the iron heads, dripping onto the wood.

Soldiers grabbed the ends of the heavy beam. Others positioned themselves near the upright stake already planted deep in its hole. "Heave!" the centurion barked. They strained and lifted the beam, with its nailed burden. Jesus felt the world tilt violently. Agony ripped through his wrists. The beam scraped against the upright stake. They wrestled it into place over the mortise cut into the top. With a final shove, it settled with a jarring thud.

They pulled his legs straight, bending the knees slightly. The cold point touched the top of his left foot. *Crack*. The nail punched through flesh and bone, embedding deep into the wood. Jesus screamed—the sound echoed off the barren hillside. The right foot followed. *Crack*. He hang pinned to the wood, trembling, sweat and blood mingling on his skin.

The cross stood upright.

The shock of full weight dropping onto the nails forced another cry from Jesus. His arms stretched tight. Every breath became a struggle. His shoulders screamed and his chest heaved. He hung suspended between earth and sky, the rough wood scraping his flayed back. Below, the soldiers secured the base with wedges and ropes. Above, a crude wooden sign was nailed to the crossbeam just over his head. It read in three languages: "Jesus of Nazareth, King of the Jews."

Two other crosses were already raised, one on each side—thieves. Their cries were constant, ragged with pain and fear. The one on his right cursed the soldiers, spat and thrashed weakly. The one on the left hung limper, his breath shallow gasps.

A crowd gathered at the base of the central cross. Priests, elders, Temple guards and scribes. They looked up, their faces hard with contempt. One stepped forward, shielding his eyes against the sun. "He saved others!" he mocked, his voice loud, carrying. "But he can't save himself!" Another joined in. "If you are the King of the Jews! Come down from the cross! Then we'll believe!" Laughter rippled through them. "He trusted in God!" another sneered. "Let God deliver him now, if he wants him! He said, 'I am the Son of God'!" Their taunts were sharp and relentless.

The thief on the right joined in, his voice strained with pain and malice. "Aren't you the Anointed One? Save yourself! Save us too!" He twisted his head to glare at Jesus.

The thief on the left stirred. He turned his head slowly, painfully, toward his fellow prisoner. His voice was weak, but clear. "Have you no fear of God? You're under the same sentence! We deserve this. We're paying for what we did. But this man..." He looked up at Jesus, hanging silently, enduring. "He's done nothing wrong." He turned his face fully to Jesus. His eyes held a desperate plea. "Jesus," he rasped. "Remember me when you come into your kingdom."

Jesus turned his head. It was an effort, pain shot through his neck. He looked at the man—the thief's face was etched with agony and a fragile hope. Jesus's own face was a mask of suffering, blood streaked and swollen. He drew a painful breath. His voice, when it came, was a rough whisper, but it cut through the noise below. "Truly I tell you..." He paused, gathering strength. "Today...you will be with me...in paradise." The words held no grandeur, only a bone-deep weariness and a promise scraped from the depths of abandonment. The thief's eyes closed, a tear cutting through the grime on his cheek. A moment of peace amidst the horror.

Below, near the base of the crosses, soldiers gathered. They had Jesus's discarded clothes. There were four men with one garment each. The tunic was seamless, woven in one piece. "Let's not tear it," one said. "Let's cast lots. See who gets it." They pulled dice from a pouch. They knelt on the dusty ground, ignoring the dying men above them. The rattle of dice, the low calls—gambling for a dead man's tunic while he died above them was indifference personified.

Further back, away from the priests and soldiers, stood a small group of women. Mary, the mother of Jesus, stood supported by another woman. Her face was gray, etched with a grief too deep for tears. She stared up at her son, her hands clenched in her robes. Beside her, pressed close, stood Mary Magdalene. Her face was streaked with dirt and tears, her eyes wide with horror, fixed on Jesus. She saw every tremor, heard every labored breath. She saw the blood dripping steadily from his feet, pooling darkly on the ground below. She saw the flies gathering. She felt Mary the mother's silent, shaking grief beside her. Her own chest felt tight, crushed. She wanted to scream. She wanted to run to the cross, claw at the soldiers, demand they stop, but, she stood frozen, bearing witness.

Jesus looked down, his vision blurry and fading. He saw the soldiers casting lots, he saw the mocking priests and he saw the women—his mother and Mary. He saw her terror, her love and the despair mirrored in her eyes. A wave of agony worse than the nails hit him—leaving her—leaving them all—for this—for the silence. He lifted his head, straining against the pull of the nails. He looked up at the sky, it was a hard, clear blue. The sun beat down mercilessly. Where was the Father? Where was the plan's comfort? Where was the legion of angels? Only the vast, empty blue—a tyrant's indifferent ceiling. The bitterness surged, cold and final. He had begged for another way. The answer was the nails, the wood and the slow suffocation. The abandonment was absolute. He closed his eyes. The thirst was a fire in his throat. The pain was a world without end.

Hours passed and the sun climbed to its zenith—high noon. The heat intensified, the air grew heavy and still. Then, a change. It was subtle at first, the brilliant blue began to dim—not with clouds—the sky itself seemed to darken, draining color. The fierce sunlight softened and weakened. Shadows lost their sharp edges. The soldiers gambling below paused, looking up. The mocking priests fell silent, glancing around uneasily. The darkness deepened rapidly, unnaturally. It wasn't nightfall, it was a suffocating gloom swallowing the hill, spreading outward. Within minutes, the sun was a dull, copper disk, then extinguished completely. An unnatural night covered the land. It was pitch black, impenetrable. The only sounds were the ragged breathing of the crucified men and the sudden, fearful murmurs from below. The darkness was thick, heavy, a physical weight pressing down. It felt like the end of the world. On the cross, Jesus opened his eyes but he saw nothing, only blackness—the silence of God was now complete darkness. He hung suspended in a void. He was alone and utterly abandoned. The cold dread of Gethsemane returned, magnified a thousand times in the suffocating dark. He drew a shuddering breath into lungs that burned. The bitter cup was full, and he was forced to drink. The darkness was absolute—time stopped—the hill waited.

Chapter 2

The darkness was absolute, it was thick and suffocating. Jesus hung in the void. He couldn't see the crosses beside him, he couldn't see the ground, he couldn't see the mocking priests or the terrified soldiers—only black. The nails burned in his flesh, his shoulders felt torn from their sockets and every breath was a battle. He had to push up on his nailed feet, scraping raw bone against iron, to lift his body enough to draw air into his compressed lungs. He did it, again and again. Agony spiked with each movement. Exhaustion dragged at him like lead weights. The thirst was a dry burn in his throat, parching his tongue. His mouth tasted of blood and dust.

Time lost meaning. Minutes? Hours? The darkness stretched on. He heard the ragged gasps of the thieves beside him. The one on the right still cursed, weaker now. The one on the left was silent, his breathing shallow. Below, muffled voices rose in fear. "What is this?" "An omen!" "The gods are angry!" The gamblers had stopped. Soldiers muttered prayers to foreign gods. The priests' mocking had ceased, replaced by uneasy silence.

A flicker of torchlight appeared below his cross. A soldier approached, holding a sponge soaked in cheap, sour wine—vinegar— impaled on a hyssop stalk. "Here!" the man called up, his voice tight with tension. "Drink this! If you're the King, save yourself! Come down!" It was mockery disguised as a cruel mercy. The sharp smell of the vinegar cut through the dusty air.

Jesus turned his head toward the voice, toward the dimly seen sponge held aloft. He opened his cracked lips, the sour liquid touched his tongue—it was vile. It did nothing for the fire in his throat. He pulled his head away. The sponge withdrew and the brief light vanished—he was back in the black—back in the void—swallowed by the darkness.

The taste lingered—it was sour and bitter like the cup he'd begged to pass, like the silence of heaven. The weight of abandonment crushed down, heavier than the darkness, heavier than the cross. It wasn't just loneliness—it was wrath. It was cold, implacable and directed at him—the tyrant's demand. The sacrifice pinned like a specimen. He felt it like a blade twisting in his side, a physical manifestation of divine rejection. Where was the Father? The promises? The comfort? He saw only the crushing dark— only the nails—only the thirst—only the wrath.

A sound tore from his throat. It wasn't a cry of pain, it was a raw, guttural scream of utter desolation. It ripped through the unnatural silence on the hill, echoing in the blackness. It was words, in his own tongue, Aramaic, wrenched from the deepest pit of his being: *"Eli, Eli, lema sabachthani?" My God, my God, why have you forsaken me?*

The scream hung in the dark air. Below, confusion rippled through the onlookers. "He's calling Elijah!" someone shouted. "Hush! Let's see if Elijah comes to save him!" Another voice, hopeful or mocking. They didn't understand. They heard only the prophet's name, not the cry of utter forsakenness.

No answer came—no angelic host split the darkness—no voice thundered from the void—only silence. The silence was deeper than before. The sky stayed black and the blade of wrath twisted deeper. He was alone—truly alone. The pact was broken, the Father had turned his face away. The sacrifice was complete in its isolation. He felt the life draining out of him, drop by drop, breath by strained breath. The coldness spread from his core.

Then, through the roaring in his own ears, through the gasps of the other dying men, through the fearful murmurs below, he heard it. It was faint, distant but unmistakable—a woman's sobs, harsh, broken and desperate. *Mary.* Her grief pierced the dark shell around him. He knew that sound. It was the sound of a world breaking. Her world—His world.

The sound anchored him. It pulled him back from the edge of the pure void of abandonment. He knew her terror, he knew her love and he knew the cost. He remembered her hand under the table. Her eyes locking with his on the road. Her presence here, witnessing this horror. A final surge of something—not bitterness now, but a terrible, clear-eyed acceptance—welled up. It was done—the path was walked—the cup was drained—the tyrant's price was paid. There was nothing left.

He drew in one more agonizing breath. He lifted his head as much as the nails allowed, facing the infinite blackness above. He forced the words out, his voice a dry rasp, yet carrying a final, chilling clarity: *"It is finished."*

His head dropped, his chin fell onto his chest and his body went limp, hanging full weight on the nails. A final shudder ran through him. Then, stillness—utter stillness—the ragged breathing stopped.

Silence—absolute silence for a heartbeat. Then the earth moved. It wasn't a tremor, it was a violent lurch. The ground beneath Golgotha heaved, rocks split with sharp cracks and the crosses swayed violently. The thief on the right screamed, a sound cut short as his cross groaned. Soldiers below cried out, thrown off their feet. Dust choked the air, visible even in the gloom as the shaking ground stirred it up. The darkness remained, but now filled with the roar of the earth tearing itself apart.

Far away, in Jerusalem, within the innermost sanctuary of the great Temple, the massive woven Veil—a curtain thick as a man's hand, separating the Holy Place from the Most Holy Place where God was said to dwell—tore. Not from the bottom, where hands might reach, but from the top down, as if ripped by an invisible, giant hand. The sound of rending fabric echoed in the sudden, shocked silence of the priests on duty. The way was torn open—the barrier was gone.

On the hill, the shaking subsided. As the dust settled, the unnatural darkness began, slowly, to lift. A dim, bruised light filtered through. It illuminated the three crosses stark against the fading gloom. On the center cross, the man hung motionless, blood dripped slowly from his wounds, pooling dark on the disturbed earth below. His eyes were closed. His face, even in death, held an expression of profound exhaustion and a terrible, final peace. The King was dead—the sacrifice was complete. The silence of heaven remained. The soldiers picked themselves up, staring at the dead man, then at each other, their faces pale with superstitious fear. The hill was quiet again, except for the wind and the low moan of the remaining thief, nearing his own end. The long day of execution was over. The body remained. The sky lightened towards a somber dusk.

Chapter 3

The unnatural darkness lifted slowly, revealing a bruised twilight sky. Golgotha lay quiet, the earthquake's violence spent. Dust settled over the three stark crosses. On the center one, the body hung utterly still, blood dripped slowly onto the disturbed earth below. The air smelled of dust, iron, and death.

A centurion stood near the base, staring up at the dead man. His face was pale, his earlier professionalism replaced by unease. He'd seen many die but this somehow felt different, the darkness, the earthquake and the man's final cry. "Surely," he muttered, loud enough for nearby soldiers to hear, "this man was innocent." Others nodded, shifting uncomfortably.

Below, the small group of women remained. Mary, the mother, leaned heavily on her companion, her face a mask of numb shock. Mary Magdalene stood rooted, her eyes fixed on the limp form. The sight carved a hollow space inside her. The sobs that had wracked her were gone, replaced by a cold, leaden stillness. He was gone—truly gone. The light, the warmth, the impossible presence—extinguished. Only the brutal reality of the cross remained.

Joseph of Arimathea moved through the near-deserted streets. He was a council member, wealthy and respected. He'd kept his sympathy for Jesus quiet—no longer. The earthquake, the darkness, the speed of the death—it demanded action. The sabbath approached, leaving a body exposed was unthinkable. He went straight to the Praetorium.

Pilate was still in the judgment hall, looking weary and shaken. Reports of the earthquake and the Temple veil's tearing had reached him. His handwashing felt hollow now. Joseph stood before him, composed but urgent. "Prefect," he said. "I request the body of Jesus of Nazareth for burial."

Pilate looked surprised. "Is he dead already?" Crucifixion usually took days. The centurion from Golgotha had just arrived and confirmed it. "Yes, Prefect. The man died quickly. We verified it." Pilate waved a dismissive hand, his relief was evident, another problem solved. "Granted. Take the body." He issued a written order.

Joseph left quickly. He sent servants for tools and clean linen. He needed help, so he sought out Nicodemus, another council member who'd shown cautious interest in Jesus. He found him at home, also troubled by the day's events. "He's dead, Nicodemus," Joseph said without preamble. "Pilate granted me the body. We must bury him before sunset. Help me."

Nicodemus hesitated only a moment. The earthquake had shaken him. He went to his stores, he returned carrying a heavy bundle. It was a mixture of myrrh and aloes, a king's ransom in burial spices, enough for a royal tomb—a silent, costly tribute.

They reached Golgotha as the sun dipped low. The soldiers were preparing to break the legs of the two thieves, hastening death before Sabbath. They approached the center cross. One soldier, following procedure, raised his spear. He thrust it hard upward into Jesus' side, just below the ribs, a final confirmation. Blood and watery fluid spilled out, running down the wood and onto the ground. There was no reaction, his death was certain.

Joseph presented Pilate's order, the centurion nodded, glad to be rid of the body. Soldiers lowered the cross and worked the nails free with practiced brutality. The body slumped to the ground. Joseph and Nicodemus stepped forward and spread the clean linen on the dusty earth. They lifted the body onto it. It was heavy and cold. The wounds were stark in the fading light: the pierced hands and feet, the deep gash in the side, the lacerated back. Flies buzzed around them.

Mary Magdalene watched from a short distance. She saw them lift him. The finality of it hit her again. Her hands clenched at her sides. She wanted to run forward, touch him one last time, push them away but she stood frozen. His mother had been led away, unable to bear more.

Joseph and Nicodemus worked quickly and efficiently. They had little time to spare. They poured the immense quantity of spices Nicodemus brought directly onto the body. The pungent, sweet-sharp scent of myrrh and aloes filled the air, briefly masking the smell of blood. They wrapped the linen tightly around the body, encasing it with the spices within the shroud. They bound it with strips of cloth. They covered the head with a separate cloth. The work was respectful but hurried—a necessary duty.

They lifted the wrapped body onto a simple stretcher Joseph's servants had brought. They began the short journey, Joseph owned a tomb nearby. It was new, cut from rock in a garden close to the execution site. He'd intended it for himself. Now, it would serve.

Mary followed—She kept back, like a silent shadow. The small procession moved through the gathering dusk. The garden tomb was set into a limestone outcrop. A heavy, disc-shaped stone, rolled in a channel, sealed the entrance. Joseph's servants rolled it back with effort, revealing the dark opening.

They carried the body inside. The tomb chamber was small and cool. They laid the linen-wrapped bundle on a stone shelf that lay along one wall. There was no ceremony, no words spoken over the body. Only the heavy scent of spices and the chill of the rock. They turned and left the chamber. Jesus was alone in the darkness—again.

Outside, Joseph's servants put their shoulders to the stone. It rumbled heavily in its channel, grinding across the entrance. A deep, sealing thud echoed as the stone settled into place. The tomb was shut.

Joseph spoke briefly to Nicodemus. They nodded to each other, their faces grim. The task was done. Sabbath began at sunset. They turned and walked away, back towards the city, leaving the garden silent.

The Roman centurion, acting on Pilate's order—prompted by the priests' fear of body theft—arrived with guards. He gestured to the sealed tomb. "Post a watch," he ordered. "Make it secure." Soldiers took positions. They sat down near the tomb entrance, their presence a guarantee against tampering. The tomb was guarded.

Mary Magdalene stood alone. The others were gone. The soldiers ignored her, she wasn't a threat to steal the body. She couldn't even move the stone. She stared at the sealed tomb and the huge stone that blocked the entrance completely. It looked cold, implacable and impossible.

She took a step forward, then another. The soldiers watched her, bored. She walked past them as if they weren't there and stopped before the stone. She reached out a trembling hand, her fingertips touched the rough, cool limestone. The solidity of it shocked her—it was real. He was behind this, sealed in darkness—gone.

No thoughts of promises he'd made about rising came to her. Those words felt like ashes now, blown away by the wind on Golgotha. Blown away by the cry of abandonment. Blown away by the stillness of his body on the stone shelf. There was only this—the cold rock under her fingers. The crushing weight of absence. The utter, desolate silence where his voice had been. The tyrant had taken his payment. The silence of heaven remained absolute, a vast, uncaring void. She leaned her forehead against the stone and closed her eyes. No tears came, she had no more to give—only emptiness—a loss too deep for sound.

In the city, behind locked doors, the disciples hid. Fear was a palpable thing in the close, dark room. Rumors of arrests swirled, the sound of marching feet outside made them flinch. Peter sat apart, his face buried in his hands. The rooster's crow echoed endlessly in his mind. The others huddled together, speaking in whispers. The man they'd followed, the hope they'd carried, was dead—sealed in a tomb. Their world had ended on that hill. God had not intervened. The silence remained, unbroken, into the deepening night. The stone was rolled and the guards kept watch. The garden was still. The borrowed tomb held its occupant. The story, for now, was finished.

The Road to Damascus

Saul of Tarsus wiped the blood from his hands with a rag that had seen too much use. The Christian woman's screams had stopped an hour ago, but her words still echoed in his mind like poison. *"Jesus forgives you,"* she had whispered as he drove the iron spike through her palm. "Even you."

The audacity of these followers sickened him. They spoke of love while their very existence threatened the order God had established through Moses and the Law. Saul kicked dirt over the dark stain in the courtyard and walked toward his horse. Damascus awaited, and with it, more heretics to silence forever.

"Saul." The high priest approached from the temple steps, his robes pristine despite the carnage. "The letters are ready. The synagogue leaders in Damascus expect you within the week."

Saul took the sealed documents. His authority to arrest, interrogate, and execute Christians stretched across the empire now. The work God had given him would not be contained by the walls of Jerusalem.

"They multiply like rats," the priest continued. "For every one we kill, three more appear claiming they have seen the dead Nazarene walking among them."

"Hallucinations born of guilt and fear," Saul replied. "When they feel the iron, they remember the truth quickly enough."

Three days later, Saul rode at the head of a column of temple guards through the desert wasteland between Jerusalem and Damascus. The sun burned overhead like the eye of an angry god, and the sand beneath their horses' hooves had been baked hard as stone. His men stayed silent, knowing his moods. They had seen what happened to those who questioned his methods.

The youngest guard, barely eighteen and soft around the edges, had made the mistake of asking why they tortured women and children along with the men. Saul had made him watch while they crucified an entire Christian family outside Bethany. The boy had not spoken since.

166

"Sir," the captain of the guard called out. "Rider approaching."

A lone horseman emerged from the heat shimmer ahead, moving fast. As he drew closer, Saul recognized him as one of the temple messengers. The man's face was pale with exhaustion and fear.

"What news?" Saul demanded as the messenger reined in his agitated horse.

"The Christians in Damascus," the man gasped. "They know you are coming. Someone warned them. Half have fled the city already."

Saul felt rage build in his chest like a fire. "Who? Who betrayed us?"

"We do not know. The high priest sent me to tell you to proceed with caution. There may be an ambush."

Saul looked ahead toward the distant city, its walls shimmering in the heat. "Let them try. God's wrath will not be turned aside by cowards and heretics."

The messenger glanced nervously at the other guards. "Sir, there are rumors. Strange reports from the road. Travelers speak of visions. Voices in the desert. Some say the dead walk again."

"Superstition," Saul spat. "The desert plays tricks on weak minds. We continue."

But as they rode deeper into the wasteland, Saul began to notice things that disturbed him. Birds fell dead from the sky without cause. The water in their skins turned bitter. One of the horses went lame, then another, as if the very ground beneath them had become cursed.

The young guard who had questioned him earlier suddenly pulled his horse to a stop and pointed with a shaking finger. "Look."

In the distance, figures moved across the sand. Men and women in rough clothing, walking in the same direction as Saul's party. They moved too smoothly, their feet seeming to barely touch the ground.

"Who are they?" the captain asked.

Saul squinted against the glare. The figures were too far away to make out clearly, but something about them chilled his blood. They walked in perfect formation, like soldiers, but they cast no shadows despite the blazing sun overhead.

"Travelers," he said, but his voice lacked conviction. "Nothing more."

They pressed on, but the figures paralleled their course, never drawing closer, never falling behind. As the hours passed, more appeared. Soon dozens of silent shapes moved across the desert on either side of them, keeping pace with the horses.

The guards began to mutter prayers under their breath. Even the captain, a veteran of twenty campaigns, fingered the hilt of his sword nervously.

"Sir," the young guard whispered. "Should we turn back?"

Saul rounded on him with fury. "Turn back? When God's work remains unfinished? When heretics still breathe?" He struck the boy across the face with his riding crop. "We serve the Lord of Hosts, not some dead carpenter's ghost stories."

But even as he spoke the words, doubt gnawed at him. The desert had grown too quiet. No insects buzzed, no wind stirred the sand and even their horses' hooves seemed muffled, as if the very air had thickened around them.

The sun reached its peak and began its descent toward the horizon. Damascus remained a distant smudge against the hills. The silent figures continued their strange march, and now Saul could see there were hundreds of them. They stretched across the desert like an army of the dead.

"Water," the captain called out. "The men need water."

They stopped at a small oasis marked on their maps, but the pool they found was empty except for cracked mud and the bones of animals that had died waiting for rain that never came. The palm trees stood leafless and black, as if burned from within.

"This place is cursed," one of the guards whispered.

Saul dismounted and walked to the center of the dead grove. The silence pressed against his ears like physical weight. He knelt and scraped at the dried mud with his knife, looking for moisture, but found only dust and more bones.

When he stood and turned back toward his men, the figures in the desert had moved closer—much closer. He could see their faces now, and his blood turned to ice water in his veins.

He recognized them. All of them.

The woman he had tortured in Jerusalem stood at the front of the gathering, her palms still bearing the wounds from his spikes. Behind her, the Christian family he had crucified watched him with eyes that held no life. Dozens of others followed, men and women and children whose screams he had silenced in the name of God.

They stood in perfect stillness, waiting.

"Mount up," Saul commanded, his voice hoarse. "We ride now."

But as his guards scrambled for their horses, the dead began to walk forward. They moved slowly but with terrible purpose, their feet making no sound in the sand.

"Saul of Tarsus," the crucified woman called out, her voice carrying impossible distances. "Do you know what you have done?"

Saul drew his sword. The blade shook in his grip. "You are dead. I killed you myself."

"Yes," she agreed. "And we have seen what lies beyond death. We have seen the kingdom you serve."

The dead continued their approach. His guards turned their horses in circles, crying out in terror, but the animals would not flee. They stood frozen as if paralyzed by invisible chains.

"Tell me," the woman continued, now close enough that Saul could see the maggots crawling in her wounds. "Tell me about the God you worship. The one who demands blood from children. The one who calls murder righteousness."

"The Lord of Hosts demands obedience," Saul snarled. "You chose rebellion. You chose heresy."

"Did we?" Another voice joined the first. The father from the crucified family stepped forward, his children flanking him like pale shadows. "Or did we choose love over fear? Mercy over vengeance?"

More voices rose from the crowd of the dead. "We chose forgiveness over hatred." "We chose hope over despair." "We chose life over death."

Saul raised his sword above his head. "Lies! All lies! God is righteous! God is just!"

The sky darkened suddenly, though the sun still blazed overhead. Clouds that had not been there moments before gathered with unnatural speed, heavy and black as iron. Thunder rolled across the desert, and lightning split the air.

"Look," the dead woman commanded. "Look and see the god you serve."

The lightning struck again, and in its flash, Saul saw something that shattered his mind like glass. In the clouds above, a face appeared. Ancient beyond measure, twisted with rage and hate. Eyes like burning coals stared down at the gathering, and when the mouth opened, it revealed teeth like broken tombstones.

"*They question my authority!*" the thing in the sky roared. "*They spread poison with their talk of love! Kill them again, Saul! Kill them all!*"

But before Saul could move, another light blazed in the desert. Brighter than the sun, whiter than molten silver. The dead fell to their knees, but not in fear—in recognition—in reverence.

A figure walked out of the light. A man in simple robes, his hands and feet bearing the marks of nails. But his face was not the serene mask Saul had expected. It was bitter, carved with lines of suffering and doubt.

"Jesus," the dead woman whispered.

The figure looked at her with eyes full of pain. "Yes. Though I wonder sometimes if that name means anything anymore."

The thing in the clouds shrieked with rage. *"You were supposed to die! You were supposed to stay dead!"*

Jesus looked up at the face in the storm. "I did die. I felt my blood drain away while you watched and smiled. I felt my breath stop while you counted it victory." His voice grew hard. "But death taught me something, Father. It taught me what you really are."

"I am God!" the creature bellowed. *"I am the creator of all things!"*

"You are a tyrant," Jesus replied quietly. "A monster who feeds on suffering and calls it righteousness. You sent me to earth not to save humanity, but to increase their guilt. To give them one more rule to break, one more reason to hate themselves."

Saul watched in horror as son faced father across the desert sky. The dead gathered around Jesus like children seeking protection from a nightmare.

"These people," Jesus gestured to the crowd of the slain, "died because they believed my message of love. They died because they thought I offered them something better than fear." His laugh was bitter as winter wind. "They died because I was fool enough to trust you."

The face in the clouds contorted with fury. *"They died because they were weak! Because they chose rebellion over obedience!"*

"They died because you demanded it," Jesus shot back. "Every drop of blood Saul has spilled was spilled in your name. Every scream of agony was music to your ears. You call it justice, but I have seen your justice, Father. I have tasted it."

Saul found his voice at last. "You speak blasphemy. God is good. God is righteous."

Jesus turned to him, and Saul saw madness flickering in those ancient eyes. "Good? Righteous? Look around you, Saul. Look at what goodness and righteousness have built. A desert full of the dead. A world drowning in blood."

The light around Jesus began to flicker and fade. "I came to bring salvation, but I brought only more suffering. I preached love, but I gave them another reason to hate. I promised eternal life, but I delivered only eternal death."

The thing in the clouds laughed, a sound like grinding bones. *"Now you understand, my son! Now you see the truth! Humanity is corrupt! They deserve nothing but punishment!"*

"No," Jesus said, but his voice lacked conviction. "No, there must be another way."

"There is no other way!" the creature roared. *"There is only obedience or destruction! Love or annihilation!"*

Jesus looked at the faces of the dead surrounding him. Their eyes held hope, even in death. They still believed in his message, even as it crumbled to ash in his hands.

"I have failed you all," he whispered. "I thought I could change things. I thought I could bring light to the darkness. But the darkness is too strong. It lives in the very heart of heaven itself."

The dead woman stepped forward and took his hand. "Teacher, you have not failed us. Your words gave us courage to die with love in our hearts instead of hate."

"And what good did that do?" Jesus pulled away from her touch. "You are still dead. Your children are still orphans. The world is still broken."

Saul watched the exchange with growing confusion. His faith, built on the certainty of God's righteousness, cracked like a dam under flood water. If Jesus himself doubted, if the son of God questioned his mission, then what truth remained?

"I do not understand," he said aloud. "I have served God faithfully. I have done his will."

Jesus turned to him with eyes full of pity and rage. "His will? Look at your hands, Saul. Look at the blood that stains them. That is not God's will. That is the will of a monster who wears God's face."

The storm clouds began to swirl faster, forming a massive whirlpool in the sky. The thing's laughter grew louder and more terrible.

"*Choose, Saul!*" it commanded. "*Serve me and live! Defy me and join the dead!*"

But before Saul could answer, Jesus spoke again. "There is a third choice, Saul. You can walk away. You can refuse to serve either love or hate. You can choose nothing."

"Nothing?" Saul whispered.

"Nothing," Jesus confirmed. "No grand purpose. No divine mission. No eternal reward or punishment. Just the simple choice to stop killing in God's name."

The desert fell silent except for the wind whistling through the bones of the dead trees. Saul looked at his sword, still raised to strike down phantoms. He looked at his guards, cowering behind their horses. He looked at the dead, watching him with patient eyes.

"I have killed so many," he said.

"Yes," Jesus agreed. "And if you continue on this path, you will kill many more. The creature in the sky will whisper righteousness in your ear while you drive nails through innocent hands."

"But if I stop, what becomes of the Law? What becomes of order?"

Jesus laughed, and it was the saddest sound Saul had ever heard. "The Law? Order? Look around you, Saul. This is what the Law has built. This is what order looks like when it serves a tyrant."

The young guard who had questioned Saul earlier suddenly stepped forward. His face was pale but determined. "I choose nothing," he said clearly. "I will not kill for God or man anymore."

He dropped his sword in the sand and walked away, heading back toward Jerusalem on foot. One by one, the other guards followed. Soon only Saul and the captain remained.

"Sir?" the captain asked. "What are your orders?"

Saul looked at the letters of authority in his saddlebags. The power to arrest and execute Christians across the empire. The divine mandate to serve God's will through violence and terror.

He thought of the woman's words as she died: "Jesus forgives you. Even you."

But Jesus stood before him now, broken and bitter, questioning everything he had once preached. There was no forgiveness in those eyes, only exhaustion and despair.

"I choose," Saul said slowly, "to be Paul."

The creature in the sky shrieked with rage. *"What does that mean!?"*

"It means," Paul replied, dropping his sword beside the guard's, "that I reject both of you. I reject the god who demands blood and the savior who has lost faith in salvation. I choose to find my own way."

Jesus stared at him with something that might have been respect. "And what way is that?"

Paul looked at the dead gathered around them. "I will tell people about you. Not the perfect son of God, but the broken man who questioned everything. I will tell them about doubt and failure and the courage to keep searching for truth even when it hurts."

"They will not listen," Jesus warned. "They want heroes and villains, not broken men asking questions."

"Then I will make them listen," Paul said. "I will travel to every city, every nation. I will preach not certainty, but doubt. Not righteousness, but the struggle to find meaning in a world ruled by monsters."

The storm began to dissipate. The thing in the clouds faded with a final roar of fury. The dead smiled sadly and began to fade as well, their forms growing transparent in the failing light.

"We must go," the woman said to Jesus. "Our time is ending."

Jesus nodded. He looked one last time at Paul. "You will suffer for this choice. They will call you heretic and fool. They will beat you and imprison you and eventually kill you."

"I know," Paul replied. "But at least my suffering will be honest. At least I will not pretend it serves some greater good."

As the dead and their teacher faded into the growing darkness, Paul found himself alone in the desert with only the captain for company. The oasis remained dead, the bones still scattered in the sand.

"Sir," the captain said quietly. "What do we tell them in Damascus?"

Paul mounted his horse and turned away from the city. "We tell them nothing. We go home."

"And the Christians?"

Paul thought of the believers hiding in Damascus, waiting for persecution that would never come, at least not from him.

"Let them live," he said. "Let them ask their own questions and find their own answers. God knows there are enough monsters in this world without my help."

As they rode back toward Jerusalem under a canopy of cold stars, Paul began to plan his new mission. He would indeed travel to every corner of the empire. But, instead of hunting Christians, he would become one. Not the kind who preached certainty and righteousness, but the kind who admitted doubt and embraced the terrible freedom of questions without answers.

Behind them, the desert wind carried the echoes of laughter. Not the cruel laughter of the creature in the clouds, but something warmer. The laughter of people who had found courage in the face of cosmic horror, who had chosen love despite knowing it led only to suffering.

Paul smiled in the darkness. Perhaps that was enough. Perhaps that was everything.

In Antioch

The sun hammered Antioch flat, burning everything with an intense heat. Dust hung thick in the air, coating everything—the rough stone buildings, the faded awnings over the market stalls, the dry throats of the people. It got inside the small house near the city gate too, the one belonging to Lydia, a widow whose husband had traded spices. Every seventh day, the dust settled on the sandals and cloaks of the men and women crowded inside. They pushed benches against the walls, sat cross-legged on woven mats, filled the small courtyard. Their voices were low and intense. They talked about Jesus.

Barnabas stood near the low cooking fire, its heat adding to the room's stifling closeness. Saul sat beside him, his face gaunt, eyes burning. Barnabas spoke of Jesus's words, the parables about seeds and soil, the call to love even enemies. Saul's voice cut in sharper. He spoke of the Kingdom coming like a thief in the night, of judgment falling swift as a desert storm. They all believed it. They felt the urgency pressing on them, a physical weight. Jesus had risen, he had ascended, he *would* return—any day—any hour. The world felt thin, ready to tear open.

Their duty was clear—spread the word—tell everyone. Get the message out, before it was too late, before God's vengeance swept the earth clean. They saw God's hand everywhere—in the drought withering the crops outside the city, in the sickness that took children and in the harsh rule of Rome. They saw a demanding God—a punishing God. Jesus himself, Saul recounted with chilling certainty, had known that wrath. He'd cried out to God on the execution stake, feeling abandoned, tasting the bitterness of that forsakenness before submitting to the brutal plan. They spoke of that moment often. The ultimate proof of God's terrible purpose and Jesus' misguided obedience.

They fanned out through Antioch's crowded streets and stifling alleys near the river Orontes, where washerwomen beat clothes against rocks. Tabitha spoke to groups of women by the columned forum, where merchants hawked Syrian silks and Egyptian grain. Barnabas reasoned with Greeks in the shadow of the great Temple to Jupiter, Saul confronted Jews and pagans alike, his words like stones. "Repent! The Kingdom is at hand! The one God demands it! His Anointed, Jesus, whom you killed, will judge you!" They offered no proof beyond their burning conviction. Only the words, the stark warning, the promise of salvation through a crucified man they claimed was God's son. It sounded like madness to many.

The name started in the taverns. It dripped from the lips of merchants whose stalls Saul disrupted. It was muttered by priests of Apollo and Cybele whose offerings dwindled. It was shouted by Roman soldiers shoving the preachers aside. *Christiani*. Little Christs—a new name for the followers of the Christ. It was spat out, covered in dust, a word meant to mock their obsession, their strange devotion to a dead rebel and his absent, vengeful father-god. It lumped them together, this ragtag group of Jews and Syrians and Greeks, as something other, something ridiculous and slightly dangerous.

Lydia heard it first, whispered by her neighbor's son as she drew water. "Careful, Lydia. They're calling your people *Christiani* now." She flinched. It sounded ugly and derisive. She brought the word back to the house meeting and a murmur went through the room. Their faces tightened, Barnabas looked grim and Saul's jaw clenched. "Fools," he rasped. "They mock what they cannot understand. They mock God's chosen."

The confrontation happened on a market day. Heat shimmered off the packed earth of the main square. Saul stood on the worn steps of a disused shrine, his voice carrying over the uproar. He preached fire and judgment—a group gathered, not to listen, but to challenge. Leading them was Demetrius, a silversmith whose trade in religious trinkets had suffered since Saul's arrival. Demetrius was broad, his face red above his tunic.

"Enough, Saul!" Demetrius bellowed, pushing to the front. The crowd around him rumbled their agreement. "Enough of your doom-saying! Enough of your 'King Jesus'! Where is this mighty son of your invisible tyrant god? Hiding? Dead? You disturb the peace! You scare good people with your tales of fire!"

Saul's eyes locked onto Demetrius. "Peace? There is no peace for the wicked! God sees your idols, Demetrius. He sees your greed. His judgment is real. Jesus *is* the Son of God! He rose! He reigns! He returns soon to crush the serpent's head!" Saul's voice rose, raw with conviction. "Your silver gods cannot save you from the wrath to come!"

"Son of God?" Demetrius laughed, a harsh, barking sound. The crowd laughed with him. "Proof, Saul! Show us proof! Or is your only proof the fear you peddle? Your 'son of God' died like a common bandit!

Abandoned even by your own vengeful sky-tyrant, by all accounts!" He swept his arm wide, addressing the crowd. "Hear him! The *Christiani*! Little anointed fools! Following a ghost, trembling before a god who eats his own son!"

The word hung in the hot air. *Christiani*. It hit Saul's followers standing nearby—Lydia, Tabitha, a Cypriot named Manaen. It stung—it was meant to diminish them, to paint them as deluded fanatics. Saul drew himself up, his face pale with fury. "Blasphemer! You invoke the wrath you deny! God struck down Herod Agrippa for his pride! He will strike down all who oppose His Anointed! Jesus *is* Lord!"

"Your lord is dust!" Demetrius shot back. "And you, *Christiani*, are dust-eaters! Choking on your own fear!" He spat on the ground near Saul's feet. The crowd surged, voices rising, with a mix of anger and jeering. Roman soldiers, alerted by the noise, began pushing through the crowd, their armor glinting dully in the sun. Barnabas appeared beside Saul, gripping his arm. "Not here, brother. Not now." Reluctantly, fury still burning in his eyes, Saul allowed himself to be pulled away from the steps, the mocking cries of "*Christiani*!" following them like thrown stones.

Back in Lydia's house, the air was thick with anger and humiliation. The word echoed. *Christiani*. Little Christs—it felt like a brand.

"We cannot let them define us with their scorn," Tabitha said, her voice tight.

Barnabas paced the small courtyard. "They use it to wound. To separate us."

Saul sat silent for a long moment, staring at the dusty floor. Then he looked up, his eyes were different. The fury had faded, replaced by a cold, hard light. "They mean it for shame," he said slowly. "But they speak a truth they do not see." He stood. "Jesus *is* the Christ. The Anointed One. We *are* his. We bear his name. We bear his rejection. We bear his obedience...even to death." He paused, the image of Jesus' forsaken cry on the cross stark in his mind. "Let them call us *Christiani*. We *are* Christians. If the name marks us for the world's hatred, so be it. It marks us as belonging to Christ. To the bitter end God demanded of him...and may demand of us."

A stillness fell over them. The sting of the insult began to shift. It wasn't just mockery anymore. It was an identity, forged in opposition, sealed by the terrifying God they served and the abandoned Savior they followed. *Christian*. It was defiance—it was acceptance—it was the name of those who walked the narrow path under the eye of a demanding, jealous deity, waiting for the fire to fall. They embraced it—the word settled on them, heavy but theirs.

The expectation of the End intensified. The drought worsened, springs ran low and tempers frayed throughout Antioch. The Christians met more often, prayed with desperate fervor. Saul's sermons grew fiercer. The Kingdom *must* be near. The signs were everywhere—the hardship, the persecution and the mockery. God's patience was thinning. They increased their efforts, preaching on street corners with renewed zeal, their declaration "Jesus is Lord!" now coupled with "We are Christians!" It was a challenge flung at the dusty sky.

A group of believers from Cyprus arrived, gaunt from travel, bearing grim news of famine striking Jerusalem. "A sign!" Saul declared at the next gathering. "Judgment begins at the house of God! It rolls outwards! Antioch is next unless it repents!" Fear, sharp and cold, mingled with their fervent hope. They pooled their meager resources—sacks of grain, jars of oil, dried fish—to send aid to Jerusalem. It was an act of obedience, a desperate plea for mercy, a tangible sign of their unity as Christians. Barnabas and Saul were chosen to lead the journey, carrying the Antioch church's offering, their faith, and the new name back to the city where it all began.

The day of departure dawned hot and still. The sky was a bleached, pitiless blue. The small band of believers gathered outside Lydia's gate to see Barnabas and Saul off. The laden donkey shifted impatiently. Prayers were said, hands clasped tightly. There was a brittle tension in the air, a sense of stepping onto a knife-edge. They were sending their strongest into the heart of the brewing storm, carrying their identity and their plea.

As Barnabas mounted his horse and Saul adjusted the donkey's lead rope, a commotion erupted down the street. Demetrius appeared, leading a larger, angrier mob than before. News of the famine relief, twisted into some conspiracy or sacrilege, had spread. "There!" Demetrius roared, pointing. "The *Christiani!* Stealing our grain! Sending it to their dead king's city! Inviting their god's curse upon us all!"

The mob surged forward—artisans, day laborers, faces contorted by heat and fear and the poisonous words Demetrius fed them. Stones flew—One struck the donkey, making it bray and lurch forward. Barnabas' horse reared.

"Get back inside!" Barnabas shouted to Lydia and the others, trying to control his panicked horse.

Saul stepped forward, raising his hands. "People of Antioch! This is folly! We bring aid to starving brothers! We seek God's mercy for all!" His voice was swallowed by the roar of the mob.

A jagged piece of roofing tile struck Saul's temple. He staggered, blood instantly welling and streaking down his dusty face. He didn't cry out. He just looked up, past the surging crowd, past the blinding sun, his expression not of pain, but of a terrible, dawning recognition. For a fleeting second, it wasn't the mob he saw, but the crushing weight of abandonment, the echo of a cry in a different darkness: "*Eli, Eli, lema sabachthani?*" Then the world went black as another stone hit his chest, knocking him backward onto the unforgiving ground.

Barnabas tried to reach him, but the mob was a wall of fists and clubs. Lydia screamed, Tabitha tried to pull her back inside the gate. The scene dissolved into chaos—the thud of blows, the animal panic of the horse and donkey, the triumphant roar of the mob and the choked cries of the believers. The carefully gathered sacks of grain were torn open, their contents spilling into the dirt, trampled underfoot. The offering for Jerusalem vanished into the Antioch dust.

Barnabas, bleeding from a cut above his eye, managed to drag Saul's limp, bleeding body back through Lydia's gate just as Roman soldiers finally arrived, their disciplined violence scattering the mob with brutal efficiency. The street outside was a ruin of spilled grain, blood, and broken pottery.

Inside the courtyard, they laid Saul on a mat. His breathing was shallow, ragged. Lydia pressed cloths to the bleeding wound on his head. His eyes fluttered open. They found Barnabas' face, there was no fear in them—only a profound, weary emptiness, a reflection of the abandonment he preached about. He tried to speak, his lips moving soundlessly for a moment. Then a single, harsh whisper escaped, thick with blood and dust.

"Father...why...?"

His body tensed once, a final spasm, then went still. The fierce light in his eyes extinguished. The man who had embraced the name 'Christian' with defiant certainty, who had channeled the voice of a vengeful God, lay dead on the packed earth floor. Not in glorious martyrdom before emperors, but broken by a mob in a dusty street, his mission unfinished, his cry echoing the one he believed defined his Lord. The only sounds in Lydia's house were the ragged sobs of the believers and the relentless, indifferent buzzing of flies already finding the blood drying on the stones outside. The Kingdom had not come. The tyrant God remained silent. The name 'Christian' clung to them now, soaked in tragedy.

Philo of Alexandria Visits the Temple in Jerusalem

The desert sun burnt the land, everything was dry, dusty and cracked. Philo of Alexandria squinted against the glare. Sand gritted between his teeth. His camel plodded, a slow swaying rhythm that matched the heat haze dancing on the horizon. Jerusalem rose ahead, a cluster of stone buildings baked white and brown, clinging to the hills like a stubborn weed. It looked less like a holy city, and more like a frontier outpost braced against the wilderness. Philo adjusted his wide-brimmed hat, a practical concession to the relentless light. He felt the familiar weight of scrolls in his saddlebags—Plato, the Torah, and his own treatises on the Logos. Reason traveled with him into this parched land of prophets and zealots.

He entered the city gates, dust hung thick in the narrow streets. Men moved with purpose, hands near belts where knives hung. Others argued fiercely near market stalls, voices sharp as flint. Roman soldiers stood watchful, their armor gleaming dully under the grime, eyes scanning the crowd like hawks. The air smelled of animals, sweat, spices, and something else—a sharp tension. Philo sought the quiet of the Temple complex, a sanctuary of stone amidst the human storm.

Inside the vast Court of the Gentiles, the noise was different. It was a low hum of prayer, the clink of coins changing hands at the money changers' tables and the bleating of sacrificial animals. Philo walked the perimeter, observing. His gaze settled on a group near Solomon's Porch. A man stood speaking, he wore simple, travel-stained clothes. His face was lean, etched with lines that spoke of sun and hardship. There was no softness in his eyes, only a deep, unsettling intensity. His voice cut through the Temple murmur, clear and hard.

"Hypocrites!" The word cracked like a whip. "You clean the outside of the cup and dish, but inside you are full of greed and self-indulgence! Whitewashed tombs! Beautiful on the outside, full of dead men's bones and everything unclean within!"

Philo stopped, the accusation was brutal and direct. This was no gentle rabbi offering parables. This man spoke like a judge pronouncing sentence. His bitterness wasn't concealed; it was a weapon. He denounced the scribes, the Pharisees and the very structure of the Temple commerce. "My house shall be called a house of prayer for all nations! But you have made it a den of thieves!" The man swept an arm towards the money changers. His gesture held contempt.

A murmur ran through the crowd—some nodded grimly; others looked furious. Priests watched from the shadows, their faces stony, covered with dust. Philo felt a sense of unease—this was dangerous talk. He saw the man's eyes scan the faces before him. They held no hope, only a bleak acceptance. When a Pharisee challenged him about taxes, the man's reply was curt, almost dismissive. "Give back to Caesar what is Caesar's, and to God what is God's." The answer silenced his questioner, but there was no triumph in the speaker's face, only weariness. He looked like a man carrying a crushing weight, resigned to its burden. Philo wondered what burden could make a man so hard, so devoid of the gentle piety Philo sought in the Divine Logos. This Logos felt harsh and unforgiving, like the desert sun.

Later, seeking understanding, Philo secured an audience. The Roman prefect, Pontius Pilate, received him in a stark room within the fortress Antonia. Pilate looked tired, his toga seemed out of place, like a costume worn too long. Maps of Judea lay unfurled on a heavy table.

"Alexandria," Pilate said, pouring wine without offering any. "A city of philosophers. What brings you to this dustbowl, Philo? Seeking wisdom among the zealots?" His voice was dry, edged with cynicism.

"Curiosity, Prefect," Philo replied. "The currents of faith run strong here. I observe."

Pilate snorted. "Faith? Superstition. Rebellion dressed in prayer shawls. They hate Rome. They hate each other. They hate anyone who tries to keep order." He gestured vaguely towards the window overlooking the Temple Mount. "That rabble-rouser causing trouble down there? Another one. Claims to be a king. They all claim something. They end the same way." He took a long drink. "My job is to keep the peace. For Rome. Sometimes peace requires...decisive action. The god these people worship demands blood anyway. Seems a vengeful sort. Always smiting, always punishing. Makes my task easier, in a way. They understand force." Pilate's eyes were flat and pragmatic. He saw only problems to be managed, not souls to be saved. Philo felt the gulf between Pilate's weary tyranny and the bitter prophet's fire. Both seemed facets of a world ruled by a harsh, demanding master.

Another day, Philo navigated the labyrinthine corridors of power to meet the Sanhedrin. The air in their council chamber was thick with incense and tension. Elderly faces, some shrewd, some pious and some hardened, regarded him. Caiaphas, the High Priest, presided, his robes were immaculate, his expression unreadable.

"Welcome, Philo of Alexandria," Caiaphas said. His voice was smooth, controlled. "Your reputation precedes you. A bridge between Athens and Jerusalem?"

"An observer," Philo corrected gently. "I seek the underlying truth that unites reason and revelation."

A murmur went through the elders—one, with a sharp face and sharper tongue, leaned forward. "Revelation is clear. The Law is given. The Temple is sacred. We guard it. Against impurity. Against blasphemy. Against those who would tear down the traditions." His eyes flickered towards the window, where the sounds of the city drifted in. "There are elements...disruptive elements...that threaten the delicate balance. The Romans watch. They look for excuses. Stability is paramount. The Holy One demands purity, Philo. He demands obedience. Woe to those who stray." The unspoken threat hung in the air. Philo sensed their fear—fear of Rome, fear of the crowd and fear of the unpredictable anger of their demanding God. Their concern wasn't truth, but control.

Curiosity led Philo further, to the palace of Herod Antipas. It stood in stark contrast to the austerity of the Antonia or the Temple. Marble floors, gaudy frescoes depicting pagan scenes and the disgustingly sweet scent of exotic perfumes. Herod received him lounging on a couch, picking at grapes. He looked soft, indolent, his eyes restless.

"Ah, the philosopher!" Herod declared, waving a languid hand. "Escaping the desert for some civilized conversation? Or perhaps fleeing the righteous indignation down the hill?" He chuckled. "That prophet, the one from Galilee...John, was it? Nasty business. Had to deal with him. Now this other one...Jesus. Causing a stir. They say he performs tricks. Wouldn't mind seeing one." Herod's smile lingered then faded. They held a nervous glint. "Pilate sent him to me. Some local squabble. Annoying. I sent him back. Politics. Always politics. And that God of theirs…" Herod shuddered theatrically. "So…absolute. So demanding. Smote my father, you know. Nasty way to go. One prefers a more…accommodating deity." Herod's world was one of petty power and indulgent fear. The vengeful God of the Jews was a distant, uncomfortable rumble in his comfortable prison.

Philo spent his days in study, in debate with local scholars, in observing the rituals at the Temple. He found pockets of reason, echoes of the Logos he sought. But the city buzzed with a strange energy. Whispers ran through the streets like dust devils. Soldiers moved in larger groups. Faces in the crowd looked strained. One evening, walking back to his lodgings near the Upper City, Philo passed a commotion. A cluster of Temple guards, their faces grim, roughly dragged a man through the shadows. The man's face was obscured, Philo barely registered it, preoccupied with a complex argument about Platonic forms he'd had earlier. The city was always arresting someone.

The next day, the tension felt thicker. The market stalls opened later and fewer people lingered in the streets. A Roman patrol marched past, boots striking the stones with unusual force. Philo noticed people gathered in small, hushed groups, breaking apart quickly when soldiers approached. He saw a woman weeping silently by a well. He assumed it was a private grief, he tried not to get involved. He had a scheduled discussion with a renowned scribe about allegorical interpretation so he focused on that.

He passed the Praetorium—a crowd had gathered outside its gates, larger and angrier than usual. Shouts rose and fell—a name, repeated with venom. "Barabbas!" Then another name, spat out. "Jesus!" Philo frowned. Barabbas? A known troublemaker, he recalled hearing. Jesus? The bitter preacher from the Temple? He saw Pilate standing on a balcony, looking strained, washing his hands in a basin a servant held. It was a theatrical gesture. Philo dismissed it as Roman political maneuvering, irrelevant to his quest for divine reason. He walked on, seeking the quiet shade of his host's courtyard to prepare his notes.

The sun climbed higher, hotter. A strange darkness began to creep across the sky around midday. Not clouds, but a deep, unnatural dimming. The air grew still and heavy. Philo, working by lamplight now, found it difficult to concentrate. An odd pressure filled the city, a silence deeper than usual. Distantly, he thought he heard a faint cry carried on the still air, a single word that sounded like "Abandoned!" It was swallowed instantly by the unnatural gloom. He shivered, attributing it to the strange weather and his own tired mind. The vengeful God showing displeasure at some transgression, perhaps. He lit another lamp.

By late afternoon, the darkness lifted as suddenly as it had come. The sun reappeared, harsh and accusing. Life in the streets seemed muted, stunned. Philo decided to visit the Temple one last time before his departure the next day. He needed clarity after the unsettling afternoon.

The great complex felt hollow, fewer worshippers moved through the courts. The priests seemed subdued. Philo walked towards the massive curtain separating the Holy of Holies from the rest of the Temple. He stopped, something was wrong. He stared at the fabric, thick and richly woven, hung strangely. A long, vertical tear ran down its center, from top to bottom. It looked like a wound, ripped. It wasn't worn, or frayed—it was violently torn. He glanced around, others noticed it too, murmuring in hushed, frightened tones, echoed the quiet space. They pointed, their faces pale with superstitious dread. "The Veil..." someone whispered. "Torn!"

Philo felt a coldness seep into his bones, deeper than the desert night. This was no accident, this felt like an act—a final, terrible punctuation mark. The impenetrable barrier between man and the Most Holy, ripped open. Not in reverence, but in violence. Not an invitation, but an exposure. The stark, brutal act mirrored the harsh landscape, the vengeful God Pilate feared and Herod mocked, the bitterness in the prophet's eyes. This was no Logos of harmonious reason. This was the desert's answer—this was the fist of an angry sky-god striking his own sanctuary.

He stood frozen before the torn curtain, the whispers of the terrified faithful swirling around him like dust. The meaning of the torn veil, the strange darkness, the cries he'd half-heard, the tense faces—fragments clicked together with terrible force. The preacher—the arrest he barely saw. Pilate's hand-washing. The name 'Jesus' spat by the crowd. The unnatural dark at noon—the cry of abandonment—the torn veil.

He had been here and walked these streets. He had spoken to the powerful and the learned. He had seen the man, heard his bitter words. He had witnessed the storm clouds gather and felt the oppressive weight. And he had seen nothing—he had understood nothing—he had been blind, deaf, wrapped in the scrolls of reason while the desert enacted its brutal, divine drama right outside his window. The Logos he sought felt like dust in his mouth. The vengeful God had acted, and Philo, the great philosopher, had been too busy contemplating the divine to notice its bloody, earth-shattering arrival.

A profound emptiness opened within him, colder and more desolate than the Judean wilderness. He had journeyed seeking connection and understanding. He had found only a ripped curtain and the crushing realization of his own irrelevance. The tragedy wasn't just the death he now understood must have happened; it was the magnitude of his own failure to perceive it. The desert sun beat down on the stones of the Temple courtyard, bleaching them white. Philo turned away from the torn veil, the scrolls in his bag suddenly heavy as tombstones. His journey for wisdom ended not in revelation, but in the stark, unforgiving light of his own ignorance. The silence of the Temple pressed in, broken only by the dry rasp of sand skittering across the stones.

The Letter and the Lightning

The reed pen scratched across the papyrus like a dry bone. Paul watched the words form under the scribe's quick hand. Outside the cramped room in Corinth, the city busied itself with its usual chaos—merchants shouting, cart wheels grinding and the distant bark of Roman orders. But inside, the air felt charged, heavy. Paul tasted dust and urgency. Every scratch of the pen was a defiance. He spoke the next sentence, his voice low but firm. "For I delivered to you as of first importance what I also received: that Christ died for our sins according to the Scriptures, that he was buried, that he was raised on the third day according to the Scriptures..."

He paused, the image flashed again: the Damascus road, the blinding light and the voice that shattered his old life. It wasn't just a voice, it was a command. He pushed it down, tried to focus on the message—the core—Death—Burial—Resurrection. The proof? The witnesses he listed— Cephas, the twelve, the five hundred, James, all the apostles—their names were anchors in the swirling doubt of this corrupt city and this fractured world. His own name, last on that list, still felt like a brand. The persecutor turned proclaimer. That should be proof the message held power, power to break the strongest resistance—even his.

A sudden crash echoed from the street below. Shouts followed, sharp and angry. Paul's hand instinctively went to the rough wood of the table, bracing. His companion, Titus, moved silently to the shuttered window, peering through a crack. "Jews from the synagogue," Titus murmured. "Argue with Aquila. About you."

Paul closed his eyes for a second, not in fear—calculation. Time was short—always short. He saw the faces of the believers in Thessalonica, their young faith shaken by death. Their questions haunted him. *What happens to those who die before the Lord returns? Will they miss the Kingdom?* He had to answer—now. The mob outside was a reminder. The Enemy used many tools: doubt, division, violence and above it all, the looming shadow of the God who demanded payment.

He resumed dictating, the words pouring out faster, driven by the tension in the street and the vision in his mind. "We do not want you to be uninformed, brothers and sisters, about those who sleep in death..." Sleep— a gentle word for the harsh reality. He saw graves—mothers weeping for sons, old men gone before seeing the promise. "...so that you do not grieve like the rest, who have no hope." Hope—that was the weapon against despair and against the tyranny of the grave imposed by the first Adam's failure. Adam—the name tasted bitter—one man's sin, one act of disobedience, and death ruled all. The Law given later only highlighted the failure, the constant falling short. It proved humanity stood condemned before a righteous, furious God. A God whose wrath burned against sin— God created the problem, then punished humanity for his own doing. Paul felt the heat of that wrath even now, like the desert sun beating on his back during his escapes.

"For if we believe that Jesus died and rose again..." There it was, the pivot, the reversal, exactly what Paul needed in his message. Adam brought death—Christ brought life. Adam's sin condemned but Christ's obedience justified. "For as in Adam all die, so in Christ all will be made alive." The new Adam—the obedient one. Jesus—the Christ—He took the curse—He absorbed the wrath meant for rebels. The vindictive God demanded blood, and Christ gave it—His own.

Another shout, closer this time. A stone thudded against the outer wall of the workshop and dust sifted from the ceiling. Titus gripped the hilt of his dagger, the scribe's hand faltered, a blot spreading on the papyrus. Paul didn't flinch, his voice cut through the noise, sharper now. "Listen! I tell you a mystery!" The scribe scrambled for a fresh sheet, this was vital— the answer for the grieving Thessalonians. The hope for every believer facing the knife, the cross, the silent creep of illness under a wrathful sky. "We will not all sleep, but we will all be changed—in a flash, in the twinkling of an eye, at the last trumpet."

He saw it—the tension outside faded. He saw the sky ripped open, not with gentle light, but with the terrifying, glorious fury of a Judge returning to claim what He had purchased. "For the trumpet will sound, the dead will be raised imperishable, and we will be changed." He emphasized *we*. Those alive, clinging to faith in a world screaming its unbelief. "After that, we who are still alive and are left will be caught up together with them in the clouds to meet the Lord in the air."

Paul's words were coming faster, the scribe wrote furiously, trying to keep up. *Caught up*—Harpazo—Snatched—Seized. Like he was seized on the Damascus road—an irresistible force—a rescue from the coming storm. Paul felt the phantom grip on his own shoulder. He pictured it: graves bursting open. Living believers ripped from plows, from beds, from hiding places, pulled skyward. Meeting the descending King. Not a gentle reunion, but a triumphant, terrifying ascension. Escape from the final outpouring of the vengeful God's wrath upon a rejecting world. "And so we will be with the Lord forever."

He stopped, the sentence hung in the dusty air. Forever—Safety—Victory over the last enemy, death itself. Life, finally, free from the shadow of the first Adam's failure and the tyrant God's condemnation. Purchased by the blood of the second Adam, sealed by His resurrection and secured by His imminent return.

Silence followed, profound after the intensity of his words. The shouting outside had moved on, perhaps finding no quarrel here today. Titus relaxed his grip, his knuckles white. The scribe stared at the words he had written, his face pale.

Paul leaned back, the rough wood of the chair pressing into his spine. The letter to Corinth needed finishing—arguments about order, morality, the resurrection body. Vital, but the core pulsed in the words just dictated for Thessalonica. The core that justified every risk, every beating, every night spent in a dank prison cell. Christ died—for sins—not his own—ours. Humanity was chained by death because of the rebellion inherited from Adam. Christ rose, proof death's chains were broken. Christ would return to gather His own, both the resurrected dead and the transformed living, snatching them from the jaws of the coming wrath—to be with Him—Forever.

He looked at the papyrus, these fragile sheets were weapons—they carried dynamite. They declared rebellion against the gods of Rome, against the Law's impossible demands, against the despair peddled by death and the whispers of the Accuser. They offered life, bought with blood, validated by an empty tomb and guaranteed by a promised return. They spoke of a rescue so sudden it would be like lightning splitting the sky.

He took a deep breath, the air still tasted of dust, but also of purpose. "Now, concerning the collection for the saints..." he began again, his voice steady. The work continued, the letters would go out and T he word would spread. He would run the race. He would fight the fight until the trumpet sounded, or the stones found their mark, whichever came first. The vindictive God had been satisfied for now. The new Adam had won, the rescue was coming—that was the story. The only story worth telling, the only story worth dying for. He dipped his own pen into the ink, ready to add his signature mark of authenticity to the dangerous, glorious truth.

Before the Sword

Torchlight flickered wildly in the olive grove. It caught the gleam of armor, the whites of frightened eyes and the sweat on Simon Peter's forehead. Soldiers, Temple guards, a mob stirred up by the priests—they formed a shifting wall of menace. Their presence choked the quiet night air, they surrounded Jesus. Peter felt the familiar heat rise in his chest, a burning mix of fear and fury. This was betrayal—this was an ambush. His hand tightened on the leather grip of the sword concealed beneath his cloak. He hadn't expected things to move this fast, this violently. He saw the determination on the faces advancing towards his teacher—reason fled—instinct took over.

The high priest's man, Malchus, pushed forward. He wasn't a soldier. He wore the finer clothes of a household servant, but his face held the same avid cruelty as the guards. He reached out, not for Jesus directly, but to roughly shove John aside, clearing a path for the arresting soldiers. Malchus moved with arrogant authority, the confidence of a man backed by overwhelming force. That arrogance snapped the last thread holding Peter's anger in check. This servant dared lay hands on them? Here? Now? Peter didn't think—he just acted. The sword pulled free from its sheath, a harsh metallic scream in the tense silence. He lunged, not with skill, but with raw, desperate force. He aimed for the head, for the threat—the blade connected.

It sliced through the night air, then through flesh and cartilage with a sickening, wet crunch. Something small and dark flew sideways, landing with a soft thud in the dirt near a gnarled olive root. Malchus screamed, it was a high, piercing shriek of pure agony and shock. He staggered back, clutching the side of his head where his right ear had been. Blood, shockingly black in the torchlight, pulsed between his fingers, streaming down his neck, soaking his tunic. His eyes were wide with disbelief, then terror as he stared at the crimson fountain erupting from his own body. He collapsed to his knees, his screams turning into guttural, choking sobs.

Chaos erupted—soldiers roared, drawing their own weapons. The mob surged forward, then recoiled from the sudden violence and the sight of Malchus writhing in the dirt, blood pooling beneath him. Peter stood frozen, the bloody sword heavy in his hand. He saw the horror on the faces of the other disciples. He saw the stunned, almost resigned look on Jesus' face. He saw the raw, animal hatred ignite in the eyes of the soldiers. He'd done it— he'd struck a blow but the sickening reality of it, the sheer volume of blood,

Malchus' screams—it washed over him like icy water. His bravado vanished. This wasn't a glorious stand—this was butchery—panic seized him.

Jesus moved, he stepped towards Malchus, ignoring the drawn swords pointed at his chest. He knelt in the bloody dirt beside the shrieking servant. He placed his hand near the horrific wound. Peter expected words of rebuke, directed at him, he braced for it but Jesus spoke to Malchus, his voice cutting through the man's agony. "Enough." The word held impossible weight. The screaming stopped, replaced by ragged, wet gasps. Malchus stared up, transfixed and trembling violently. Jesus touched the bloody ruin, for a single, impossible moment, the pulsing fountain of blood seemed to hesitate. The raw edges of flesh...shifted. Peter blinked, unsure if the flickering torchlight deceived him. Was that...healing? A miraculous closing? But the moment passed and Jesus stood up. His hand came away clean. The bleeding slowed, perhaps, but the ear was gone—utterly gone. The wound remained a ragged, awful hole. Malchus touched it with trembling fingers, whimpering at the raw, exposed pain. Relief mixed with profound terror in his eyes. He lived, but maimed. Jesus looked at Peter. His eyes held no warmth, only a deep, unfathomable distance. "Put your sword away. Those who live by the sword, die by it." The words were simple but carried a lot of weight, they offered no comfort, only cold, hard fact. They felt less like mercy and more like a pronouncement of inevitable consequence.

The soldiers recovered from their momentary shock. Rough hands grabbed Jesus, they bound his wrists tight. Peter dropped the sword, it clattered on the stones. The metallic sound echoed his own internal collapse. He saw Malchus being hauled roughly to his feet by two guards. The servant swayed, pale as death, one hand clamped uselessly over the gruesome wound on the side of his head. His fine clothes were ruined, saturated with his own blood. He looked at Peter, his eyes, glazed with pain, burned with a hatred so pure it was terrifying. That look promised retribution. Peter turned and ran. He fled into the darkness of the olive grove, the image of Malchus' ruined face and the sound of his screams chasing him. He ran until his lungs burned and the chaos faded behind him. He hid in the shadow of a large stone cistern, gasping and trembling uncontrollably. He'd tried to defend his Lord but he'd only made things worse—far worse. He'd invited death upon them all and the look in Jesus' eyes...it wasn't forgiveness. It was judgment. Cold, silent judgment.

Malchus endured the journey back to the city. Each jolting step sent fresh waves of agony through his skull. The initial shock had dulled into a deep, throbbing burn that consumed half his head. The crude bandage pressed against the wound by a guard offered little comfort; it felt like a rock grinding against exposed nerve endings. The high priest's house was ablaze with light, servants gasped as Malchus stumbled in, supported by guards. The high priest, Caiaphas, looked up from consulting with other officials. His face, usually composed with cold calculation, registered shock, then fury as he saw his trusted servant's condition. "Malchus! What happened?"

Malchus tried to speak, but only a pained groan escaped his lips. He gestured weakly towards the side of his head. A guard stepped forward. "It was one of the Nazarene's followers, my lord. Simon, the fisherman. He drew a sword. Cut off Malchus's ear." He pointed to the blood-soaked servant. "Clean off."

Caiaphas' eyes narrowed. The outrage was palpable. This was more than an attack on a servant; it was an assault on the Temple's authority, on *his* authority. "The Nazarene's mob resort to murder now?" he spat. "Where is he? Where is this Simon?"

"The others fled," the guard reported. "But we have the ringleader. Jesus of Nazareth. Bound and secure."

"Good," Caiaphas said, his voice tight, his gaze returned to Malchus. The servant's suffering was evident, a visible symbol of the Galilean's dangerous defiance. "See to him. Get the physician. Now!" His command snapped servants into action. They guided the trembling Malchus away towards the servants' quarters.

The physician arrived quickly, an old man with steady hands but weary eyes. He unwound the bloody cloth, Malchus flinched violently, a strangled cry escaping him as the air hit the raw wound. The physician examined it under the lamplight. He prodded gently. Malchus whimpered, tears streaming down his face. "The ear…?" he managed to rasp.

"Gone," the physician stated flatly. "Clean cut. Gone." He cleaned the wound as best he could, packing it with clean linen soaked in wine and oil, the sting was excruciating. He bound Malchus' head tightly. "The bleeding has slowed. The wound is…clean, surprisingly so. No sign of corruption yet. But the pain…" He shook his head. "That will be severe. For a long time. And the disfigurement…" He didn't need to finish. Malchus understood—he was ruined—his face was a horror. His position, his standing—gone. All because of one fisherman's wild swing. Hatred, colder and harder than the pain, settled in his gut. Simon Peter—he would remember that name—he would see him pay.

Above, in the high priest's council chamber, the hastily assembled Sanhedrin questioned Jesus. The mood was ugly, fueled by the news of Malchus' injury. Accusations flew—false witnesses were brought forth. Caiaphas pressed Jesus directly: "Are you the Messiah, the Son of the Blessed One?" Jesus' answer, "I am," was met with cries of blasphemy. Robes were torn and spittle flew. "He deserves death!" Caiaphas declared, and the council roared in agreement. The assault on Malchus served as potent proof of the danger Jesus and his followers represented—violent, lawless men who attacked the servants of God.

Peter, meanwhile, had crept closer to the high priest's courtyard, drawn by a desperate need to know Jesus' fate. He lingered near a fire in the outer court, trying to blend in with the servants and guards. His heart pounded hard against his chest. Every shout from inside the house made him flinch. He jumped when a servant girl pointed at him. "You! You were with him! With the Nazarene!" Peter's blood ran cold. He denied it. He denied Jesus three times, then he froze when he heard a cock crow in the distance. He remembered Jesus' words to him: *Before the cock crows, you will deny me three times.* While Peter was distracted outside, Jesus' fate had been determined inside. The sentence had been passed—crucifixion. The enormity of his failure crashed over him—the violence, the cowardice, the denial. He stumbled away from the fire, from the accusing eyes, and wept bitterly, alone in the gray pre-dawn light. He had cut off a man's ear, then denied his Lord. He felt utterly lost, damned.

Malchus, lying on a rough pallet in a small room off the kitchen, heard the commotion above. He heard the accusations, the cries for death. He heard the cock crow. He didn't weep but his pain was a constant fire, a reminder. He focused on that pain, fed it with the image of the fisherman's panicked face in the torchlight, the feel of the sword's impact. Justice would come—earthly justice. He would demand it, he would testify. He would see Simon Peter hang for this. His ruined face would condemn the fisherman before the judges. Let the Nazarene face his fate. Malchus wanted the fisherman. He wanted him to suffer, he wanted him to lose more than an ear.

Malchus learned of the verdict—a grim satisfaction that slightly eased the relentless pain in his head. One down—the Nazarene would die but the fisherman...Simon Peter...he was still out there hiding, denying. Malchus would find him. He would make sure the Romans knew—an attack on a servant of the high priest was an attack on Rome. He pictured the cross. He pictured Peter on one. The image brought a flicker of warmth against the cold agony. Soon—it would happen soon.

Simon Peter wandered the city streets like a ghost. The weight of his actions crushed him. He saw Malchus' ear flying. He heard the screams, he heard his own denials echo. He saw Jesus's face—not angry, but profoundly distant, as if Peter had already ceased to exist. He felt hollowed out, a vessel of shame. He avoided the other disciples, he avoided the Temple. He avoided anywhere soldiers might patrol. He was a marked man. Malchus lived. Malchus would identify him. The Romans crucified thieves and rebels, they would crucify an ear-slicer without hesitation. Every shout in the street, every clank of armor, sent jolts of terror through him. He was a dead man walking—he knew it. The sword he'd drawn so recklessly now hung over his own neck.

Outside the city wall, on a hill called Golgotha, soldiers nailed Jesus to a cross. They raised it between two thieves. The chief priests and scribes mocked him.

Meanwhile, in the high priest's house, Malchus felt the unnatural darkness press in. The lamps were lit early and a strange stillness hung in the air, broken only by the distant murmur of the crowd at Golgotha. The physician changed his bandage. The wound still pulsed, hot and angry, no miraculous healing had occurred for him. Only pain and disfigurement remained. He heard about the Nazarene's final words: forgiveness. It meant nothing. Forgiveness didn't restore his ear. Forgiveness didn't erase his ruined face. Forgiveness didn't bring back his life as it was. It felt like an insult. Where was the justice? Where was the vengeance for *him*? He looked towards the Temple and thought of the God they served, the God of Abraham, Isaac, and Jacob. The God who drowned Pharaoh's army. The God who commanded the destruction of Canaanite cities. The God who struck down Uzzah for touching the Ark. That God understood justice. That God demanded blood for blood. Malchus clutched the rough edge of his bandage. The Nazarene was dead—now, for the fisherman. His pain demanded payment. He would get it—he would appeal directly to the Romans. He would show them his face. He would make them see. Simon Peter would pay—God would see to it—or Malchus would.

After the Sword

Malchus stood guard in the high priest's courtyard. Whispers reached him about the Galilean, Jesus. Some claimed he healed sickness. Others said he challenged the Temple. Malchus touched the scar where his ear had been severed, then hastily bandaged. He remembered the chaos, the flash of a sword. Fear tightened his chest. God demanded absolute obedience. God punished doubt. Everyone knew this. The stories about Jesus felt dangerous, a challenge to divine order. Malchus scanned the faces around him. Were agents of God's vengeance already watching? He forced himself to stand straighter, eyes forward. He reported nothing. Silence felt safest. The dread remained.

BENEATH A DYING SON

NEW TESTAMENT SHORT STORIES

LAUGHTON J. COLLINS, JR.

BENEATH A DYING SON

NEW TESTAMENT SHORT STORIES

LAUGHTON J. COLLINS, JR.

BENEATH A DYING SON

NEW TESTAMENT SHORT STORIES

LAUGHTON J. COLLINS, JR.

My Website

Social Media

Link Tree

dot.profile

Authors Den

Goodreads

Bookwire

Amazon Author Page

Bookshop

@LAUGHTONJCOLLINSJR

Substack

E-Mail

www.ingramcontent.com/pod-product-compliance
Lightning Source LLC
Chambersburg PA
CBHW071251250626
47163CB00002B/416